AF

W9-BTS-738

QUIET MEG

Other books by Sherry Lynn Ferguson:

The Honorable Marksley

QUIET MEG

•

Sherry Lynn
Ferguson

AVALON BOOKS
NEW YORK

Published by Thomas Bouregy & Co., Inc.
160 Madison Avenue, New York, NY 10016

Library of Congress Cataloging-in-Publication Data

Ferguson, Sherry Lynn.
  Quiet Meg / Sherry Lynn Ferguson.
      p. cm.
  ISBN 978-0-8034-9906-5 (hardcover : acid-free paper)
1. Landscape architects—Fiction. 2. Aristocracy (Social
class)—England—Fiction. I. Title.

  PS3606.E727Q85   2008
  813'.6—dc22

                                    2008005925

PRINTED IN THE UNITED STATES OF AMERICA
ON ACID-FREE PAPER
BY HADDON CRAFTSMEN, BLOOMSBURG, PENNSYLVANIA

For Charlotte and Audrey

Chapter One

The proprietors of grand estates usually adopted a formality and consequence comparable to their surroundings. Never before had Charles Cabot been asked to share refreshments out on the lawn.

The invitation from Sir Eustace Lawrence K.C. caused a comical consternation amongst the household staff. A hastily assembled table, offering drinks and cold savories, soon claimed the long shadow of a beech trunk, for the avenue's ancient trees had not yet leafed out to dense shade. But the amiable Lawrences, displaying a fondness for the open, bravely settled themselves in the bright March sun. There they persisted, though a fickle breeze threatened to topple their charming party.

By backing his chair to the same massive tree that sheltered the luncheon, Chas gave himself what little cover was to be had as well as a view of the long stretch of turf abutting the river. His thoughts had focused entirely on the

1

prospect before him—on Selbourne, his newest project, for which he knew he scarcely had time. If Bertram Lawrence had not chanced upon him in town and pressed him to render an opinion, Chas would have considered himself more than reasonably occupied. Still, improving the estate's grounds had its challenges. There was a promisingly pictur-esque pool of water in back, and the low hill directly across from him had possibilities . . . But young Lucy Lawrence's anxious complaint put an end to his musings.

"Why must Meg rush home *now*? She's been happy with Bitty! Just weeks ago she wrote that she would stay through the summer!"

"She had no choice." Louisa Ferrell, Lucy's older sister, reached to rescue a fluttering letter from the girl's hand. "Aunt Bitty's new home in Cheltenham is half the size of Tenby's. With Mrs. D— sharing, it's unthinkable that Meg should move with them."

"But we shall be departing for town by mid April! Surely she can't intend to stay here alone?"

"And why should she stay here at all, young lady?" Sir Eustace asked abruptly. Confined to his Bath chair, the burly gentleman still managed to fidget, as though he denied his limitations. Certainly nothing else about the forceful Lawrence patriarch was limited in any way. The glare he sent his youngest was a reprimand in itself. "Margaret is your sister. She is welcome to join us in town."

"But she won't want to, Papa! Not after . . ." Lucy bit her lower lip and glanced toward Chas's spot in the shade. He directed his gaze once again to the river. "This is my come-out. She knows what this means to me! It would be too—too much to have everything tattled about again!"

"And aren't you just too, *too* particular," Bertram teased. "Are you afraid Meggie will squash your expectations? Perhaps spirit away some of your suitors?" He smiled affectionately at his sister. "Don't be bird-witted, Luce. You shall be the toast of the season. And attention is the last thing Meggie wants."

"But she draws it. She cannot help it. She . . ." Lucy again looked Chas's way. "Mr. Cabot will think me most ungracious."

"Mr. Cabot," he assured her, "is only ever charmed by Miss Lawrence."

"Coming at it a bit too strong there, Cabot," Bertie laughed. "Since you've known Lucy all of an hour."

"Our guest is too kind, my dear," Sir Eustace said. "I will not have such talk about Margaret. I'd wish her home today. I have missed her. You should be mindful of my ill health and advancing years."

Lucy looked concerned, but the others grinned.

"I thought Meg was expected last Christmas," Mr. Ferrell volunteered.

"Oh, but Ferrell, you must remember!" Louisa said. "I did tell you . . . How Meg stayed on, because of Bitty's concerns about the move? It's been most distracting—"

"Margaret's been away almost ten months," Sir Eustace told him. "'Tis long enough. She must stop hiding."

"Meggie doesn't hide, father," Bertie said. "She could not hide even if she wished to."

"And that is just what I dread," Lucy said.

"Oh come, Lucy," Louisa said. "Having Meg back will not make one whit of difference to your season. You shall see."

"We are boring you, Cabot," Bertie claimed. "Here you sit suffering our domestic squabbles, when we sought your help with problems out-of-doors! I cannot believe this aids you in your planning."

"Only if you habitually entertain on the lawn," Chas said mildly.

"Never," Sir Eustace conceded. "Uncomfortable business. With all the bumping and rolling to set up here on the grass—what there is of it. Groundskeepers have slacked off for ages. And look at that copse of pines by the river! Grown so tall now they block half the view. Time was I could sit right where you are and see clear to Milford."

"I can still make out a good bit of the far bank, sir. But if you prefer to see more of it, something could certainly be done."

"By no means let *my* preferences guide you, Mr. Cabot. I am not long for this world—" This time his family protested, "So you must listen only to the desires of my son and my daughters."

"I hope to accommodate all of you," Chas said. "Perhaps you might each choose a direction—east, west, north, and south."

"And you mustn't forget Meggie," Bertie added. "She is a direction all her own."

"She might be our pole-star, then," Chas suggested, battling an unreasonable dislike for the absent 'Meggie,' "and set our direction when the sun is down."

Sir Eustace shot him a swift, keen look.

"You are a poet, Mr. Cabot. I fear you plan to clutter the place with posies and showy statuary."

Bertie laughed.

"That is not his interest, father."

"Nor is it my intention, sir," Chas assured him. "I have a fondness for parks. Had your estate here at Selbourne not had sufficient scope, you would have found me unsuited for this commission."

"Perhaps you'd have found *us* 'unsuited,' young man," Sir Eustace observed, too astutely. "Mind you're not presumptuous."

"You cannot snap at Cabot now, father," Bertie told him cheerfully. "You signed the papers yourself, and you are the jurist! Since he's pledged to the Duke of Clare come May, you must pocket your pride and let him get on with the matter."

"Bertie," Louisa cautioned, "you sound most uncivil."

"I don't suppose you'd take my daughter Lucinda here off my hands, would you Mr. Cabot?" Sir Lawrence offered blandly. "'Twould spare me the expense of her season, and help defray some small portion of your crew's excessive costs."

"Papa!" Lucy cried.

Chas smiled at the girl.

"Miss Lawrence would be a rare prize. But I fear I would have little to offer her at the moment."

"Did not your uncle, the Duke of Braughton, just make over Brookslea to you, Cabot?" Bertie winked at him. "With such a sweet property in the family I would be pleased to claim you as a brother-in-law."

"Do stop this, Bertie," Louisa said. Young Lucy's color was high.

"Were you raised at Braughton, then," Mr. Ferrell asked, "in Leicestershire? Is it your home?"

"I spent many summers there, sir, and now exercise some oversight at Braughton. But before school I lived on the Continent, in Austria and Italy. And since university I've traveled a good deal. I've been back in England only these past two years."

"You knew Bertie at university?" Lucy asked.

"Yes, Miss Lawrence. Your brother made quite an impression on me. 'Twas Mr. Bertram who convinced me my path lay in designing landscape."

"And how was that?" Sir Eustace asked, his eyes twinkling.

"Your son required a golf course early one morning, sir. Unconscionably early, I regret to say, since he was a bit bosky, the result of a lucky win—" As Bertie grimaced and shook his head, Chas smiled. "In any event, he wished to celebrate. I convinced him that I'd devised a course, thus keeping him from a more ambitious public display. He's claimed to be in my debt ever since. And I found my calling, which demands more of persuasion than architecture."

The others laughed. The tale was a stretch, but held enough of the truth to be credible. It dismissed all the hard hours of study, and all the years of tiring application. His distinguished clients did not wish to hear about the cultivation of his competencies, they wished only to enjoy his cultivated landscapes.

"You needn't persuade me *this* time around, Cabot," Bertie said. "You can see for yourself the place needs attention."

"I frequently must persuade even eager clients, Lawrence. The most unlikely objects can rouse unlooked for loyalties. These beeches, for example," and Chas gestured to the dignified gray row behind him. "You'd probably resist their removal."

The group looked predictably shocked.

"Surely . . . surely you jest, Mr. Cabot," Louisa Ferrell said in a strangled voice.

"Yes, Mrs. Ferrell. But I make my point. You may believe you give me license, but I know that in your hearts such is far from the case, hence the many hours to survey what now exists and to obtain your approvals. Nature is resilient, but does not adjust well to abrupt changes." He patted the smooth gray trunk behind him. "Before I tear down your copse of offending pines, Sir Eustace, I shall try to give you some concept of the likely result—so you might object."

"Do you make the drawings yourself, Mr. Cabot?" Lucy asked.

"Many of them, Miss Lawrence. But I have draftsmen do much of the preliminary recording from surveys, to line and rule measurement. 'Tis painstaking work, and I have done enough of it in my day. Now I prefer to render the visuals." Even as he spoke, he pulled a folded piece of paper from his waistcoat and, placing it on his knee, rapidly sketched the view to the river in a few bold pencil strokes. He passed it toward Sir Eustace and Miss Lucy.

"Astonishing," Sir Eustace murmured.

"Why, you've simply removed the lower branches of the pines, so that Papa can see Milford," Lucy exclaimed. "How clever!"

"Cabot has always been clever," Bertie said with satisfaction. "I told you so."

"Perhaps less clever than cautious, Lawrence. As you see, I move in increments."

"Margaret draws," Louisa remarked idly, as she fingered the sketch that had been passed to her. She had not addressed anyone in particular, so Chas did not respond. He was developing an antipathy to a complete stranger—to Margaret Lawrence, who sounded so willful and proud. The girl's preferences seemed to demand too much consideration from her pleasant family.

"Come, Cabot," Bertie said, rising purposefully from his seat. "We have at least another hour left of good daylight. Let us make an effort to see a bit of the place before you head on to town."

"You must show him the office as well," Sir Eustace said. "Mr. Cabot, I have arranged for you to stay with us when you are here. 'Tis an apartment in the East wing. We must not have you languishing at the Buxley inn. You will always be welcome to join us."

"I thank you, sir. Ladies—Mr. Ferrell." Cabot bowed. "It has been a pleasure."

"Oh, but Bertie, I wish to come as well," Lucy protested.

"Perhaps next time, Luce. We are riding, for which you are neither dressed nor much inclined. I promise nothing momentous will be decided this afternoon. Father, Ferrell." With a salute to his family, Bertie led Chas away from the table and a pouting Lucy.

"She was welcome to join us," Chas told him.

"Lucy is a pest, Cabot. You will find her constantly underfoot. I advise you to discourage her early and often. The little minx is already half in love with you. Did you not see her making sheep's eyes at you across the table?"

"As a gentleman I would never say . . ."

"Oh, you saw all right. Don't let her start. Else in a

week's time you'll be running to me begging, 'Oh, what is to be done with little Lucy?' "

They laughed as they reached the stable and their mounts.

Chas was at home in the saddle; he had been riding all his life. He was surprised that Bertram Lawrence did not appear as thoroughly at ease.

"I know you are a bruising rider, Cabot, but I'm only minimally better on a horse than the average," Bertie confessed. "Father was a legend, as you must know, and now Meggie matches him. But I consider myself a fair hand with the ribbons, if you recall."

"I do indeed. And now may I express a preference for starting off down the avenue to the gate? 'Tis the equivalent of opening the front door."

They set off along the carriageway, between the magnificent beeches. Chas would have preferred to tour alone, but the suggestion would have seemed churlish. Bertram Lawrence was, and always had been, genial company; he would ramble on with only the occasional acknowledgement.

Chas was largely free to do what he did so well—listen to the land. After years of practice his ability to absorb a place was intuitive. His eye quickly gauged elevation and hollow, sun and shade, exposure and shelter. In a familiar county like Berkshire, where he knew the soil and flora, he could save himself and his men weeks of measurements and testing, simply through close observation on a few pleasant walks or rides. Only bad weather had ever made such initial tasks uncomfortable.

They rode to the gate, went out along the road paralleling the river, considered the hedges and trees hiding the house from public view, then reentered the grounds to set off across the deer park. Chas realized the property was more extensive than he had at first supposed, and said as much to Bertie.

"It's about twelve hundred acres, Cabot. But we don't intend you to do much over to the west, the grazing and so forth, and certainly not the tenant farms," though Chas knew full well that alterations to one area tended to require answering attentions in others, even those a landholder might dismiss.

As they rode, Chas' imagination was engaged at least once in attempting to picture the wayward Margaret Lawrence.

"Is Miss Margaret your older sister?" he asked.

"Meggie? Oh no, Meggie is the middle—between Louisa and Lucy. She'd be—twenty now. Just this month, as a matter of fact." Bertie fell silent. Again Chas had the impression that the young lady, or at least the thought of her, oppressed the family.

"Miss Lucy seemed upset at her return," he prompted, irritated with himself for troubling to pry.

"Lucy is a silly goose who can think only of her come-out. Even if Meggie's letter did just arrive today, Lucy should not have been quibbling. Meggie will not return for weeks yet, I'll wager. Probably not before you've finished with us."

"Lawrence, I mentioned this project will continue long after my planning is over. Well into the fall, at least."

"I know, I know. But I meant you are unlikely to cross paths with my sister this spring."

Bertie sounded relieved, but Chas had to wonder if that was the assurance he had sought. He still could not picture the creature.

"Meggie planned the kitchen garden for our cook many years ago. Should you wish to change it, Cabot, you may face some opposition there. Come to think of it, I might object to that myself! But I shouldn't imagine you will wish to change it. 'Tis the only comfortable spot out-of-doors. I'll show you before you leave this evening."

Chas halted his horse to look toward Selbourne from the height they had reached about a mile from the house. The small hill afforded the finest vista he had yet seen of the place, but there was no easy route from the house and no spot of repose from which to enjoy it.

Selbourne itself was imposing, with its weathered gray stone and sturdy formality. Chas appreciated that it was properly scaled for its site. In the shape of a flattened H, with east and west wings, twinned chimneys and limited ornamentation, the house had clean, pleasing lines. Jones was said to have designed at least part of it; the family was not certain. It had been built for the ages, regardless. But the best views at Selbourne, as Chas had reason to know, were from inside the house—to this promontory in the east, across the park to the river in the south, past the rolling fields and farms westward, and back to the flanking wooded hills of Buxley to the north.

He asked Bertie about the uses of the property—the paddocks and stables, the farms, and the family's own entertainments—all of which he supplied with humorous asides and a degree of frustration.

"'Tis a bit of a ruin, Cabot. I told you so in town. You must consider it yours! No one has done much to the place since the lanes and gates went up with the house. The head gardener is elderly and tyrannical. I await his abdication.

Anything you find acceptable is probably mere happen-stance."

"Does your father take a daily constitutional? He says he cannot run the chair out on the lawn."

"He goes to the stables, to see his pets. On occasion he has ventured down to the river gate, but he is otherwise re-stricted to the house. His confinement is a great distress to him, Cabot. He was always a vigorous man, and a devoted horseman."

On the way back to the stables they passed the entrance to the kitchen garden at the northwest corner of the house. Though the light was fading, Bertie suggested they take a quick look. Chas handed his reins to a groom, then fol-lowed Bertie to an iron gate set in a high stone wall.

He was astonished by what lay beyond—easily five thou-sand square feet of carefully plotted *parterre*, lime and dwarf fruit trees, clipped box hedges, trellises for vines, a small central pond and, along the north wall, a tiny teahouse—shielded from stronger winds, but open to the sun. The kitchen garden, cradled within the old walls of a former sta-ble yard, was a surprising, welcome relief from the rest of Selbourne's spare setting. Even now, in early March, low bulbs and sweet peas bloomed amidst subtly hued cabbages and herbs, adding vitality and color to the gray surroundings.

"You say your sister Margaret designed this?"

"Every inch of it, except the walls of course. But she laid out the planting beds and the pond, and had the teahouse and trellises built, and has instructed cook and anyone who will lend an ear in how to keep it up. 'Twas her project, you see—though it has not seemed to give her as much pleasure since—well, for some years." His lips set grimly. "You shall have some difficulty wresting it from her."

"I shouldn't wish to. 'Tis charming."

Chas thought he must revise his opinion of Margaret Lawrence. Her garden had been artfully arranged. Perhaps her seemingly self-indulgent ways had a positive side; he valued that kind of determination in himself. But he still wondered what the young woman had done to so unsettle her worthy family.

With a promise to Bertie that he would have men out by the end of the week, Chas returned to town in the Selbourne coach. As was usual at the start of any endeavor, he was intensely focused. That night he made notes and scribbled letters to growers whose stock he knew he would wish to guarantee. But such activity did not entirely absorb him. Visiting his grandmother's house in town the next afternoon, he broached a subject that was beginning to annoy him.

"Sir Eustace Lawrence has several daughters, *Grand-mère*, in addition to his son, my friend Bertram." He gazed out at the rainy London streets. "The eldest is married—to Thomas Ferrell, the MP for Kitchley. The youngest, Lucinda, will be out this season. Do you know anything of the other, the one named Margaret?" He did not look at his dear *Grand-mère* as he asked, and he made an effort to inquire in as casual a tone as possible. Yet still she clucked at him.

"Ah, *mon pauvre* Charles. Meg Lawrence!"

He turned from the window to frown at his tiny, silver-haired relative.

"Do not take on so, *Grand-mère*. I have not yet met the woman."

She smiled in some amusement, and arched her brows.

"*Mon pauvre* Charles," she repeated, in an entirely different tone. "I do not know, my dear one, which fate I would choose for you. To meet her, or not to meet her."

"You needn't be so coy, *Grand-mère*. I probably shall never meet her, as she has been away from Selbourne much of the past year, and promises to return only once I've finished. I am due at Abbey Clare in Kent this May, if you recall." He had moved away from the windows and back toward her chair. At better than six feet tall, he loomed over her in any event; when his grandmother was seated he had to look that much further down.

"Come sit, *mon petit*," she said now. "I do not wish to break my neck. And you must hear of your Meg Lawrence."

He sat, resting his arms on his knees as he leaned forward. He was always conscious of the incongruity whenever he was in the presence of his adored *grand-mère*—his own large, male self and her frail, pale and perfect femininity. But she was his closest relative, his mother's French mother, the dowager Duchess of Braughton. She was also his wisest counsel. He never failed to visit her often when in town.

"I shall not describe this girl to you, Charles. You must see for yourself. But I will tell you of the past, the *on dit*, yes? Because the family will expect that you know, and perhaps also Miss Meg will expect that you know. And yet you, *mon cher* Charles, never know such things of the world. You see only the buttercups, yes?"

"I am not such an innocent, *Grand-mère*, as you well know, though you do introduce this topic in such an alarming fashion. And if you no longer wish me to bring you the occasional flower from the glasshouses at Kew, that can be arranged."

"Ah! The dear boy is impatient, so he threatens the old woman. We have a word for you. It is termed *le brimeur* . . . the bully."

"*Grand-mère . . .* "

"Yes, yes. So you were in Vienna three—yes, three years ago, when this girl had her debut. Miss Margaret Lawrence, just seventeen. Very young, you see, but *extraordinaire.* Most—appealing. With the poise, *la contenance,* unique— ah! elegant, perhaps. And here is her sister, engaged to the new member of Parliament, Mr. Ferrell. And her father, Sir Eustace, the respected barrister, a baronet who has wealth, and property, and horses, and is most strong—he is walking then, *tu comprends?* Yes, your *Grand-mère* found him always most handsome! So, Miss Margaret is introduced and within one week, her father has ten offers for her hand in marriage."

"Ten offers! On so little acquaintance? 'Tis like the bidding on a rarity." He smiled indulgently. "Now I know you are inventing."

"As you wish." She looked offended.

"*Grand-mère,* I must reconsider my arrangements with Sir Eustace. The family's standing is not quite that elevated. He must have immense riches."

"Shhh," she advised with a finger to her lips. "You think this is for the portion, for the pieces of silver? Did I not say the girl was appealing? Well, but of course this was absurd. Meg wishes to enjoy the season, to see the town and the entertainments. But now the other young ladies think this is not so *convenable*—to have their escorts wish to dance with Meg, to ride with Meg, to *wed* Meg. So some few—the young ladies can be most spiteful, no?—they bring Miss Meg to Vauxhall, to a fete. And they leave her to Sutcliffe."

"Sutcliffe? The Earl of Sutcliffe?" Chas knew the man. He had seen him on occasion—a dark, striking man of stern features and uncertain temper. "Sutcliffe would have been considerably older than Meg Lawrence."

"*Mais oui*. Though this is not always so much an obstacle, if there is love. But with Sutcliffe there is only the passion. He covets the girl. She would be his. This he would say from the first moment he sees her. He is a *connoisseur*; he will have the best. Only he can appreciate Meg. He will not be one of many. He must possess! Charles—I knew a man once, who sold all his family's ancient vineyards for one superior vintage. Such is Sutcliffe's desire! Yet the Earl of Sutcliffe was married."

Chas leaned back in his seat.

"Surely Miss Meg did not . . ."

"Never! Not at all. This is not proper, Charles. Meg is good. The family is good. The father most honorable, commended by the king! And the earl rages all the more. He cannot wed her. But he must have her. He plans that she should be abandoned at Vauxhall. So that he might steal her away."

"Steal her? *Grand-mère*, do you mean he *kidnapped* her?"

"*Oui, mon cher*. But there is no disgrace to the girl. Because Sir Eustace, and the brother—they stop this crime, this outrage! They find the coach, *tout de suite*! There is a battle, a small battle, but still. And Sutcliffe, or one of his men, fires a pistol. This frightens the horse of Sir Eustace.

He falls, he is crushed, he will no longer ride his superb horses. He loses the use of his legs forever. And Meg, who is so protected, so loved by her family, she is *recluse*—she is in retreat. She cares for her father, that is all." She cautioned silence, a finger to her lips, as Chas moved to comment, "But there is more, Charles . . .

"Miss Meg, she thinks to stop this madness in Lord Sutcliffe, who still sends the gifts and pays the spies. He must know where she is, what she does, all the day, always. She accepts an offer from the son of my friend Lady Kenney. You recall Lady Kenney?" Chas nodded stiffly. "Lady Kenney's boy, Douglas, has an estate far away, in Scotland. Miss Meg, I think, does not love him. But she wishes to escape. And he is *l'adorateur*, adoring. They plan to wed. Then this devil, this Earl of Sutcliffe, who has no soul, no honor, no stop to his desires—he kills the boy."

"Sutcliffe murdered him?" Chas asked sternly. He sat forward and frowned at his *Grand-mère*, who was relaying all this much too calmly. If she were not inventing, he thought her guilty at least of considerable embellishment.

"There was a duel, *mon cher*. The boy, the fiancé Douglas—he challenges for the honor of his Margaret. Yes, it is said Sutcliffe murdered him. With swords. For there could be no contest. He knew how it would be."

"Miss Margaret must have been . . . in shock."

"*Précisément, mon petit*. Of this horror one cannot say so much in words. The offers cease! In another age perhaps, a king might have stopped such as this—put an end to this—banished Sutcliffe, perhaps. Or taken Margaret for himself. But not now, this is not done, and with your patron, this Prince Regent! Ah—he is too silly!"

"He is not entirely silly, *Grand-mère*. He has some admirable sensibilities. But he lacks direction."

"And you, *mon cher*, you have too much direction—you work all the days, when you need not work at all."

"I must, *Grand-mère*. I cannot be merely the idle gentleman. I would not have you term me 'silly.'"

"Never. My Charles is not a silly man. But now, I must finish—Miss Meg comes to town once more, for her sister's wedding to Mr. Ferrell. She stands up for her sister. And the brother—your friend, Mr. Bertram—has prepared carefully, and has many men to guard the ceremony. An army, yes? And still Sutcliffe dares to invite himself, and look on Margaret." His grandmother reached to touch his arm with her delicate fingers. "I have seen this look, Charles. It is not the look of a man, but of the beast, who knows only the need—not love. Miss Meg flees London; no one has seen her for almost a year. Has Sutcliffe forgotten? *Peut-être.* But now he is a widower. He is not a man to woo, but to demand! And you tell me the Lawrences come for the season and I fear—I fear this is not good news. *Mon petit* Charles asks about Meg Lawrence! This I fear as well."

Charles patted her thin hand.

"She designed the kitchen garden at Selbourne, *Grand-mère*. Rather beautifully, as it happens. My interest is professional."

"Oh, Charles . . ." She shook her head at him. "And you have not met this girl! Perhaps that is for the best. You must finish your work before she returns."

"I cannot and will not order the sun and moon for Margaret Lawrence."

"*Non. Mais Charles—le destin! Je voudrais.*"

"*Grand-mère*—please. You have lived here more than fifty years. You must not abandon your English."

"It does not express my heart."

"You express yourself very well, particularly when you are angry. And I will always understand you in any language. Perhaps best when you are silent." She clucked. "If you now believe me at the risks of fate, why did you not steer me away from Sir Eustace and Selbourne?"

"Last week you spoke only of your plans for the Duke of Clare at the Abbey. That is the great estate that takes all of your attention, yes? You make favorites of dukes, is that not so, *mon petit*?"

"I would be a fool if I did not, *Grand-mère*. You, after all, were the favorite of a duke."

She smiled, but was not to be distracted.

"So, last week you make only the hasty mention of a property in Berkshire. You do not say Lawrence! You do not say Selbourne. If you do not inform me, I can do nothing. And then, if I had spoken of these matters before, you would only have laughed. As I believe you laugh now. *Tu es obstiné!* You are always like the mule, Charles."

"And you should not wonder from whom I claim that trait, *Grand-mère*." He kissed her goodbye. "Do not worry. *Ce qu'il plaira à Dieu.* 'Twill be as it pleases God." Yet he muttered "ten offers" to himself as he departed.

Chapter Two

Joe Coachman told her he had been followed on leaving Selbourne, and that after collecting her the carriage had also been followed from Bristol, and Meg had no reason to doubt him. She had fostered some faint hope that after all this time the Earl of Sutcliffe would have forgotten her. But the earl's obsession had become an object in itself, needing no encouragement from her other than her existence.

Her own life was too dear to her to surrender any more of it to such a madman. She now believed that if Sutcliffe trespassed again she would be quick to counter him, in much the same manner that he had harmed her family, for the man was proving impenitent.

Meg thought of Douglas Kenney. She had not loved him years ago. She had liked and respected him, but she had come to love his memory. He had sacrificed all for her, bravely and in vain. Meg had corresponded with his mother, and Lady Kenney's notes had helped to ease her conscience.

Lady Kenney had not blamed her, wisely claiming that no civilized being could have gauged Sutcliffe's depravity. Meg understood it now; she was determined never again to risk another's life.

She frowned as she stared out at the passing countryside. Lucy's come-out worried her. Others, especially Louisa and Aunt Prudence, would shepherd Lucy about town; Meg hoped she herself need appear only at her aunt's. But she could not trust that Sutcliffe would leave her family in peace. Bertie clearly did not trust as much—he had sent two outriders, armed, to accompany the coach. He had written that the occasional stranger had made too many inquiries outside Selbourne's gates; he had relayed that Louisa's town house had been broken into and searched. And he had dismissed a housemaid who had not told him her sister worked for the earl.

Meg knew Sutcliffe would have been stopped long before this had he not been a peer—and had he not been as wealthy as he was deadly. Though the *ton*'s sympathies were with Meg and her family, the privileges of rank were unquestioned. If the daughter of a commended king's counsel should be inconvenienced—that was something only to remark and regret. Sutcliffe had troubled to leave the country for some time after Douglas's death, but he had not been exiled. He might receive few invitations, but he would not be dropped. The *ton* was most estimably tolerant of its own.

Meg turned to her maid.

"Annie, coachman told me at the break that we have been followed. I fear the Earl of Sutcliffe may be contemplating mischief again. You might wish to return to your family up north. I would not keep you. Not in these circumstances."

"I wish to stay, Miss Margaret," the older woman claimed. "This earl canna frighten me. I think mayhap he should meet with an accident."

"If you stay you must promise me to be cautious. I know you want to help me, but you do not know Sutcliffe. He is dangerous. I shouldn't wish you to come to harm."

"You must not worry for me, Miss Margaret. 'Tis enough to be watching for yourself. But I feel I can help you, and so I shall stay."

Meg thanked her and briefly squeezed her hand. She had not wanted to lose Annie, whom she would trust with her life, but she felt it fair to warn her.

Shortly before they reached Selbourne's gates, the carriage pulled up sharply as a lone rider galloped past. Through the carriage windows, Meg glimpsed a dark shape and a piercing glance from a shadowed face—the rider determining, perhaps, that the occupant was indeed Margaret. This scout would be informing Sutcliffe that his prey had returned. Despite Meg's resolve, that impression chilled her.

"Looked like the devil himself with his black coat and horse," Annie said.

"'Tis but a taste of what I fear is in store for us, Annie. But you must not be so fanciful. Sutcliffe and his henchmen are only men, after all."

"Yes, Miss Margaret. And someday may they all bleed like men."

Meg could not reprimand her, given that she herself had contemplated Sutcliffe's end on more than one occasion.

"We are home, Annie. See the beeches."

The two score of distinctive trees, sporting their light green April foliage, graced the avenue, their upper branches meeting in a high arc above the carriage's path. A morning rain had darkened their smooth trunks, though the sun now lent the year's earliest flickering shade to the roadway. Meg's relief was more than physical as she caught sight of Selbourne's stone façade. Yet for all its familiarity there was something different about her home—something that she could not define. Selbourne looked warmer and more inviting.

The horses drew into the forecourt, the coach's wheels ground finally to a halt in the gravel, the grooms jumped down to steady the team and open the carriage door. Meg was aware that activity at the entrance had ceased with the arrival of the carriage; some groundskeepers had been digging a shallow trench at the yard's edge, where a mound of rich brown earth waited to be spread upon a new planting bed. She noticed several things at once—that at a nod from a tall man on the drive the others resumed their work, that the man who had nodded was dressed as a gentleman, and that sunlight spilled across this front portion of the house, where it had never before fallen in the afternoon.

Meg stepped down from the coach with the help of an instantly attentive footman. Once she stood on the gravel she glanced again at the workmen. The tall gentleman was looking at her in a manner that would have seemed forward even for an acquaintance.

He was perhaps ten yards from her. Limned as he was against the late afternoon sunlight, she could not read the expression on his face or the color of his eyes, but it was a handsome face and a direct gaze. His shoulders were broad, his hair shone bronzed blond in the sun. Meg should have found his fixed regard impertinent. Instead she fought the impulse to curtsy.

He bowed. The slight, restrained movement broke the unusual spell he had cast upon her. Meg looked to the steps up to the door. She had not felt unsteady when she left the carriage, but she did now. And she realized for that moment of mutual scrutiny she had been holding her breath. As she breathed now she could smell the day's earlier rain and a freshness that must have been spring itself.

She felt the gentleman's gaze as she ascended the steps; she had to will herself not to look to him again, lest she stumble. And then Bertie was at the door.

"There you are, Meggie!" Bertie grabbed her and kissed her before she was even over the threshold, then pulled her into the hall. "Let's look at you. Why—I do believe you've grown!" They laughed together. It was what their father used to say to them, whenever he'd been away.

Meg removed her bonnet and traveling cloak and watched Annie disappear toward the back of the house.

"Father?" she asked with concern, even as Bertie drew her into the drawing room.

Sir Eustace had been maneuvering his chair toward the hall. Meg hurried to meet him and kneel by his side.

"I've missed you so," she said, taking one of his broad hands in both of hers. Once more she felt that regret, that he would never again be as he had been.

"This has been too long, Margaret. You mustn't leave again."

"No, father." And when she released his hand he ran it fondly over her hair and cheek.

"Are you well, girl?"

"Yes—I am always well."

"Let us hope that will always be the case, my dear. And my sister?"

"Aunt Bitty sends her love. She tells you not to trouble her further about Grandpapa's portrait, as she refuses to trade it for anything you might offer." Meg rose to her feet but leaned to kiss her father lightly on the top of his gray head.

"Not for anything, ha! Elizabeth will rue the day. The stubborn woman must saw it in two to fit it into that mouse-trap of a home in Cheltenham."

"I believe she and Mrs. D— intend to employ it as a screen between the dining room and the parlor, father. Or should I say, to create a dining room and a parlor?"

They laughed. But even as quick steps in the hall announced Lucy's arrival, Meg spared a glance out one window. Two men were still digging by the drive, but the tall gentleman had disappeared.

As Lucy ran to meet her, Meg opened her arms.

"Oh, Meg! I have so much to tell you! You will never believe all that has happened even since I last wrote! I did see the Brathwells at the Buxley assembly, though Mary Pickens took all their time to herself, of course. And you will want to hear the plans for town and see the newest patterns from Madame Corinne. She has consulted *La Belle Assemblée* and all the latest . . ."

"Lucinda," her father warned, "you must take a breath."

Meg hugged Lucy. Her sister had grown prettier since the previous spring; her confidence had grown. Yet she was still just as much of a chatterbox.

"Lucy, I hope you won't think ill of me for coming home just now. You must know I only want you to enjoy town. I will not burden you."

"Why, Meg! Of course you shan't burden me. I am happy you shall be with us. Have I not said so, father?"

Sir Eustace eyed Lucy with a raised eyebrow.

"You were always a good girl, Lucy, but you do carry on. I cannot believe any young man will long tolerate such unbridled jabber."

Lucy tossed her blond curls.

"There is only one man who matters, father. The one I have chosen."

"If you have chosen, daughter, perhaps you can spare us the expense and inconvenience of town. Why does the young fool not come speak to me?"

Lucy blushed.

"Well, he . . . he does not yet know I have decided."

Bertie shook a finger at Lucy.

"I know what you are thinking, Lucinda Lawrence, and it's very bad of you. You've been making a nuisance of yourself. Leave the poor man alone." He looked at his father. "She's been pestering Cabot, father."

"Umph! Mr. Cabot is not for you, Lucinda. Leave him be. When we get to town you shall find suitors enough."

"Who is Mr. Cabot?" Meg asked curiously.

"Charles Cabot, the architect," Bertie said. "I thought I mentioned him in my last letter?" When Meg shook her head, he added, "I knew him at university. He is much in demand—revised the grounds at Hume-Wilcote last fall, and the Duke of Clare has claim on him come May, for improvements to his estate at Abbey Clare in Kent. Cabot's stopping here as a favor."

"'Tis an expensive favor, Bertram," Sir Eustace remarked.

"Oh, stop it, father. You may tease him all you like, but you know he has worked wonders here. I thought I saw him out front just before you arrived, Meggie. Let me see if I can't tow him in for you." Bertie stepped swiftly into the hall.

"I must . . . I must go change from all my travel dust, father. You mustn't wait supper. And Lucy, I have a gift for you from Aunt Bitty."

"You needn't rush, Margaret," her father advised as she moved toward the door. "You know we do not bend to the hour."

"I have been traveling since five this morning, father. I confess to some fatigue." But her shoulders relaxed as Bertie returned alone.

"Apparently he's suddenly ridden off somewhere." Bertie looked puzzled. "I thought we were to ride together tomorrow morning. Well, no matter. You shall meet him at supper, Meggie."

She smiled wanly and excused herself. She could not have explained her panic. To have that stranger—staying here. With her family at Selbourne. Sitting down with them to supper! She had come home to uneasy shelter.

Chas had turned and fled. He had watched her up the steps, but as soon as Bertram had reached to pull her indoors, Chas had turned abruptly and walked rapidly away.

He had slipped in through the gate to the kitchen garden and leaned against the cool stonewall, closing his eyes and listening to his heart pound. Appealing. *Appealing!* His grandmother had known how it would be. *You must see for yourself*, she had said. And now he was struggling for composure while hiding in the kitchen garden.

Even that had been a poor choice, for when he opened his eyes he still saw her—in the garden she had planned. This would be no sanctuary. And at any moment someone might move to a west window and spot him.

He thrust himself away from the wall and hastened across the garden, her garden, to the west gate and the stables. He quickly saddled a horse himself—the same bay stallion he had grown to appreciate over the past few weeks. Then he set out on a tear for the north boundary. He had intended to go the next morning; he would have to revisit the site with Bertram on the morrow. But just now he needed to escape the house. From any other direction he could still see at least part of Selbourne's gray stone. In his present mood he would seek it out and stare at it—and he knew he could not stare at it.

Meg Lawrence was not for him. Yet in those few seconds on the drive he had felt an instant, fierce urge to claim her.

Chas let the horse have his head, racing toward the woods at a run. The drumming of the bay's hooves echoed his heartbeats. Only as they reached the trees did he pull up and move carefully amidst the branches and tangles. Fallen leaves and pine needles were soft beneath the horse's hooves; the late afternoon shadows were long. Chas was acutely aware of the scent of the woods, the growing chill in the air, the occasional calls of birds high overhead. As his agitation eased he was alerted to something else as well—in the shadows of the trees, not more than two hundred feet from him, another rider observed him.

The man was trespassing. Having worked with the survey of the entire estate, Chas knew well where Selbourne's boundaries lay. This intruder was a good quarter mile within the estate's northern border. There was no reason for a tenant or neighbor to be visiting the property at this hour, or by this route.

He thought of a poacher—but a poacher would have fled at his approach. A poacher could not have afforded such a horse. And a poacher would not have been studying him, as though seeking to identify him. Chas set the bay to run at him.

Instantly the rider wheeled his mount, urging the animal to a dangerous gallop through the undergrowth. Chas chased him far enough to know that he had left Selbourne land and headed to the main road and the local town of Buxley. There were any number of places for him to hide on that route. And he had already vanished into the trees in the gathering dusk.

Chas drew his horse to a walk and turned back. The furtive rider's presence had to be linked to the arrival of Meg Lawrence. And that led him to think of Sutcliffe.

Chas had thought at first to excuse the earl. After his own extraordinary reaction to the girl, Chas had been inclined to forgive the man's enchantment. But now he suppressed all sympathy. Sutcliffe had stolen her once; he might be contemplating a second attempt. He had pursued her here on the very day of her return.

Chas's immediate desire to protect her was intense. It

served as a reminder of his sole image of her, standing by the coach in the sunlight, more dazzling than the sunlight. And though he had never proposed building an impassable moat on a property, he wondered if he should devise one for Selbourne.

Meg watched him return in the half-light of dusk. He had superb form—he was an excellent rider. Better than excellent, for he was riding Arcturus, her father's former favorite.

She wondered where he had learned to ride. Taller men sometimes looked awkward in the saddle; Charles Cabot was not one of them. Her father must have seen him astride. She knew her father would term him a natural.

And Arcturus! Never had the spirited bay looked so docile.

Meg moved away from the window. Her room had always provided refuge—after her mother's death, after the disastrous weeks in town for her come-out, after Douglas's duel. Now that Charles Cabot was working in the suite below, Meg found it less of a haven.

She carelessly pulled some items from a satchel. One look on the drive, when she could scarcely distinguish his face, when she had never heard his voice, when she knew little of him—one look could mean nothing. She had been tired from her journey, that was all, and disturbed by the unexpected presence of Sutcliffe's agent. She promised herself that when she went down to dinner she would find Mr. Charles Cabot did not appeal in the least.

She felt brave until she met an excited Lucy on the stairs.

"Oh Meg, you must promise me. Promise me, please, that you will not . . . that you won't . . . encourage him to . . . Oh, you know what I wish to say! It is so important just now that he . . ."

"Lucy, dearest. I have no interest in attaching your Mr. Cabot. I only hope that he deserves your regard. After all, sweet, a gardener . . ."

"But Meg, he is so much more! Just wait, you will see. Father and Bertie like him. He was with Bertie at university. And he has traveled everywhere! You must not judge him so Meg, for he might be, that is, I *think* he might be . . ."

"I shall not harm him, Lucy," Meg assured her with some amusement. "I am in no doubt of your esteem for him. I only hope that he returns your sentiments. Father and Bertie have counseled you to leave him be."

"They do not know what it is to . . . to care. But Meg, *you* do, so I am glad you understand."

Even as she kissed Lucy on the cheek, Meg knew her sister was mistaken. She did not know what it was to care. She had never had that experience. She had only begun to live her life when others had been forced to lose theirs.

Bertie entered the hall and spotted them on the stair.

"What are you two doing up there? We've been waiting to go in to supper. You can have your natter later. Meggie, come meet Cabot."

She linked her arm through Lucy's as they descended the last flight of steps, ashamed that she should cling to her little sister as though to a crutch. But she kept her chin high.

He was standing at her father's side, in front of the fire. She noted everything about him at once—his height, his shoulders, his face, his eyes. For a second the drawing room, so familiar to her, seemed foreign. *I have never been here before*, she thought, lost in his deep brown gaze. Then she looked away, and smiled at her father.

"Meg, may I present Mr. Charles Cabot, architect and landscaper without equal. Cabot, this is m'sister, Margaret." Bertie had somehow managed to pry her from Lucy and push her forward.

"How do you do, Mr. Cabot," she said. She found herself unable to raise her gaze above his neckcloth.

"I am delighted to make your acquaintance, Miss Lawrence." His voice was low and calm. This time he bowed formally, gallantly. She noticed that his dark blond hair caught the firelight. But his gaze shot up to capture her own. "I have admired your kitchen garden."

"Oh—" She struggled with the compliment, even as she watched a slow smile grace his face. "You must not make too much of a few herbs, Mr. Cabot. They grow almost like weeds." As he straightened, her attention fled once again to his neckcloth.

"They are most agreeably placed weeds, Miss Lawrence."

Meg focused on her father.

"Father, you must tell Mr. Cabot how *dis*agreeable the process was by which we planted that garden. I believe you thought me stubborn."

"Indeed. You were a terror, Meg. You had the entire staff trembling for months. I shall never recover. But you were only sixteen, m'dear. And as Cabot says, the results were well worth it. I am only thankful"—and he winked at Cabot—"that his own improvements have not been as disruptive."

"Perhaps they will be—now that Meggie is home," Bertie suggested.

All of them laughed.

"I would appreciate Miss Lawrence's advice," Cabot said politely.

"Ah, do not wish it, my boy," her father said. "Not if you still intend to finish by the end of the month."

So soon! Meg hoped her face did not show her dismay. Yet she should have been glad.

"I would like to see your plans, Mr. Cabot," she said, this time looking to the fire instead of his neckcloth.

"I would like to show them to you, Miss Lawrence."

"But not just now," Bertie said, "for I am famished," and grabbing Meg's hand he drew her quickly across the hall to the dining room. "What do you think?" he asked as he hovered next to her.

She had no time to respond, as her father and Lucy and Cabot had followed them into the dining room. Lucy sat directly across from her. Cabot kindly helped position her father's chair at the head of the table, then took the seat to Lucy's left.

"I understand you rode up to the north park this afternoon," Bertie quizzed Cabot. "I thought we were to do that on the morrow?"

"We shall, Lawrence. Naturally I—was unable to address the task we'd discussed."

"What do you intend with the north woods, Charles?" Lucy asked, and Meg stared—surprised that her sister should address him so casually.

"It could use some thinning to open cross views to the surrounding countryside. Just now it is quite a wilderness. A difficult ride, much less a walk. I wished your brother's thoughts regarding its best use. The house cannot be seen from its furthest reaches, nor"—he paused—"can it be seen in its entirety from the house."

"Perhaps we should take Meggie tomorrow morning as well," Bertie suggested.

"I shouldn't think that at all advisable."

He spoke so abruptly that Meg forgot she was studiously avoiding his gaze. His own attention to her was very direct and serious.

"Margaret is an excellent rider, Cabot," her father said. "You needn't fear she will hold you up—as Lucy did the other day."

"I do not question her skills, sir. I fear for her safety."

Bertie cleared his throat.

"I have not told you yet, father, that Joe Coachman said they were followed from Bristol, and then from the posting house at Marlborough, and that a rider passed them just shy of our gate. He peered in at Meggie."

"The devil you say!" Her father looked livid. "One of Sutcliffe's?"

"I fear so, father. The earl has not forgotten."

"Neither have I! Of all the impudence . . ."

"Father, please do not excite yourself," Meg said, reaching for his hand. "He is all bluster and bark, not bite. He would not dare approach me again."

"Miss Lawrence, I must disagree." Cabot drew her gaze once more. "For I startled a rider inside Selbourne's north boundary this evening. And he was not neighborly."

"That is . . . that is why you do not wish me to ride with you tomorrow morning?"

He nodded briefly.

"Mr. Cabot, this is my home. I refuse to be intimidated by Lord Sutcliffe or his lackeys." She raised her chin. "I shall ride with you tomorrow."

Cabot's gaze held hers for a moment, then he looked across at Bertie.

"Well then, Lawrence," he said with a tight smile. "Tomorrow we ride armed."

"I told you Meggie was a direction all her own, did I not?"

"This is not a humorous situation, Mr. Cabot," Meg said, daring to glare at him.

"I understand that, Miss Lawrence. But do you?"

As she met his gaze, Meg realized she resented him for what he had just accomplished. He had reminded her that she placed others at risk; he had reminded her that she was a prisoner in her own home. Nothing, it seemed, had changed.

"You will be able to ride out once we've assured ourselves that no one is lurking about, Margaret." Her father took her hand. "It is too soon. Let Bertram and Cabot reconnoiter on their own tomorrow."

Meg swallowed her pride. She concentrated on the meal, until a discussion of Lucy's little mare lacking exercise prompted Meg to look to Cabot once more.

"Where did you learn to ride, Mr. Cabot? I saw you return this evening on Arcturus. He is not an easy mount."

"No, I would never describe him so. But he is also a joy, as I gather you well know. Your father recommended him to me. I learned to ride when very young, at my grandfather's stables near Milan. He was Italian, Miss Lawrence. From the Piedmont." He added the last with pride.

"And his grandfather raced many of the horses," Lucy added. "And there was also a castle, a—a *castello*! Did I say it correctly, Charles?"

Meg's eyebrows rose.

"You speak Italian, Mr. Cabot?"

"Oh he does, Meg, *and* French *and* German *and* Spanish," Lucy offered, as though she'd had a hand in the accomplishment. "Oh, and English too, of course."

"You must have a talent for languages," Meg said.

"You are kind. But 'twas rather a need to understand my family—an Italian grandfather, his English and Austrian wife, my French *grand-mère* and her English husband . . ."

"The late Duke of Braughton," Lucy hastened to supply.

Cabot smiled at Lucy before looking at Meg once more.

"There is only just enough there to make me an Englishman."

"And where is your home, Mr. Cabot?" she asked.

His reaction surprised her. For a moment he looked disconcerted. Surely the man had a home?

"Cabot's been granted Brookslea, in Hampshire, by his uncle, the present Duke of Braughton," Bertie said. "I say again—a fine place that, Cabot."

"So you live at Brookslea?" Meg asked.

"Not yet, Miss Lawrence. I visit on occasion. I have rooms in town, on Bond Street. And my work takes me— well, to Selbourne, for example."

"He will live at Brookslea when he settles," Lucy said.

"Ah! You have plans then?" Meg asked, though she feared the answer.

"No," he said shortly, and his brown eyes looked almost black. "No plans."

"None of us ever does have plans, my boy," her father said. "But the devilish things pop up and take over."

"Father, you are describing the opposite of plans," Bertie laughed. "Now I remind you, Cabot, after supper I'd like Meggie to see the drawings."

"Of course," he said, and smiled at Bertie before turning his attention to his meal. Meg noticed that Cabot smiled easily at every other member of her family; indeed, he was treated almost like one of them. But he did not smile at Meg. Despite his compliment of the kitchen garden, she sensed a distance in him, as though he disapproved of her. Such disregard was new to her—she seemed to have developed a desire for masculine praise. Perhaps she had spent too much time with her elderly aunt in tiny Tenby. But she did not want the man's favor, she told herself. Even if Lucy had not set her cap for him, Meg would not have sought his notice.

She stole glances at him as he ate.

"Papa," Lucy said. "Charles says he may be in town late May, so I have invited him to my come-out ball."

"Cabot, you must stop humoring the girl," her father said. "Of course you are most welcome—whatever the date or engagement. But you must feel no obligation. I still hope Lucinda might learn some manners. She is a bit of a romp."

"Papa!" Lucy cried.

"Meggie, you must help us keep Lucy in hand," Bertie said.

"I suspect Lucy needs only an extensive wardrobe and three months in town." She smiled across at Lucy, who sent her a grateful look.

"How you females do pull together," her father said, but

he patted her hand. 'If Louisa were here tonight we would be reduced to discussing the trimming of bonnets."

"It would serve you right, father."

"Ah, Margaret! It is good to have you home." He kept hold of her hand. Meg noted with a pang that he looked grayer than when she had left the previous May.

He spent some time inquiring after his sister Elizabeth and discussing her move to Cheltenham. But they did not tarry over the meal, for Meg was tired after her journey, and Bertram and Cabot wished an early start in the morning. Mr. Cabot, Meg learned, would be leaving the next day to visit other properties. He would be away most of the week.

"Oh, but that is *ages*!" Lucy protested.

"I have my commitments, Miss Lucinda, and promises. My foreman and crew and your father's gardeners will still be working to plan in my absence."

"That is not what I meant!"

"Well, it should have been," her father countered. "Mind yourself, young lady. If you carry on so in town, our stay may be briefer than anticipated."

Lucy looked sulky, but she settled into silence.

"Let us show Meggie your plans now then, Cabot," Bertie said, "so that she has some notion what is going forward while you are away."

When Sir Eustace pushed his chair from the table, the rest of them rose. Meg accompanied her brother to the rooms allotted to Cabot's use, while Sir Eustace kept Lucy behind—for what Meg suspected would be rather a severe scold.

There was no evidence that anyone was residing in the east rooms, apart from the large table now dominating the center of the parlor. The table was covered with papers, but Meg's quick glance around revealed little of a personal nature upon the shelves or other furniture. She was beginning to comprehend that Mr. Cabot was a model of transience. But there was nothing flighty or superficial about him. Indeed, his demeanor, with her at least, was most serious.

He walked over to the table and pushed several scrolls of heavy vellum to the side, revealing underneath a layout of Selbourne in its entirety. Though Meg had never seen such a rendition of her home, she knew it immediately by the shape of the house alone, depicted at center. But much else about it surprised her.

"Why, 'tis Selbourne as a . . . a wheel," she said.

Cabot's glance at her was pleased.

"It is indeed, Miss Lawrence. I've laid out the grounds largely on a radial plan. That is unusual, but Selbourne, as you can see, lent itself to it rather well. I had only to work with what was in place. See here," he leant one hand upon the table as he took up a rule to point to the plan. "The house itself is the center, or hub. The beech avenue in front is one spoke of your wheel, and the other spokes are sight lines from the house or, as in this case"—he drew his forearm out from the house to the east—"a new walk. The wheel's rim consists roughly of the river, the paddocks and farms beyond the stables, the north woods, and here—the rising ground I term the knoll. We are trenching a ha-ha along the line of this dry rill, with a culvert either end . . ." As he moved his arm across the page Meg leaned forward.

"With the pathways, father might move about more."

"Yes, I was thinking of your father," Cabot said, "when I set the route to the knoll. And there is a possibility for something similar here to the lake and out beyond these pastures." He opened one of the scrolls and showed her a drawing, a detailed drawing in pen and ink and the faintest of colored washes, depicting the anticipated view from the house looking toward the river and the knoll. An inviting path advanced through open ground toward a belt of trees, disappearing at last in the distance. The drawing was simple, beautiful, yet so convincing that it took her breath.

"It is . . . extraordinary, Mr. Cabot," she said. "Father will be able to move with ease where he once rode. And yet 'tis still the park as he has always loved it. It looks . . . so natural." She reached to touch the page, as though to satisfy herself of a dream's veracity. In doing so, her arm brushed Cabot's sleeve.

The contact startled her. Yet she knew it should not have. It should not have affected her in the slightest.

As though aware that the enthusiasm had suddenly stilled, Bertie pointed out a few items on the larger plan.

"Look, Meggie. There will be a terrace to the east of the house, to balance your kitchen garden. And you haven't noticed that Cabot removed some of the tallest pines beside the stables."

"I did notice . . . I noticed the light," she said softly. "The sunlight at the front of the house. When I arrived . . ."

She vividly recalled the unexpected light and warmth when she'd arrived. And Cabot was looking at her in such a way—such a way that she could not meet his gaze. She took a step away from him.

"Your plans are very promising, Mr. Cabot." She did not recognize her own voice. "I look forward to seeing them— seeing them in place."

"That will take some time, Miss Lawrence. Your men and one of my crews will be working into the autumn, and some aspects of execution will move into next year. I hope, though, that you will find a moment to review these plans, and the start of some of the work, while I am away this week. All of these papers and drawings are at your disposal. You must question, or suggest, anything you wish."

"I . . . thank you. I must apologize now, but I am quite fatigued."

"Of course." He bowed to her as she took Bertie's arm. She thought he must realize the effect he had on her. He had to.

"How early, Cabot?" Bertie turned to ask.

"At first light, if you don't mind, Lawrence. I should like to reach Surrey by late afternoon."

"Fair enough. I shall sleep all the rest of the day, while you head off on your jaunt."

"Have a safe journey, Mr. Cabot," Meg managed.

Again he bowed to her, but held her gaze. She was treating him as coldly as she could; she sensed that he knew she made an effort.

She forced herself to turn away, and left the room.

Chapter Three

Her father's greeting the next morning did not surprise her.

"I thought some stranger posed as my daughter—that you should miss a ride your first morning back. I hope you've not acquired such lazy habits from my sister."

"No father," she told him, leaning to kiss his cheek. "I thought it best to unpack first. Has Bertie returned?" She knew very well when Bertie had returned.

"Back by nine. And we saw Cabot off early as well. They spent two hours up in the north park, nosing about, with nary a sight of a mysterious rider. But I would still prefer you take a groom with you, my dear, if you do not ride with Bertram. Just for a while. I would feel easier."

"Yes, father," she said, though she chafed at the restriction.

"What do you think of his plans then? Did Cabot show you all?"

"He showed me much, though I should like to review the drawings. His work is most impressive."

"I find it so, Margaret. I am very happy with it. And pleased that Bertram finally brought us a friend who does not spend his days sleeping and lounging. Not another useless fribble. Now come across here and take a look at my terrace."

They moved to the east window and gazed out at the stakes and cleared earth marking the limits of the planned addition. It would be of smaller dimension than the kitchen garden on the opposite side of the house. Apparently Cabot intended that this large window in her father's sitting room should become a door.

"I shall find it easier to steal a whiff of air now and then," her father said.

The notion was simple and sensible. They should have thought of it years ago. Yet a stranger had had to suggest it.

"Look across there." Her father pointed to the eminence to the east. "As you know, 'tis more than a mile away. Cabot's calling it the 'knoll.' He intends I should be able to wheel out to it—and up to it. I shall have to get stronger."

Meg smiled, pleased to hear him sounding so determined. She had much for which to thank Charles Cabot.

From Sir Eustace's rooms, it was possible to see down the shaded avenue, across to the river, where the tall pines had lost their lower limbs. Meg had not seen the river's far bank from the house since she was a child.

"I'd like to walk out a bit and survey the work, father. Shall I have you brought out front with me?"

"No, no. You must go at your own pace. There is too much of the business going on out there at this time of the day for me to tolerate. But I shall be watching you when you come into view, so mind you try nothing reckless—like removing Cabot's carefully placed markers." He winked at her. "He does fuss."

When she exited the house five minutes later, she waved to her father behind his sitting room window, then set off along the marked path to the knoll.

She had thought to walk all the way, but the path did not advance directly—it dropped and turned, at one point apparently leading instead toward the river, such that the knoll seemed ever more distant. Meg wondered just how that illusion had been achieved. But given the number of workmen busy on the earthworks just then, and the noisy level of activity, she decided to leave further exploration to morning rides.

That her father should have consented to any alteration in his beloved home surprised her, but she had no doubt the impulse to consult Mr. Cabot had been Bertie's. With their father's injury, Bertie had assumed the practical supervision of Selbourne. Though other matters had never interested him greatly, the running of the estate and prospects for improvement had focused his most earnest attention. And Meg allowed that Bertie must do as he thought best for Selbourne, since it would eventually be entirely his responsibility.

Their neighbors had begun to seek Bertie's advice regarding the latest agricultural innovations. Meg supposed Cabot's transformations were but one more step in her brother's enthusiasm for the latest trends, but there was nothing merely fashionable about them. Indeed, Cabot's revisions enhanced what made Selbourne so special, adding perspective and, for her father, access. The result was ingenious. She had thought her kitchen garden an enterprise, yet Charles Cabot worked routinely, masterfully, on a grand scale.

She continued on her circuit of the house. Large areas had been leveled smooth and sodded. At the east side, masons worked on a foundation for the terrace. Around to the north, the courtyard between the wings looked unchanged, but Meg noticed variously painted stakes placed out on the lawn.

At last she turned into the lane between the garden wall and the stables. She crossed to the stalls to greet her favorites, particularly Arcturus and her own dear Paloma, and to tell the head groom that she would ride at dawn the next morning. Then she stopped in at the kitchen garden.

It looked untouched, which relieved her. But as she crossed to the south gate, she noticed a single stake planted near the teahouse. She was frowning as she reached the front court, where Cabot's men were again employed with the planting beds outside the windows of the drawing room.

She did not pause even to remove her bonnet before hurrying to compare her observations with Cabot's plans.

Her father came to join her.

"Trying to understand it, are you my dear?"

" 'Tis a great deal, father."

"Indeed, though he assures me he will not change fundamentals. We were spared much worry and expense on tedious items like drainage. I fear we've not been enough of a challenge for Mr. Cabot. No doubt he hoped to inspire us to building canals and cascades."

She smiled.

"You are certain—that he is reliable?"

"My dear Margaret, I can vouch for the man's honesty. What would be his motive in damaging our home? He is rumored to be capable of purchasing several Selbournes, should he wish it. I am not inclined to contest the details." He watched her as she concentrated on Cabot's sketches. "You do not mind, my dear, that Bertram furthers such changes—without your consultation?"

"I trust Bertie, father. He loves Selbourne more than any of us. And he appears to trust Mr. Cabot." She looked again to the plans. "Most of this seems plain enough, but the rest . . . Has he explained his painted stakes? I regret I am not an instant architect."

"Should you wish to be, Margaret?" She avoided her father's too discerning eye. "You must quiz him, daughter. Something about sight lines, if I recall. And some of them are for trees. Perhaps Lucy will remember—she is most attentive to Mr. Cabot," he smiled. "I hear her across the way with her confidante, Miss Burke. No doubt they will demand your company for tea. But I"—he was already signaling a footman—"have most pressing correspondence."

His hasty departure was no surprise, since Lucy was prone to chatter even more incessantly with her doting friend Amanda Burke. Indeed, Meg clearly heard Lucy's excited tones before they entered the room.

"Oh, Meg," Lucy said. "Mandy wanted to see Charles's drawings as well, so we're having a tea tray brought in here."

"How pleasant," Meg said, though she would have preferred the quiet. "Are you well, Miss Burke?"

Lucy's faithful shadow mumbled something before bobbing a curtsy.

"Don't be so shy, Mandy," Lucy admonished. " 'Tis just Meg. Look here, these are Charles's drawings, first his maps to show where everything will go, and here his pictures of how everything will look when he's finished— although I do not intend he shall ever be *finished* here!"

"Really, Lucy," Meg protested, with a glance at Amanda's pink cheeks.

Lucy tossed her head.

"Mandy knows how I feel about Charles."

"Let us hope *he*, at least, does not," Meg said. "Now come tell me what he means by these painted stakes."

For all her infatuation, Lucy had paid less attention to her chosen one's methods than Meg found instructive. And having the two younger girls in the room with her proved to be trying. As Lucy, holding her tea, moved to lean over Cabot's master plan, Meg could no longer restrain herself.

"Do be careful, Lucy! You will spill tea all over his work!"

"I shan't! And even if I did it would not matter. He has another tiny one he calls a 'thumbnail' that he carries about in his waistcoat pocket. He says it's his insurance."

"I can see that he needs it! Can you not imagine the hours of effort to reproduce this? You would not want Mr. Cabot to be compelled to repeat it."

"Oh, wouldn't I?" Lucy declared archly. But she and Amanda, mutely munching a biscuit, dutifully stepped back from the table. "I intend to keep Charles here forever," she said boldly.

"Do you?" Meg asked. "The gentleman might object.

And so might father and Bertie. You're much too forward, Lucy." The girls made Meg feel prim. And since just last night she had suffered a similar impulse with regard to Mr. Cabot, she also felt a hypocrite. She pointed to the sheet before her.

"Do tell me what this symbol means. 'Tis for a stake in the kitchen garden."

Her little nose held aloft, Lucy returned to the table.

"I don't recall that. In fact, I have not seen it before," she said airily. She glanced only briefly at the plan. "Everyone has been most insistent about preserving *your* kitchen garden. I am surprised he would dare."

With a sigh, Meg rolled the plans back up and stored them to the side of the table.

"It is frustrating," she said, "not to understand this code. Would Bertie know?"

Lucy shrugged.

"Charles has explained everything, and father and Bertie think it is all wonderful and tell him to get on with it. When he is here he goes out all day and comes in only to supper. I hardly see him. And when he's away, he's gone days at a time."

"It is his task, Lucy. 'Tis why he is here. And Selbourne does not command all his attention."

"That should have changed."

Meg had to smile.

"Because *you* did? I see."

"Oh, I thought you understood! About love."

Meg glanced at Amanda with embarrassment. But apparently young Miss Burke was privy to all irrepressible Lucy's secrets.

"I cannot claim your wisdom, Lucy," Meg said lightly. But she excused herself and went to share her own tea with Bertie and her father, who restored her to some equanimity.

The next morning she headed to the stables at dawn. A cool breeze blew off the river, setting the fresh new leaves of the beeches dancing. No crews were working at this hour. Riding astride in Selbourne's privacy, Meg raced Arcturus across the deer park.

They leapt the rill and carefully skirted the earthworks for the expanded ha-ha. At the first evidence of the path up to the knoll, Meg slowed the stallion and had him ascend at a walk. Instead of proceeding directly uphill, they traversed the slope in a series of wide turns, presumably intended to ease the climb for her father's chair. At the top, Meg noted a roughly square layout of flat stones.

She retraced the path down, then skirted the wooded base of the knoll to reach the enlarged lake. On its shores many trees had been planted, the banks reinforced, and the shrubbery thinned. Much had been accomplished in little more than a month. Despite the evidence of considerable activity, the ducks, coots, and other water birds still found the site congenial, waking noisily in the reeds and osiers at water's edge.

Meg urged Arcturus to a quicker pace. As they traced the edge of the woods bordering the north slope, she glanced into the dense growth of trees—and spotted a shadow moving parallel to her own.

At once sensing her tension, Arcturus shied and broke stride. Meg had to struggle to control him. As she did so she noticed that the other rider was moving toward her, with growing assurance.

She relied on Arcturus then, giving him his head, assured that very few horses off a track could hope to catch him. As they plunged ahead and cut diagonally away from the woods, her heart beat so wildly she could not be certain whether she heard hooves behind her. As they neared the stables she slowed and looked back. Nothing and no one followed. Yet she had been certain the rider had started to approach.

She was breathing quickly, though Arcturus hardly seemed exercised. Patting him on the neck she walked him a while in the lane beyond the stables, then turned him back to the groom. She said nothing to the lad about the other rider, but she determined to request the groom's company in future.

Chas rushed through his work with plantsmen in Fulham. He made fleeting calls at two properties where work neared completion. He accomplished in two days what he would normally have set out to do in twice the time, all so he could manage a lightning visit to town.

There he spent an impatient morning at his tailor's, then moved on to the boot maker's. He stopped for a shave before finding his cousin at his club.

"Didn't expect you in town just now, Chas, it being spring, with the plowin' and all." Myles Trent, the Marquis of Hayden, waved him to a seat. "And I'd heard you'd promised the best of the season to gouty old Clare. You need a new coat, by the way." His Resplendence, fastidious dresser, prosperous gambler, and acknowledged out-and-outer, felt it within his purview, indeed entirely his obligation, to comment on such matters.

"I have just seen to it. And yes, I'm promised to Clare, but for this summer. I may find myself delaying for a couple of months."

"Delaying? You?" Hayden's lazy blue eyes widened. "What the devil is wrong?"

"I need to ask a favor of you, Hayden."

"Now *that* is such a rare event I'm tempted to grant your request without inquirin'. But I s'pose I ought to see if it's in me power."

"I would be truly astounded if it were not. I should like to be assured of a welcome—at Almack's."

Hayden stared at him.

"For some chit, d'you mean?" he asked at last.

"No, for myself."

His cousin grinned.

"*Incroyable!* You! Dangling after some milk-and-water miss! And Almack's—I might as easily picture an oak in a hothouse!"

Chas had to smile.

"Shall they admit me, though?"

"Good heavens, Chas. Their little hearts will be aflutter. They'll have you trussed up and on the block the moment you're through the door! Why submit to it?"

"I'd like to help a friend. Some friends, rather. And it occurred to me that this is the way to set about it."

"Even more interesting! 'Tis quite an undertaking. Would I happen to know the beneficiaries?

"Possibly. Have I mentioned Bertram Lawrence to you? We were at university together."

"Bertram Lawrence . . . Now where have I heard that . . . ? Percy Laurens . . . Lawrence Howell . . ." As Hayden tilted his famously fair head to the side, Chas forced himself to relax. Why shouldn't Myles know the truth of it? His cousin knew him very well indeed. " 'Tis most familiar. 'Twill strike me later. And I will see that the ladies are alerted. You shall face no impediment—I guarantee it. Indeed, I'm like to be trampled, merely deliverin' notice. When are you planning this sortie?"

"Not for some weeks. Don't tax yourself. There is another matter, though. At Almack's, if my behavior is not quite—acceptable should you mind very much being barred from the place for a spell?

Hayden's grin widened.

"What are you contemplatin', Chas? I believe I must brave the place with you. Haven't pranced about there in years. Probably please ol' *Grand-mère*. Why not ask for her aid with this silliness, by the by? No doubt she has vouchers papering her walls."

"I . . . haven't been to see her this trip. I just arrived late last night, and must be off again early tomorrow."

"Not been to see *Grand-mère*?" Hayden's gaze assessed him. "Then you are hiding something, Chas. Must a' been afraid she'd wheedle it out of you—or box your ears. Last time I was by she spent five minutes abusin' me. Confound that tongue of hers! And she pinched my ear so hard it's smartin' yet." He rubbed his right ear. "Never thought the Frenchies were s'posed to be such prudes."

"I appreciate the sacrifice. If she's after you for your infractions perhaps she will let me be."

"All the same the next time you are in town you must see her. And I cannot lie to her—if she asks—about your visit today."

"I would not ask you to, *my lord.*" When Hayden smiled, Chas asked, "What do you hear from David?" Hayden's younger brother, Lord David, Major Trent, had served with Wellington on the Peninsula for five years.

"You've had the news from Paris, then?" Hayden's glance was sharp. "No doubt Wellington will stay while they discuss the peace. But David shall have a dilemma. He complains there's little to do if he comes home. He's not certain he'll sell up. Father wants him back—wants him to consider marryin' the neighbor—Caswell's chit. Remember the Caswells? Guess you aren't the only one with marriage on your mind."

"Don't start, Myles. 'Tis always those who jest who tumble furthest."

"You sound like *Grand-mère*, Chas. 'Tis the quaintly Continental in you, I s'pose. At least you don't shriek it in French. Do remember to invite me to the wedding." He was laughing as Chas left him.

Meg noticed the wagons, loaded with greenery, rolling up the front lane. She watched them long enough to be certain Cabot did not accompany them, then turned her disappointed attention to helping Lucy pack for town.

Her father had determined they would travel the end of the following week, a decision that set off a flurry of preparation. The intention to go to London might have been dropped out of the blue, so frantic and total were the efforts to speed them on their way. But Meg would preferably have stayed at Selbourne. She had no interest in the upcoming season. And there was that small possibility, scarcely admitted, that Cabot would return before the end of the month.

When she raced down to dinner after the second bell, she was startled to find him being seated at the table.

"Oh, Mr. Cabot," she breathed, moving to her father's right side. "I did not know you had returned."

"Just this evening, Miss Lawrence."

"You were with the wagons then?"

"They preceded me."

Her gaze wanted to devour him. Indeed, only a glance at Lucy, who was looking as Meg felt, recalled her to her senses.

"Where did you get this lot, Cabot?" Bertie asked.

"Some plantsmen in Fulham. I wanted some good-sized trees. There is one item I hope will interest Miss Lawrence."

Meg had to look at him, at his direct gaze and gleaming, candlelit hair. "I brought you a silverbell tree for your garden." He sounded pleased.

"Silverbell," Lucy repeated. "Doesn't that sound lovely, Meg?"

"I have not heard of such a tree, Mr. Cabot."

" 'Tis native to North America. Collinson has the *Halesia* only rarely. This is the sole specimen he will have this year—a charming little tree, Miss Lawrence, with unusual bell-like blossoms in early spring. 'Tis aptly named."

"Is that what the symbol on your master plan meant then, for the stake by the teahouse? That you planned a tree?"

"Should you desire it—yes."

"You think my . . . the garden needs something?"

"It needs nothing," he said, trapping her gaze. "It wants nothing. This is merely an ornament."

"I regret then, that I . . . do not want it."

Meg heard her father draw a sharp breath, but he stayed silent.

Cabot's lips moved as though he would smile.

"I assure you it will not grow much taller than the garden walls. And it would give your teahouse some welcome afternoon shade."

"I know you've considered every aspect, Mr. Cabot. But I do not feel another tree would suit the garden." She did not want his gift, which was what this was. She did not want a unique and thoughtfully appropriate gift from him. It was best that he know that now.

For a moment his gaze darkened. Then he smiled and shrugged.

"'Tis no matter. I shall find a spare little corner at Brookslea in which to tuck it away. 'Twill do nicely."

A spare little corner! He knew how to hurt her as well.

"Honestly, Meggie," Bertie protested, "balking at a little tree."

"Why must you be so mean?" Lucy asked. "It's not like you at all!"

Trust Lucy to betray her, Meg thought, catching Cabot's considering gaze. She had wanted him to believe there was nothing unusual in her response.

Her father was studying his dinner plate, with an amusement that Meg could not fathom.

"Would you like me to have the tree, father?" she asked.

"Not at all, my dear. You must do as you wish. Though I might ask what particular objection you have to an inoffensive twig."

"It is simply— It is not what I planned."

"I certainly understand, Sir Eustace," Cabot said. "One's plans can become inviolable."

Meg looked at Cabot with some impatience. How dare he defend her!

"Is that what the stakes on the north lawn mean then? That you plan to plant trees there as well?"

"No." For a moment he met her challenge with silence. "I shall be happy to show you what they mean."

She did not want him to show her anything. She wanted him to leave her in peace.

"Perhaps, Meg," her father said, "we can take a look at the plans again after supper—so that there will be no further surprises. After all, Mr. Cabot must be entrusted to decide for us while we are away. We cannot be reduced to planting and removing the same herbage repeatedly—even if such activity did line Mr. Cabot's pockets."

"Papa!" Lucy cried. But the men were laughing. And Meg felt a stranger to her own family.

She said little as the discussion moved to the arrangements for town. Cabot volunteered that he had just visited, and Meg looked at him in astonishment. To travel so much and accomplish so much in such a short time was extraordinary. He did not appear unduly tired, but perhaps the candlelight was kind.

He caught her gaze, and seemed to address his next question directly to her.

"Have there been any more uninvited guests?"

"Not a one," Sir Eustace said with satisfaction.

"No," Bertram agreed. "And I searched the north woods just yesterday."

Meg looked not at Cabot but at the tablecloth.

"There has been a rider in the north woods every morning," she said softly.

"What?" Her father reached to grab her left hand. "Why did you not tell me?"

"I did not want you to worry. I . . . have not acknowledged him. And I have taken the groom with me."

"Every morning, you say? How close then? How did you spot him?"

"The first morning I rode—I took Arcturus, on a circuit. I ran him along the edge of the woods and noticed movement in the trees, at some distance. But then the rider must have realized it was I, and not Mr. Cabot—on Arcturus. When he started toward me, I gave Arcturus his head and raced back to the stables."

"But what of the groom?" Bertie asked. "This rider ran at you even with Dobbs along?"

"He wasn't with me. Not that first morning."

Her father pressed her hand, hard.

"Margaret," he admonished. "You had assured me."

"I know. But it was so early. I stayed within view of the house, in the open."

"Father," Bertie said, "we'll have everyone out to comb the woods tomorrow morning. If this fellow thinks us complacent he's in for a shock."

Cabot had been observing her very closely, and very seriously.

"If you'll pardon me, Lawrence," he said. "Your visitor will simply wait until you tire of deploying an army, however many days that may take. Miss Lawrence has been wise to ignore him. Indeed, I fear I blundered in chasing him last week. I should have predicted he'd remove himself before our search. You might consider surprise now, instead. After attracting him with his objective."

"You mean let Meggie continue this risky business? As bait?"

"Not unguarded. Tomorrow morning, you or I should accompany your sister. Curiosity might draw him forward, whence he might be caught from the sides or behind. A couple of men sent well before dawn, to hide themselves and wait, might check him."

"We cannot be certain there is only one," Bertie said.

"It . . . it always looks like the same man," Meg said. "The same horse, the same dark clothes as the rider at the gate that first day."

"And no doubt he will be cautious if Dobbs is not along," Sir Eustace said. "How would you address that, Cabot?"

"Perhaps we shouldn't try. Perhaps I should simply escort Miss Lawrence tomorrow, and ride Arcturus. This spy has seen me before on the same horse, and I appear to interest him. If Miss Lawrence and I were to act as though unaware of his presence, he might be caught."

To act as though unaware of the spy's presence! When Cabot had proposed it, Meg had wondered how such calculated ease was to be achieved. But once out with him in the morning air she found that goal not at all difficult to attain. When riding with Charles Cabot, one thought entirely of Charles Cabot.

"Where would you like to lead us this morning, Miss Lawrence?" he asked as they left the stables. "Your father is watching us through a field-glass—a most effective monitor, if we stay in view."

She smiled.

"I suggest you show me some of your work sites—what you are calling the knoll, perhaps. And the lake."

He nodded, and they turned down the beech-lined avenue. The days were beginning to warm, most of the trees were full foliaged, and a scattering of early white and purple blossoms lit the green sward. Arcturus chomped at the bit, but he clearly knew his rider was a master.

"Arcturus likes you," she observed.

"I like Arcturus." Cabot smiled at her. "Your mare looks strong and speedy. She is Arabian?"

"She is." Meg reached to pat her neck. "Paloma is second only to Arcturus in speed, and she is actually quicker to turn and respond. Arcturus is difficult to stop."

"I haven't tried to."

Meg laughed.

"We shall see you then at supper, when he finally winds down." On a whim she touched her crop to Paloma's flanks, knowing the mare was eager for a run. She also knew they had the advantage—at least for a few seconds—and she urged the mare in a race toward the knoll. Meg felt the sting of the air and the wild delight of freedom—a joy she had once taken for granted. Arcturus soon pounded behind them, drawing even on the rising ground. She was pressed to hold the lead. But Arcturus did slow sooner in order to stop at the top, and Meg and Paloma nosed forward the last few feet to claim the promontory first.

"Cleverly raced, Miss Lawrence," Cabot said as he walked Arcturus at her side. "You know your horses."

"They are family, after all. 'Tis almost impossible not to learn their habits. I must grant you a handicap, though, and declare the match a tie." She was flushed from the run, breathless. She found it difficult to meet his intent gaze. Instead she turned to the site. "What do you intend to build here?"

"What would you like?" He asked sincerely, not flippantly, but Meg knew the incident with the silverbell tree was not far from his mind.

"I would truly like to know what you envision, Mr. Cabot, as you have taken such care to consider my father's situation in planning this."

"Well then, something to catch the eye here in the distance, at your highest point. I've a fondness for trees as subjects in themselves, but I've not yet determined."

"Perhaps a Grecian ruin, or an obelisk?" Meg suggested playfully.

"I shouldn't have thought that your preference. But by all means. A temple of reverie—if it appeals."

"Not at all. I was . . . teasing you, Mr. Cabot." She looked away as his gaze caught hers too warmly. He turned to explaining how the zigzagged course would ease her father's ascent up the steep slope; he had demonstrated a commendable sensitivity to her father's condition. Listening to him, Meg grasped that in working on a property, Cabot made it uniquely his own, that he found something of his own ground in the process—much as a farmer might claim sustenance from his acres.

"Whose is the property below here?" Cabot asked, indicating the fields and brick walls of the residence beyond the hedges toward the east.

"Oh that's Havingsham. Havingsham Hall belongs to Mr. Wembly, a good friend of my father's, and for many years master of the local hunt. 'Twas assumed my sister Louisa and the Wembly's son Walter would wed, but she chose Thomas Ferrell. Mr. Wembly was disappointed, and my father has not seen him since—not since just after his accident. The Wemblys leased out the Hall and moved to town. I've not met the current tenants. But Lucy and the youngest son, Harris Wembly, were once firm friends. I hope the rift will not last. The Wemblys are very good."

"They have no son for you though, Miss Lawrence?"

She looked at him sharply.

"Are you hoping to combine the properties for yet a larger park, Mr. Cabot?"

He laughed, so easily that she could not maintain her pique.

"That is a thought, Miss Lawrence. Though I admit I am not accustomed to planning on such a dynastic scale." He patted Arcturus's neck. "Come, let's to the lake before the horses cool." He urged the bay to an easy canter down a newly sloped trail through the trees. Meg followed reluctantly. She had thought she might have a civil conversation with him, but the man had an extraordinary ability to discompose her.

They startled a host of waterfowl as they broke from the trees at the side of the lake. Extensive labor had excavated and reshaped the north bank, lending the water a beguiling curve. The result was very visible from this side, and magical in its effect, which was to entice one's gaze in two directions. A new clump of willows on the restored bank appeared to have been in place for years.

They trotted the horses at the water's edge, while Cabot silently considered the house in the distance. Then he chose to canter again on the gradual rise to the north lawn. As they neared the back courtyard, he at last slowed Arcturus to a walk.

"Do you now see the meaning of these stakes, Miss Lawrence?"

She had been studying him as he rode, not contemplating the scenery. As she looked to the house, the stakes, and the lawn she had to shake her head.

Cabot dismounted abruptly and moved to her side.

"Come," he said, raising his arms to help her down. "Let me show you."

The request was so unexpected that she did not think to protest, merely let him grasp her waist and swing her from the saddle. But his touch, his nearness, acted upon her immediately. She could not breathe. As he looked down at her, Meg met his gaze. In that second his fingers released her waist and he stepped back.

"If you would, stand here and look directly toward the blue stake, and tell me what you see."

Meg did as he asked, her thoughts in a wild turmoil that had nothing to do with the north lawn, but as she looked she saw what he intended—a direct view to one of the oldest beeches on the property, a tree that amongst the family had earned iconic status.

Cabot grasped her shoulders lightly from behind, and neatly shifted her to stand looking along another blue stake—she would have turned somersaults if those warm hands had commanded them. This time the object was not quite so clear, but along the same line of sight stood a huge, gnarled oak, partially obscured by the company of lesser trees and in need of considerable pruning, but a magnificent giant indeed. New eyes had discovered in the oak as striking a tree as the beech.

Again the warm hands moved her, this time backwards. For one moment Meg thought Cabot meant to pull her against him. She closed her eyes in anticipation. But he released her shoulders.

"Now," he said, "look toward the red stake." His voice was rough, as though he had tired of instructing her.

She did as he directed, and saw at once the two grand trees, the lake, the knoll, and a corner of the house, in one sweeping panorama. For the first time, she noticed that the lake appeared set in a natural amphitheater.

"'Tis how I keep things in scale and balance, as though framing a picture. Do you see it?"

Meg nodded in silence. She had thought her home beautiful, but she had never viewed it in its entirety, not in just this fashion.

She wheeled to him.

"'Tis fascinating to think that—"

"Shhh." He grasped her gloved hand and raised it to his lips. "Do not look toward the woods, Miss Lawrence," he said softly. She did not need the warning; she could not have looked away from his lips on her hand. "Our visitor has come forward, and I believe your brother is about to pounce."

At a shout from the woods they turned. A rider was fleeing the trees, racing toward the lane skirting the stables, but Bertram was almost upon him, and two grooms were in a direct line to head him off. Cabot released Meg's hand and moved to Arcturus, but even as he raised the reins, the others had trapped their prey and pulled him from his horse.

"Enough of that! Bring him here." At her father's call, Meg spun around to face the north terrace. She glanced at her father, being wheeled outside, then looked to Cabot. She could feel the color mount to her cheeks. Apparently she alone had forgotten the morning's mission. They must think that she had played her part superbly.

Bertram and the two stable hands brought the stranger stumbling forward.

"Dobbs, run along next door and fetch the magistrate—fetch Jefferies." At the order from Sir Eustace the young groom at once set off at a gallop.

"Now let's look at you. Bertram, stop strangling the man."

Bertram released his hold on the man's neck scarf.

He was a rough-looking fellow, what little Meg could see of him beneath his cap and copious worn clothing. His thin cheeks were grizzled, his hands and nails grimy. But despite his lowered head and shaded face, Meg was conscious of those glittering, watchful eyes. She recognized that bold gaze.

"You'd best come inside, Miss Lawrence," Cabot said, reaching for her arm.

"No, I'd . . . I'd rather stay. He's the same man, father, who passed the coach the day I returned."

"What do you mean, sirrah, spying on my daughter?" Sir Eustace demanded.

The stranger stood silent.

"You've been trespassing."

Again he stood silent.

"I promise you none of what happens to you will seem worth what Sutcliffe pays you."

"Th'earl has naught to do with this."

"Hasn't he? Yet you know Sutcliffe is an earl?"

The man swallowed and set his jaw belligerently.

"Father," Bertie growled, "let me take him aside and knock some sense into him . . ."

"I've no doubt you have many creative inducements in mind, Bertram, but I, at least, must answer to the Bar. If the man chooses to remain mum, that is his right. He will still be charged, he will still be convicted, and he will still be imprisoned for a very, very long time. He is clever enough to know that if he gives us the information we seek, matters will go easier for him. Our magistrate is not persuaded by obstinacy."

Again the man swallowed.

"You've been here for a week, man. Are you staying in the village?" At that the intruder at last nodded. "Alone?"

"Aye," he said. "In the stables at the inn."

"Bertram, you'd best get on at once to Meakin at the inn. Make certain no one else is lurking about and most of all that no one departs without our knowledge. We don't want Sutcliffe to learn anything's amiss. He's apt to send rein-forcements. And have that big fellow Finch come from the stables to lend Nichols a hand."

Bertie helped Nichols secure their captive, then quickly mounted and raced away.

"Now Cabot," Sir Eustace said, turning back at last to face them. "I thank you for a good morning's work. I've no doubt Jefferies will deal with this fellow creditably. But I must ask one more favor of you—that you join my family for breakfast."

Cabot smiled as he bowed. Then he offered his arm to escort Meg into the house.

"Your father is enjoying this," he said to her.

"Yes." Meg was surprised to find she was trembling. "He likes to arrange things."

"The magistrate will no doubt help reveal the man's purpose," Cabot said, as though to reassure her.

"I know his purpose, Mr. Cabot." As she laid her gloves and hat on the table in the hall her fingers were still unsteady. "What I do not understand is Lord Sutcliffe's persistence. He has had years now . . . to forget. Yet he cannot let me live as I wish. Even here at my home. Quietly . . ."

"*Quietly?*" Cabot repeated the word, with such disbelief she was compelled to turn to him. "You cannot live *quietly*. Even if Sutcliffe had never existed you could not have lived quietly. The idea is preposterous." He eyed her impatiently, as though frustrated by her incomprehension. "Perhaps it's time, before your departure for town, that you realize just what you are. You were not put on this earth to live quietly, Miss Lawrence. You were created to cause havoc. You should heed those who recognize it, for there will always be a Sutcliffe." His words were uncompromising, strangely bitter, and struck Meg as entirely unwarranted. She would have welcomed his comfort. But his attack seemed a betrayal.

"You overstep, sir," she said coldly, holding his grim gaze. "What do you know of my situation, of my behavior? And what can you possibly know of Lord Sutcliffe? I'm obliged to heed my father, out of affection and duty, but I am not obliged to mind the presumptuous rants . . . of a *gardener.*"

"Margaret!" Her father's unexpected roar chased her up the stairs.

Chapter Four

Lucy had accused her of woolgathering. For three weeks—through the packing and removal to town, through the first mad days of settling in at Aunt Pru's town home, and through Lucy's ecstatic introduction to the modiste, the milliner, the theater, museums, musicales, dinners, parties and picnics—Meg's mind had indeed been almost entirely elsewhere. Even tonight, awaiting Lucy's debut at Almack's, Meg found herself sitting alone in her darkening room.

She had wanted to apologize. But at the last moment her courage had failed her. And she had not seen Cabot since.

Meg had watched him, surreptitiously, for much of the day following her outburst. She had watched him ride out early to the lake, with one of his wagons of greenery. She had watched him order the removal of the stakes in the north lawn. And she had watched him at last out in the sun with a crew of workmen, installing the path to the knoll. He had thrown himself into that labor as though he were one of the menials, as eager as they to finish a rough and tiring job. Indeed, he had removed his coat; Meg had even seen him wielding a shovel, with a strong and practiced economy and seeming resolution to flaunt his ability. Such disrespect for his standing was not proper. It was not done. He had known it was not done and had not cared. It was a deliberate reprimand. When he had walked back toward the stables, across the front courtyard, Meg had rushed to the hall, intending to call to him. But she had stood silent.

He had continued past the open door—and her. He who had always proved the gentleman had discarded his usual attentions; his boots and breeches were spotted with soil, his shirt clung damply to his chest, a simple broad-brimmed hat shaded his face. As she waited and watched him walk by, she might have thought he did not even see her. He had not looked toward the doorway. But at the last moment he had acknowledged her, by touching the brim of his hat. The pride in the gesture had been unmistakable. He had not, at the last, found it within his power to be quite as rude to her as she had been to him. He had passed on without her response.

Charles Cabot, gardener, had continued on as though he were master of Selbourne.

She might easily have summoned him, but guilt had restrained her, and now she had her silence as well to regret. She had, in effect, cut him. He had left the next morning for the southeast and Kent, and had not returned to Selbourne before their own departure for town.

Lucy burst into the room only to halt abruptly in the unexpected dimness.

"Why Meg, what are you doing here in the dark? We're leaving shortly. Are you ready? I wanted to ask you about my hair."

Meg rose from her seat and walked toward the hall.

"I am ready, Lucy pet, just gathering my courage."

"Your—oh, Meg, I hadn't thought! I suppose you think—you think Sutcliffe might be there?"

Meg shook her head. She had been tossing all Sutcliffe's gifts and flowers away.

"I shouldn't think he would. It was never his preferred venue. I imagine it even less so now. No, I was just remembering all those people. It is quite a crush. But you, my darling sister, shall stand out like a beacon. You look lovely, Lucy."

"My hair—do you think it will do?" Lucy spun around before Meg, her fresh white gown, trimmed in blue ribbon, floating about her, her blond curls caught up in an intricate arrangement of tiny white silk flower buds.

"You know it will. Peters has an expert's eye and hand with such arrangements."

"We will be late, Meg, if you don't come down with me now. Are you quite ready? Don't forget your dance card."

Meg would happily have forgotten it. She did not look forward to the ogling gazes and hot press of hands she would associate forever with Almack's. But for her sister's sake she would make efforts to enjoy it.

"The dress suits you very well," Lucy remarked as Meg moved into the hall. "I am glad I insisted you have it done up with this gorgeous emerald trim and sash. Just don't— please do not stand next to me all the evening."

"And why is that, you minx?"

"Because you are so very beautiful, Meg, that I should never have a chance."

Meg kissed Lucy on the cheek.

"No one will spend two seconds looking at an old spinster like your sister—and I'll wager you will be on the dance floor all the evening in any event. If you were any more popular than you are, Lucy, doorways and drawing rooms all over town would have to be widened to accommodate your followers."

Lucy laughed.

"I am having such fun! I pray that it will never end. I think Aunt Pru shall have to have me for years and years and years."

Which would rather defeat the purpose, Meg thought as they descended the stairs. Just because she herself had been so notoriously unsuccessful was no reason for Lucy to believe such solitude preferable to a happy match.

"Father would want you home," she said instead.

"And why should father want that?" Sir Eustace asked from the drawing room door. "Ah! Well you do both scrub up nicely, though if I am not mistaken, Lucy, you have a smudge of cocoa on your chin." As Lucy raised her fingers to remove the nonexistent smudge, Sir Eustace winked at Meg. "It's gone now, poppet. Must've been a trick of my eyes. You look a treat. The young men won't know what they are about."

"But Papa, I think I do want them to know what they are about!"

" 'Twas just a figure of speech, child."

Louisa and Ferrell came to the door of the drawing room to admire Lucy's dress. Bertie was just starting down the stairs with Aunt Pru, a process that required some patience, as she had grown rather plump and insisted on leaning on Bertie's arm much more heavily than on the banister.

Meg was watching the two of them fondly when her father drew her attention.

"Margaret, I would wish you to remember something tonight." He nodded toward the large portrait in the hall. Painted eight years earlier, it showed Louisa, Meg, and Lucy with their mother. Meg had always loved the portrait of her mother, but after her death, Sir Eustace had wanted the reminder away from Selbourne. Aunt Pru had claimed her sister's image for her town home. "You are still a young woman, only twenty. And to me you will always be younger." Again he looked to the portrait. "Do not be too eager to dismiss a youth you have hardly experienced. If you are not happy, my child, what has everything been for?"

She moved to place her hand on his shoulder, where he clasped it. He had noticed her mood; she had not explained to him her remorse over her treatment of Cabot. But tonight was a night for festivity. If nothing else, her father's comment reminded her to make more of an effort.

"I am happy, father. I am simply—nervous. I want everything to go well for Lucy."

"You know Joe Coachman will have three riders with the carriage. Nothing will occur."

"I know that. I am easy in my mind about that, father. You needn't fret."

"I do not fret, my girl."

"Yes, I know," she actually laughed. "You are usually too busy with your preparations to fret."

"Off with you, then," he grumbled. "I wish to have some

peace. Bertram, Ferrell—I expect a report regarding the ladies' conduct."

"Do not carry on so, Eustace," Aunt Pru chided him as they donned their wraps. She favored her late sister in spirit if not in looks. "Anyone would think you were in truth itching to accompany us."

"Of all the hare-brained notions," he muttered as they left the hall. "Such trouble for a glass of ratafia!"

It was a tight fit for the six of them in the carriage and an even tighter fit outside Almack's, where all the early arrivals appeared to have converged at once. Meg smothered her flutters as they passed through the initial greetings and perusals with the patronesses, thanking the two most directly responsible for their attendance, thanking all of them for their kindness and indulgence. Lucy's manner, Meg noted, was confident and engaging—she would pass with warm approvals. Meg's relief for her sister did not extend to her own ordeal.

"We have not seen you in London for some time, Miss Lawrence." Sally Jersey's gaze was boldly assessing. "Have you been abroad?"

"I have been in the country, milady."

"'Tis a long time to rusticate, Miss Lawrence. Much has changed here in town." She eyed Meg's gown as though it could not possibly be the latest fashion, which in fact it was. "I do hope you enjoy yourself. I believe Lord Sutcliffe attends tonight."

Meg stiffened. But she thanked her and moved on, thinking that some fixtures of town—waspish Lady Jersey, for example—had not changed one whit.

"She is odious," Louisa whispered. "And as much of a

gossip as ever. Do not mind her. She envies you rather too obviously, Meg. Ferrell believes she will spill state secrets and be banished to the Continent." As Meg smiled they made their way through the crush of people to the dancing hall.

Meg still remembered what was most attractive about Almack's: the cavernous, mirrored long hall, reflecting the light of a host of lanterns, and the exceptional music, pleasing even when the company was not. She felt again the impolite stares, heard the trail of whispers. The appraisals were almost a weight upon her. But she continued to smile.

They moved closer to the roped off area where Aunt Pru could find a seat. Louisa also took a seat, claiming, to Meg's surprise, that she did not feel in the least like dancing, but she turned with such energy and enthusiasm to speak with some of her acquaintance that Meg had to wonder at the decision.

"She thinks herself noble," Ferrell told her. "By freeing my time to circulate on business. But do not worry—I shall lure her on to the floor at some point. Now Meg, you must allow me to lead you out for the first two dances. And Lucy, you must permit me at least one following. Miss Burke," he acknowledged Lucy's friend, who had come up to them immediately, "would you be kind enough to grant me an early dance?"

Amanda Burke blushed, but nodded an assent.

Bertie claimed the very first dance with Lucy, even as a number of admirers in fancy coats and cravats presented themselves as potential partners. Lucy was busy scribbling names on to her dance card as one darkly handsome young man turned from her to Meg.

"Miss Meg—do you remember me? Harris Wembly." He bowed.

"Oh, Harry! Of course—how are you? How is your family?"

"We are all well. Here in town now these two years. Though I am usually up at Oxford. I am studying to take orders."

"That is excellent news, Harry. I am so glad to see you. It has been too long. You used to ride over often."

"Yes, Miss Meg. I have missed that as well. Though I have had some word through mother's correspondence with Miss Lucy."

Meg glanced over at her surprisingly secretive sister, who had never mentioned she had regular contact with Mrs. Wembly.

"I hope you have successfully obtained a dance or two with Lucy, Harry."

"I have indeed, Miss Meg, and I hope to be equally successful with you—if you would grant me that pleasure." Meg did so, just as the music started up.

Ferrell led her out for the first set. He was a fair dancer, careful and attentive, and thankfully never given to chatter. Meg, who loved music, considered that trait most agreeable. She had been to very few dances in the past three years, only occasional Buxley or Tenby assemblies, which were in the nature of community constitutionals. Though she had always enjoyed dancing she had feared she might forget the steps. But by the time she and her brother-in-law had completed two dances she felt relaxed and cheerful. She wondered if he and Louisa had intended as much.

Her limited surveys of the crowd had failed to reveal any sign of the Earl of Sutcliffe. Perhaps Sally Jersey had spoken purely from spite.

Bertie claimed her for the third dance.

"Little Lucy is thrilled beyond measure," he told her with some impatience. "'Tis impossible to make a peep of one's own! I hope she lets some of the chaps open their mouths now and then, or she will frighten them away. What a rattle!"

"She is excited, Bertie, and you are her brother. Naturally she will be easy talking to you."

"Perhaps. I see she's a bit more subdued with Ferrell, but not much. It's good to see Harry here. He'll keep her steady."

"Yes." Meg eyed the young man as he regarded Lucy. "Did you know Lucy and Mrs. Wembly were corresponding?"

"What?" Bertie shrugged. "Well those two were always matched in zeal. Stands to reason they'd stay close, even though Wembly and father fell out."

Meg wondered. Harry Wembly was a serious young man, and though he moved to stand up with Amanda Burke for the following dance, his gaze remained on Lucy.

"Lady Jersey told me Lord Sutcliffe might be here tonight, Bertie," Meg told him. "Though I haven't seen him."

"Sutcliffe can do naught here, Meggie. We've seen to that. He'll approach you at his peril." Bertie's lips set stubbornly.

"I shouldn't want a scene at Lucy's come-out."

"Won't be any scene, Meggie, as he'll simply be removed from the scene." Bertie gave her hand a squeeze. "Father insists you enjoy yourself."

"I will, Bertie. I am." She was silent for the rest of the dance, content to watch Lucy's smiles, her aunt's nodding pleasure, the shifting reflected light against the floor and the dancers. She stood out the next dance to speak to Louisa and Aunt Pru. Two young friends of Lucy's asked for dances; Meg wrote them on her card, suspecting Lucy had put them up to the invitation as a test of their devotion— for they seemed not the least inclined to remain in her company. Meg was not surprised. Though she had hoped she would no longer be considered worthy of remark, she caught enough averted glances to realize that Meg Lawrence was still infamous. She was certainly not being pressed by potential partners.

She was impatiently tapping her foot to the music when Louisa said,

"I see Mr. Cabot has come."

Instantly Meg's tapping stopped. She followed Louisa's gaze to the other side of the room, where Cabot had indeed made an appearance. His hair shone in the lights. He was dressed superbly, his shoulders hugged by a coat that could only have come from Weston. In the dark, formal clothing he looked devastatingly distinguished, and far removed from the laboring man she had last seen in his shirtsleeves. Meg's gaze locked on to him as he conversed with his companion, a man as tall as himself and with similar features, but thinner and fairer. All her thought and attention focused on Cabot, until she overheard the conversation beside her.

"Who is this Mr. Cabot?" her aunt asked.

"The architect that father and Bertie have had out at Selbourne. I'm certain Lucy has mentioned him."

"Oh, yes. Apparently much sought after. That's Hayden with him you know, Louisa."

"Yes, I see. I shouldn't have thought the marquis was a regular attendee here at Almack's."

"No indeed. Quite the contrary. Most unusual. He must be here because of your Mr. Cabot. They are friends?"

"Relatives, auntie. Cousins."

"Indeed? Cousin to the Marquis of Hayden, heir to the Duke of Braughton? That is very good *ton*."

Meg did not care for the gist of the talk. She waited impatiently for Cabot to look their way—she had seen him notice Lucy; he had smiled and bowed. When his attention at last found her, Meg met the force of it with as much steadiness as she could summon. So many yards across the hall she could not read his gaze, she knew only that it was hers. Even that tenuous a contact made her tremble. As Cabot briefly inclined his head to her, Harry Wembly blocked her view, claiming his country dance.

Meg reluctantly let him lead her out. They found an opening at the far end of the room. Meg had planned to quiz him further about his plans to join the clergy, but awareness of Cabot had robbed her of any other direction or purpose.

When Harry returned her to the circle of the Lawrences, Lucy was taking an enforced rest.

"You saw that Charles came, Meg?" she asked. "I thought he might."

"You thought he might! Why on earth should you think so?"

"Because I asked him. He told me he liked to dance, so I asked him. If he were to be in town of course. You knew he said he would try to attend my ball. But it's even better that he should be here tonight as well."

"Lucy, you shouldn't have. You do not ask a bachelor—a man who is a virtual stranger . . ."

"Don't be silly, Meg! It's just Charles."

Meg's attention again shifted to Cabot's spot across the way. A lovely redhead, older than any ingénue, was now conversing with him. The lady's gold and white gown, trimmed in the finest lace, boasted a scant bodice that was shockingly immodest.

Meg's face warmed as the woman placed a hand on Cabot's shoulder and pressed her generous bosom against his arm. Meg could tell the two had been close, in a manner that she could only imagine. That such intimacy could be so apparent somehow hurt her.

"Who is that . . . that *woman* clutching Charles?" Lucy asked.

"I do not know, Lucy," Meg said faintly. "You must ask our aunt."

"She is positively brazen! I wonder how he can bear it!"

"He does not appear to mind," Meg remarked, rallying as she realized that was indeed the case. Her agitated reaction was absurd, missish. Cabot was certainly free to choose his own company. He was older than Bertie, and had traveled the world; she should have expected as much.

"The Countess d'Avigne," Aunt Pru told them disapprovingly. "Formerly Vanessa Paxton. You will remember, Louisa. Her husband, the French Comte Thibault d'Avigne, took his own life."

"Oh, how awful!" Lucy said, sincerely shocked. And Meg's gaze returned pensively to the couple.

"You look well, countess," Chas said as she leaned into him.

"As well as 'La Lawrence'?" she asked archly. "Ah, do not be surprised, Chas. You see, I am well used to men's consideration. Of me . . . or of others."

Chas schooled his features. He was tempted to ask her why she would choose to give herself more pain. Instead he said affably, "There is no comparison."

Vanessa smiled and playfully tapped his arm with her fan.

"You are wasted on this insipid place, Chas."

Chas looked at her more closely. She had been several years older than he, but now he would have guessed considerably more. When, fresh out of university, he had first met her, Vanessa d'Avigne had been married a decade. She had chosen, early and avidly, to live freely. Though young and admiring, Chas had not chosen to join her. But he had thought of her again while living in Vienna, when he had heard of the count's suicide over gambling debts. How the countess had managed since he had not heard, but he had known her well enough to be certain that she would.

"Why are you here, Vanessa?" he asked softly.

"This is my stepdaughter's first season. I . . . superintend." She smiled, as though the thought were absurd. "You would be doing me a kindness, and no doubt thrill the child, were you to ask her to dance." She nodded toward a petite brunet standing in a cluster of similarly gowned debutantes. "Candace d'Avigne."

" 'Twill be a pleasure," Chas said, though he regretted the distraction from his own purpose. Again his gaze drifted unwillingly to Meg.

"You were always a good boy, Chas," Vanessa said, "and now it seems you have become a good man. So I must warn you to watch yourself. Lord Sutcliffe does not care for attentions to Meg Lawrence."

Chas looked out over the dancers.

"Then he must be a most unhappy man."

Vanessa laughed.

"I believe he must be. But you understand me. And now because you've promised to be kind to Candace I shall be kind to you. Who knows?" She gave a very Gallic shrug. "Perhaps such knowledge will be useful someday. I had it from a friend of d'Avigne many years ago, a friend who had reason to know." Again she pressed herself close. "Should it come to it, Chas, you must choose pistols. The Earl of Sutcliffe shoots high—by one or two inches. Though he may compensate, those two who have survived him avow it. Yes, I thought that might interest you." She shrugged once more. "Be careful, *mon brave*." She squeezed his arm hard before taking herself off to livelier entertainments.

Chas's attention again sought Meg as she moved to the dance floor with a dazzled mooncalf. The youngsters seemed to be the only ones approaching her. Perhaps they had not heard—or Sutcliffe did not concern himself with the minnows.

He indulged himself by letting his gaze rest on her as she danced—noting the lustrous dark curls against her forehead and nape, the cameo pure skin, the slight flush to her cheeks, her soft curves in the new gown . . .

"D'you mind telling me, Chas, why I'm dawdling here—a mere spectator?" Hayden had returned from his conversation with one of his friends. "If you've no intention of dancing I'd prefer to take myself off."

"A moment, Hayden. There is one more favor I would ask you." Chas' attention still followed Meg as she gracefully dipped and twirled on the other side of the room.

Hayden traced his interest.

"Oh *mon Dieu . . .*" He actually groaned. "You are a rogue! When you ask a favor of me . . ." His gaze fixed on Meg's dark head. "Why did I not recognize the name? Chas—you must listen. She is Sutcliffe's."

"She is not. The devil may stake a claim, but it needn't be honored."

"But *think,* Chas. Sutcliffe has killed others for less. Can you not . . . find someone else?"

Chas turned to look at him. Whatever Hayden read on his face must have convinced him that the possibility was remote.

"I shan't be able to have her for myself, Hayden. But I need to do this. Do you understand?"

Hayden shook his head. For a brief moment he examined Meg Lawrence through his quizzing glass. Then he asked wearily,

"What d'you want?"

"Go put our names on the Lawrences' dance cards. You, at least, shall lend them considerable countenance, Hayden. Assign me an early dance with Lucy, whilst you dance the same with Meg. Just choose whichever event you feel you can endure—no doubt she will appreciate one partner older than twelve. You might oblige me by dancing as well with Lucy later, if you can. But with Miss Lawrence . . . On Meg's card, be most particular to write yourself in a second time, for the waltz."

"Two dances with Meg Lawrence, and one the waltz! But you know I don't waltz, Chas. I can scarce abide the romp through a country dance."

"You won't waltz, Myles." Chas held his cousin's blue gaze.

"Ah! I see. Well." Hayden raised his chin. "Now we are for it." He did not dawdle. He walked around to the Lawrences, stopping only twice for acquaintances—which must have been a record in alacrity. Chas watched him pay his respects to the family, saw the plump aunt's eyes goggling and Lucy's mouth agape. They had probably never before seen quite as exquisite a creature as the Marquis of Hayden. Meg curtsied as Hayden asked for her card. As Chas sensed her gaze lift to his own he quickly looked elsewhere. He must remember to pay that little attention to Candace d'Avigne.

At the next pause in the dancing, Hayden returned to him.

"All is in hand, Chas. You have the dance after this with Miss Lucinda while I lead out Miss Lawrence. The waltz is the last dance in the next set. And you should know that Sutcliffe has just arrived with his hell-hound, Mulmgren."

Chas nodded and quickly crossed the floor to be presented to Candace d'Avigne. The girl was shocked at his request, but at a nudge from one of her companions assented at once to the next dance. Chas suspected he had demoted some earnest youngster.

As he led little Candace through the steps, his gaze

found Sutcliffe. The earl's manner commanded attention. Though he was only of an average height, he had all the arrogance and haughty demeanor of station—the disdainful set to his lips looked cruel. His dark hair had grayed at the temples, his sternly chiseled face was thin. His late wife's dowry had made him one of the richest men in England, but apparently he never had enough—if the hungry manner in which he stared at Meg Lawrence were any measure.

Chas almost missed a step with Miss d'Avigne, so focused was he on the Earl of Sutcliffe. The poor girl blushed, and Chas forced himself to attend. He chatted amiably in French, to put her at ease, and was most complimentary as he took his leave. Before the next dance he waited just long enough to watch Hayden lead Meg to the floor, noticing that they made a striking pair—Hayden so blond and Meg so . . .

"Charles," Lucy hissed, moving to his side, "do hurry or we shall miss the set!"

Chas drew her quickly into the dancing. That he should have permitted her to manage him spoke volumes about his distraction.

"You look tolerably well, Miss Lucy. I note you are the belle of the ball."

"It is so much fun!" She laughed. "I have been seeing everything you told me to see, and more besides! And we have been here scarcely two weeks! You should come to visit us at Aunt Pru's. You will have to present yourself to her, you know; you should have before. She will forgive you, though. She is in alt over your cousin. Isn't he just magnificent? Why, the sapphire in his cravat alone must be worth a fortune! And isn't he brave—to dance with Meg? I shan't know what to say to him." For a second, little Lucy worried her lower lip. Chas suspected he had been supplanted in her affections.

"You shall be most compatible, Miss Lucy, for Hayden loves attention, and you seem happily willing to give it."

"He's getting attention now, but not the sort he probably wants." Chas looked toward his cousin, only to find himself watching Meg yet again. Just at the edge of the set, Sutcliffe stood seething. His bold look was possessive.

"That hateful man," Lucy complained. "Brother Ferrell says he believes in senior—no, *seigniory*," she said loftily.

Chas stifled a laugh.

"No doubt. I would not relay that outside the family, though, Miss Lucy. You would not wish Mr. Ferrell to face political troubles."

"Oh no!" she said. "But the earl is beastly, isn't he? Why must he ruin everything?"

"You must not permit him to ruin anything, Miss Lucy. You must enjoy yourself. The Sutcliffes of this world always come to a bad end."

"Do they, Charles?" she asked hopefully, her wide blue eyes raised to his. "That's rather a nice thought."

He kissed her hand in the midst of the step, which threw her into confusion, and thankfully kept her quiet.

Chas returned her to her brother and quickly took his leave before Meg and Hayden returned. He wended his way amongst the bystanders so that he might observe Sutcliffe. As Hayden led speechless Lucy onto the floor, Sutcliffe approached Meg.

Bertram and Ferrell moved to either side of her, as though suspecting the earl would contemplate stealing their sister in view of Almack's attendees. Seeing her so promptly protected gratified Chas. Indeed, he wondered why he should trouble to involve himself. But he knew the answer to that particular puzzle—as little happiness as it brought him.

Sutcliffe bowed low. He clearly requested a dance from Meg, which she as clearly refused. Chas watched the man's face redden, his fingers clenching before he snatched the dance card from Meg's hand. He perused it as Bertram protested. Sutcliffe handed it back and turned to pin Hayden with his glittering gaze. The satisfied twist to his thin lips made Chas wish to strike him right there. But it was enough to observe how little mastery Sutcliffe had over his passions. That flaw, Chas imagined coldly, would always prove to the earl's disadvantage.

Sutcliffe strode angrily away to join his slight and sullen friend, whom Chas assumed to be the Baron Mulmgren.

Chas suspected Meg Lawrence could hardly enjoy the evening, with such a war going on about her. Indeed, assurance of her unhappiness, of her *de facto* imprisonment, was much of what had impelled him to this present course.

Hayden found him during the next dance.

"I am taking myself off to the refreshment room, Chas. Sutcliffe and Mulmgren cannot follow me without deserting Miss Lawrence. You may find me there later—if Sutcliffe leaves you ambulatory." He raised his glass to one eye and lazily surveyed the room. "I do not know whether I have done you a favor or not, cousin."

"You have. I am eternally grateful."

"I might wish that promised to be longer." But Hayden smiled at him. "By the by she is a diamond."

"I only wish she were hard as one. She has been hurt, and she will be again."

Hayden nodded and departed. Chas looked for Sutcliffe and failed to spot him. The earl would not leave before the waltz, that was a certainty, though he was no doubt pleased by Hayden's absence from the hall.

Chas danced again, with Lucy's young friend Amanda Burke and once more with Candace d'Avigne, ascertaining before both dances that Meg was already partnered. During the break he removed himself from the Lawrences' view. When the next set began he spent his time in conversation with some of his grandmother's acquaintance, well aware that she was bound to hear all in any event. Noting that Sutcliffe was nowhere to be seen, Chas wondered if Hayden had been pursued to the other room. But it was too late to check—the orchestra was tuning up for the waltz. Chas strode over to Meg and bowed low. In her presence he wished almost to kneel.

"I believe this dance is mine, Miss Lawrence."

"Your cousin . . . Lord Hayden . . ."

"Lord Hayden regrets that he's been detained. Would you do me the honor?"

"I . . . yes, of course."

The music had started. It was one of his favorites. With a brief nod to Bertram, Chas swung Meg onto the dance floor.

Chapter Five

For some time he did not look at her, merely led her effortlessly through turn after turn, in a smooth and rhythmic spell. But as his gaze at last settled on her face Meg knew she had to speak.

"I know 'tis you I must thank. Your cousin . . . so attentive to Lucy . . ."

"Hayden chooses his own partners," he said softly. "As do I."

Meg had to glance away.

"Where did you learn to waltz?"

"In Vienna, Miss Lawrence. I told you I have Austrian relatives."

"You must have waltzed every day?"

"Morning, noon, and night."

She turned again to his quick smile.

"Sir—I owe you an apology." Just then he spun her about, robbing her of breath.

"For what, Miss Lawrence?"

"For . . . calling you . . ."

"A gardener. Which is what I am. You needn't apologize. Though I might wish you had shown the profession a bit more respect." Despite the dismissal, something of anger lingered; his hold on her waist tightened. But as Meg continued to gaze silently up at him that temper seemed to fade. Their gazes locked as surely as their hands and arms.

Again she yielded to the spell of the dance. It was best that it should be the longest waltz ever played—the waltz without end. She knew she should speak, that they should both be speaking, but she was as loathe to break the silence as his touch.

A smile lit his eyes.

"What are you . . . pondering, sir?" she asked warily.

"Trees." Again they whirled about.

"I doubt many women have been so complimented," she said at last.

"Only one, Miss Lawrence. Your eyes are unique. I cannot decide if they are green as fresh leaves, or blue as the deepest ocean. But yes—I think of trees."

Meg knew she was blushing. The arm circling her waist again tightened, but this time not in anger.

"You are holding me too close, Mr. Cabot." But he did not loosen his grasp.

"I would ask you to attempt a smile, Miss Lawrence. Just for a few seconds here, as we come into this turn. 'Twould do my reputation a world of good—amongst Miss Lucy and her friends."

The thought that he should need any help in that sphere was laughable. She could not help but smile. Cabot wheeled her around once again. As the music ended he loosed his arm from her waist and bowed very low—right under the Earl of Sutcliffe's nose.

Meg froze. To move from such joy to such fear in an instant was more than she could manage. She watched numbly as Cabot stood erect and started to take his leave.

"One moment, sir," Sutcliffe hissed. "I would speak with you." He would have forced an introduction. But Cabot, who was a few inches taller, merely looked past the fuming earl and departed into the crowd.

Meg had not realized Cabot had left her so close to her family. Bertie was at her side at once, just as Sutcliffe's jealousy flared.

"Such a display has never before been admitted in this hall, Miss Lawrence," he bit out. "I imagine that even now your privileges are being revoked."

"So let them be," Bertie said. "M'sister has done nothing wrong, Sutcliffe. And you have no right to speak to her so."

Meg laid a hand on Bertie's arm. She feared her brother would provoke more than he anticipated.

"Let us leave here, Bertie," she said softly. "We need not answer to Lord Sutcliffe."

"Need not, miss?" Sutcliffe repeated, his gaze trapping hers. "The time will come when you will wish to."

She followed Cabot's example and turned her back on him, compelling Bertie to follow suit. Had Cabot known how it would be? Why then, had he deserted her to face Sutcliffe alone? She felt that the extraordinary pleasure and freedom of the waltz had been stolen from her, like so much else.

Even as her family rose to leave, Meg was conscious of

the whispers around them. She kept her chin high and clung to Louisa's warm hand. To her credit, Lucy did not look dejected or disappointed, but left the hall as proud as any other debutante who had 'taken.' Once that achievement had been acknowledged it could not be withdrawn.

Louisa squeezed Meg's hand.

"Ferrell believes he intends to elicit a challenge," she whispered as they donned their wraps.

"Who?" Meg asked, her voice strained and equally low. "Sutcliffe?"

"Mr. Cabot."

The thought shocked her. Meg had great respect for her brother-in-law, but she hoped in this instance that Ferrell was wrong.

They made their way together outside. As Aunt Pru passed Meg to step up into the carriage she looked closely into her face.

"Are you quite all right, Margaret?" she asked. " 'Twas a spirited waltz."

"I am fine, Auntie," she assured her, following her into the carriage. Meg imagined she must look pale as death. It occurred to her to wonder what possible remedy Pru might have suggested had she not claimed to be fine.

Louisa squeezed in next to Meg facing forward, then Bertie, Lucy and Ferrell sat opposite. There seemed to be even less room in the carriage for this return trip—or else Meg was too conscious of the concerned attention of her family. Expectancy kept them silent. But they did not disapprove. Quite the contrary. They all appeared to be trying very hard to stifle smiles. For a while they heard only the horses' hooves and sounds of the street.

Lucy, sitting directly across from her, finally burst out, "Oh, Meg! To see you! It was so—so glorious!"

The others seemed to expel a collective sigh. Ferrell smiled out the window as Louisa again pressed her hand.

"Lucy is right," she said. "You deserved that, Meg. Almack's has never seen its like."

"And probably never will again," Aunt Pru observed sagely. The prospect of surrendering their privileges did not appear to trouble her, because she laughed. "The Countess Lieven and Princess Esterhazy were positively green. They have never danced as well."

"Do you think . . . do you think father will . . ."

"Father will wish he had been there, Meggie," Bertie assured her, "to laugh in Sutcliffe's face."

Meg was less confident of her father's good humor. Sir Eustace was keenly aware of the very real danger of taunting Sutcliffe. She thought her father might share some of her fears for Bertie—and for Cabot.

"Will this gentleman be paying his addresses to you, Margaret?" Aunt Pru asked.

In the light from passing lanterns Meg stared at her in dismay.

"Oh no, nothing like that," she said at last. "He . . . simply enjoys the waltz. He told me he learned in Vienna."

Ferrell again turned to smile out the window as Lucy frowned at her.

"Well, I should think that after something like that you might have to be, to be at least *promised*, or . . . or . . ."

"Lucy," Louisa interrupted, "you spent considerable time with young Harry Wembly this evening."

Lucy tilted her little nose.

"Why shouldn't I speak with him, since he was kind enough to come? He is our neighbor—and a friend."

"Kind enough to come!" Aunt Pru exclaimed. "Did you invite him, young lady?"

"Why, yes. And Charles too, for that matter. Though they'd have had to obtain their own vouchers of course . . ."

"Lucinda," Aunt Pru sniffed. "It is not done."

Silence again descended in the carriage. Lucy glared accusingly at Louisa's corner, but Meg could only be grateful for the respite.

Sir Eustace wished to see them immediately upon their return home.

"So, my children—did Lucinda Lawrence take the place by storm?"

"She did indeed, father," Louisa said.

"Lucy did very well," Aunt Pru supplied. "Though she must work on her deportment."

"Oh, Papa," Lucy knelt before his chair. "You would have been most impressed! With all the lights, and the ladies and gentlemen all beautifully dressed. The music was exquisite—would you not say so, Meg? And I danced every dance but two, because Aunt Pru insisted I must rest, and one was a waltz, but Meg will tell you about that. Harry and Charles came just as I asked and I danced with them and with ever so many other gentlemen and—and several peers, too, including the Marquis of Hayden. Oh, he is just top of the trees, father! He's Charles's cousin and he wore a sapphire as large as . . . as large as an egg! I would have had more dances only Lord Sutcliffe made such a fuss after Meg and Charles waltzed . . ."

"They waltzed, did they?" Sir Eustace asked, looking to

Meg's spot by the piano. "Did you enjoy the waltz, Margaret?"

"It was most pleasant, father."

"He did not stomp on your pretty toes, then?"

"No, father."

"It was a very graceful exercise, Eustace," Aunt Pru inserted. "And the two of them were enchanting to watch. But I fear there may be repercussions."

"From Lord Sutcliffe?" Sir Eustace asked quickly.

"From Almack's patronesses."

"Bah! What do we care for that?"

"I rather think you might care, Eustace, with two daughters not yet wed. This Mr. Cabot did not present himself to me."

"He is known to us, Auntie," Louisa said.

"'Twould rather have spoiled the enterprise, Lady Billings," Ferrell added.

"What enterprise, Thomas?" Sir Eustace asked sharply. But Ferrell merely grinned.

"I don't care whether he is Braughton's nephew. Mr. Cabot was most abrupt," Aunt Pru said.

"A little abruptness now and then suits a young man, Prudence."

"I really don't see what was so abrupt about 'im . . ." Bertram protested, only to be shushed by his aunt.

"His cousin Lord Hayden, on the other hand, was impeccable," she continued.

"Impeccable or no, 'tis not his *lordship* I'm trusting to revise my scenery," Sir Eustace growled. "Leave this be, Prudence. I shall request that Mr. Cabot bend a knee to

Lady Billings when next he is in town. Is that acceptable?"
Even as Aunt Pru smiled, Sir Eustace added, "But I warn
you—he is very busy. He's been twice at Selbourne in the
past two weeks. I've had it from my steward. I do not ask a
hardworking man who is doing as he ought to come running to town to pay homage to you . . ."

"He had time enough for a waltz," Aunt Pru said under
her breath, but Sir Eustace ignored her.

"And you should know as well, that he has promised his
efforts to the Duke of Clare this summer. I think you would
have to cede that Clare is impeccable *ton*. Polished enough
even for you, Pru! I'll not have you troubling this young
man."

"Father," Meg said, "perhaps it would be best if Mr.
Cabot were to avoid town for a while. Lord Sutcliffe was
most unpleasant. There is no need to revive this business."
She sent a pleading glance at Louisa and Ferrell.

"My daughter must be allowed to dance without Lord
Sutcliffe's say-so."

Meg rubbed one palm against the piano's smooth ebony
finish. All at once she felt exhausted. The waltz played repeatedly in her head. And given her father's pride and her
aunt's persistence another confrontation with Sutcliffe
seemed inevitable.

"We must be going, father," Louisa said, observing her.
"Meg and Lucy must be tired."

"Of course, m'dear. We will talk more tomorrow."

"And there will be callers tomorrow," Aunt Pru noted
with satisfaction. "And we must also complete our plans
for Lucy's ball."

"Can we not attack one item at a time, Prudence?" Sir Eustace asked with irritation. "I swear you wish everything to happen yesterday!"

Aunt Pru chuckled as she led the way out of the drawing room. Louisa kissed Meg's cheek, whispering "courage" into one ear before departing. As Meg moved slowly upstairs to her room, Lucy confidingly linked one arm through hers.

"I am so pleased, Meg. I could not have asked for more. Lord Hayden dancing with us! I shall never forget it. And Charles was simply splendid, don't you think so? He looked so very fine. Almost—almost too fine for us. Lord Hayden told me Charles will be an heir to . . . to . . . oh, some place in Austria. A lake I think—when some old grand uncle dies. Not that I would wish his uncle to die, of course . . ."

"Lucy, I truly am fatigued."

"Oh yes, Meg, I won't keep you, only I wanted to say that I . . . that you and Charles . . . that the waltz was . . . Oh! That you must have Charles if you wish." And with a quick kiss Lucy darted off to her room.

"Well," Hayden said pleasantly the next morning. "The betting is running four to one that Sutcliffe will kill you."

Chas continued to tie his cravat as he viewed Hayden's reflection in the mirror.

"You are the gambling man, Hayden. You must place your blunt where you will."

"Oh, I have," his cousin said, dropping his quizzing glass to fuss with the faultless fall of linen at his own throat. "Why they all focus on you I cannot fathom, since I danced with Meg Lawrence as well. Although, in all fairness, we probably made a less spectacular showing . . ."

"This is one attention you needn't envy, cousin," Chas said. "Unless you find the odds more promising than I do?"

Hayden smiled.

"Who taught you to dance so anyway?" he asked. "Not that stuffy old dancing master you used to moan about. Hasefuss. No, Heizfast . . ."

"Herr Fass," Chas corrected, yanking his cravat free to begin anew. "No, not Herr Fass. But his *daughter* . . ."

Hayden laughed.

"Chas, I shall miss you." He realized what that implied. "Only for the nonce, of course. You are certain you must be off to Kent today?"

"I must see Clare. I'm thinking I might need his help in some way."

Hayden's eyebrows rose.

"Surely me pater . . . Braughton . . ."

"No, I cannot ask him. I owe Clare my time. If I start what I can, perhaps he will more equably bear with a delay. And if I am not long for this world," he turned from the mirror, "at least I shall leave the plans for Abbey Clare as a legacy."

"Most men might leave offspring as a legacy," Hayden suggested mildly.

"I fear that is beyond my present capability."

Hayden laughed again.

"Only if one has your preference, of course—for sowing cedars instead of wild oats."

Chas smiled.

"You are planning to call on the ladies today?"

"Of course. I don't need instruction in manners, Chas, though you appear to. You don't wish to make your intentions clear to Sutcliffe by accompanying me?"

"I made my intentions very clear last night. The gentlemen at White's seem to have understood."

"And Miss Lawrence—does she understand?"

Chas shrugged.

"It does not signify," he said, though he was conscious of an uncomfortable pressure in his chest.

Hayden eyed him.

"There is some speculation I have an interest in the youngster—Miss Lucinda," he drawled. "The attention cannot hurt the chit. She's a spirited little thing. It might be some sport to elevate her prospects. Though I believe she already has a *tendre* for the Oxford boy—same year as Clare's brat, by the by—that studious Mr. Wembly."

"*Lucy?*" Chas asked incredulously.

"Yes. She had that funny little way of dismissin' him and invitin' him at the same time. I tell you I know these females, Chas. Usually on to 'em within a few minutes at most. Little Lucinda Lawrence I can understand. Not at all like your Meg—with those big eyes all sincere and soulful. I tell you, it's not to be borne. Better to have as much deception on a woman's part as a man's. Otherwise there's no fun in the game." He spoke with unusual heat.

"If I did not know you very well, Myles, I might think you protest too much."

Hayden waved a languid hand.

"Merely observin', Chas."

"All the same—should you win your bet—Meg Lawrence might do worse than the Marquis of Hayden."

For a moment their glances held.

"Come to think of it," Hayden said, "you've that same look in your eyes, Chas. It asks too much of a chap, I tell you. You two are better off gazin' at each other than anyone else. 'Twould solve the problem." He rose from his seat. "I might wish to know your plans with regard to Sutcliffe. Not that I intend to do anything about 'em, mind."

"I shall let him stew. Time is to my advantage."

"You've no fears for the girl?"

"Yes." Chas drew a breath. "Yes, but there's nothing else to be done. Her father and brother have looked after her until now. They must do so a while longer."

"The stakes have been raised. Sutcliffe may press."

"I shall be away a week at most. Do not let him know where I am. 'Twill keep him off balance. When I return I shall tweak his nose a bit more. Sutcliffe has no discipline—at least as regards Meg Lawrence. Eventually he will pop."

"Guard your back in the meantime, Chas, for that serpent Sutcliffe may not pop just when and where you wish. And there is Mulmgren."

"Point taken, cousin. And now I must stop off briefly to see *Grand-mère* on my way. She will have heard of this . . ."

"Ah, Chas!" Hayden shook his head. "Now I *know* you are braver than I!"

Meg and Lucy were at home to callers later that day. A host of young men came by to pay their respects, to sample the offerings of Aunt Pru's chef, and in general to strut, preen, and talk a great deal of nonsense.

Meg had suffered it for more than an hour and was about to surrender her seat to yet another caller when Thwaite the butler announced the Marquis of Hayden, accompanied by the Viscounts Demarest and Knowles and the Honorable Mr. George Gillen.

The marquis, adorned most elegantly, strolled in, to the stupefied amazement of the drawing room's occupants. He acknowledged first Aunt Pru, then Meg, then Lucy, and proceeded to repose himself on the settee by the front window. The several lesser luminaries who had followed him in then began conversing in an acceptably lively and courteous manner, which Meg was gratified to note pleased her sister and aunt immensely. The other young men present knew Lucinda had been singularly honored.

Meg contented herself with as little conversation as she felt she could spare. Lord Hayden's visit was proper and welcome, but most unexpected all the same. Knowing that the man had played an essential role in the previous night's ruse made Meg both curious and anxious. She wondered if it were true that Cabot wished to provoke Sutcliffe in some manner—even to the extreme of a duel.

Though the marquis sat quite a distance away from her, Meg was aware that his gaze was often fixed upon her. He was Cabot's cousin. Was he his confidant? And where was Cabot?

The marquis's interest turned again, as it had several times before, to the street outside, where a fine afternoon drizzle had just begun. Meg looked for similarities with his cousin. Apart from sharing height and an attractive self-confidence, their features were also much akin. The nose, certainly—and perhaps something in the forehead and line of the jaw. At last conscious that she searched for a resemblance because she missed the original, Meg pointedly applied herself to the chatter of the visitors seated nearest her. Lord Hayden rarely spoke, and then only to utter a *bon mot* worthy of laughter. Meg thought him rather an extraordinary personage.

When Aunt Pru signaled that the session was at an end by rising and moving to the door, Meg and Lucy went to her side to accept their callers' farewells.

Hayden and Lord Knowles were the last to rouse themselves for departure. Lord Hayden flattered Lucy and then Aunt Pru with his compliments on their company and their household, watched them curtsy and turn toward Knowles, then looked to Meg.

"Mr. Wembly is a fine young man," he said softly.

"Harry Wembly?" Meg asked, startled because Harry had not been among their guests that afternoon. "Yes . . . Yes he is."

"I understand he means to take orders."

"That is what he has told me, milord."

With a considering glance at Lucy, in animated conversation with the garrulous Knowles, the marquis said, "That would be most suitable."

Meg stayed silent as Hayden's gaze returned to hers. "M'cousin regrets he could not attend this afternoon. He hopes he did not offend last night?"

"No. No of course not." Meg managed somehow to hold his discerning blue gaze. But she asked low and urgently, "Where is he?"

"Kent," he said. "He has gone to Clare. He will be back," he smiled, "shortly."

Meg gently shook her head.

"You must . . . keep him away."

For an instant the blue gaze was even sharper. Then he smiled broadly.

"I regret, Miss Lawrence, it cannot be done."

With a very low bow he took his leave, trailed by the still voluble Knowles. As the two reached the front door, Bertie, damp from the afternoon's rain, bounded in at the doorstep.

"Ah, my Lord Hayden, Lord Knowles. How d'you do?"

"I wonder, Lawrence, if you would stop outside here with me a moment?" Hayden asked as he donned his cloak and hat.

Bertie looked surprised but quickly assented, and the men stepped out into the rain. Mystified, Meg remained in the hall after her aunt and Lucy retired. Two minutes later her brother returned, shaking himself like a wet puppy. As he yielded his cloak to Thwaite and said something low he noticed Meg lingering at the drawing room door.

"Allo, Meggie!" he said, rather too cheerfully.

"Bertie—what did the marquis want?"

Bertie glanced at the floor, straightened his cuffs, and cleared his throat.

"Just . . . a small matter . . ." His gaze shot to her face and steady regard. "Dash it all, Meggie! You're not 'sposed to know!"

"If it concerns me, Bertie, don't you think I *should* know?"

"I hate it when you sound like father!" he objected. "'Tisn't . . . 'tisn't natural, Meg." But he told her, "Sutcliffe's men have been following him all day. They've been watchin' the house from across the street. Lord Hayden saw them arrive just after he did."

"Why would Sutcliffe hound the marquis? He cannot

hope to intimidate every person in London who dares speak with me . . ."

"Lord Hayden was followed from Cabot's, Meg."

Abruptly she sat down on a hall chair.

"Bertie . . . Bertie, I must not be hemmed in so. I have not set foot outside this house for two weeks now without Annie and Aunt Pru and Lucy and Louisa and half a dozen grooms! One more packed evening party or tedious reading and I vow I shall embarrass all of you. At least in Wales— at least with Aunt Bitty, Sutcliffe did not know where I was. But here! There might as well be bars around this house. And for him to pursue our acquaintance! I shall go mad. Bertie, you must help me . . ."

She had not been aware of wringing her hands until Bertie clasped them.

"Calm yourself, Meggie. Father and I have seen to it. We've had Paloma and my Sam brought to town. They're quartered over at Ferrell's near the park. We'll go riding first thing tomorrow morning. Father says as long as we vary the time and the place we need take only one groom. 'Tis little enough, I know, but 'tis something. Father says no one can catch you on Paloma anyway."

Cabot on Arcturus can, Meg almost advised him. But she kept that knowledge to herself, and welcomed the prospect of escape.

Daily rides restored her to some passing contentment. Several times she and Bertie left before dawn from the back of the house, only returning when screened by trades-mens' or grocers' deliveries later in the morning. Defeating

Sutcliffe's cordon lent Meg a heady sense of satisfaction. Only the absence of Charles Cabot spoiled her happiness, but she could not very well bemoan what she had determined was her preference.

She and Lucy joined Louisa each day to pose for Monsieur LeBecque, who was painting their portrait for their father. Aunt Pru had thought it time to reprise the family grouping she displayed in her hall, and the three girls had agreed enthusiastically. Sir Eustace would be surprised and pleased; the painting was also a charming way to commemorate Lucy's season. So most mornings Meg and Lucy departed for almost two hours, telling their father they were exploring London, which in some manner they were—if only by driving past a number of landmarks in transit.

"We shall make certain you see everything properly later, Lucy," Louisa told her. "There is plenty of time." And Lucy, still enraptured with the city's many offerings, had not objected.

This morning, though, Monsieur LeBecque had claimed he had other tasks to which to attend; they would see on the morrow, he boasted, how very well the portrait progressed. Though Aunt Pru and Lucy had rushed eagerly to an additional fitting at the dressmaker's, Meg had stayed behind. A family outing to Vauxhall was planned for that evening, so she was just as glad to rest undisturbed at home.

Vauxhall would unfortunately be associated forever in her memory with her own painfully curtailed season three years before. But her father had planned the evening's entertainment himself, and Meg reasoned that if Sir Eustace could tolerate it for Lucy's sake, then she could as well. Nothing untoward would occur, for she would remain close to her family. Vauxhall gardens, after all, had never been the problem; the problem had been two deceitful, envious girls—and Lord Sutcliffe.

Meg opened the piano in the drawing room and started to play. She had played often on her Aunt Bitty's upright in Tenby. Her Aunt Pru, though not a pianist herself, had a finer instrument—one of the newest and grandest pianofortes. Anticipating that, Meg had brought her music with her, but she reminded herself to visit Hatchard's for more. She would look for one piece in particular.

She slowly picked out the tune of the waltz she had danced with Cabot the previous week. One lilting section in a minor key had remained with her, haunting her. She found it now, slowly, one note at a time, even as she heard Thwaite admit a visitor to the hall. As footsteps passed the open door Meg stopped and glanced up from the keyboard. Cabot stood silently, listening, in the doorway.

At first she meant to rise from the piano bench—she wanted to run to him. But in the same instant reason stayed her. He looked at her steadily; he would have heard what she played, yet he did not appear to recall the tune with any joy. As Meg's fingers abandoned the keys to seek the sanctuary of her lap, she remembered she wore only a simple shift and that she had not put up her hair. She was at home, after all. No one called before noon.

"I have come to see your father," he said at last, and paused. Her whole body welcomed his voice. "Regarding Selbourne."

At his pause, Meg's breathing had stilled. It resumed in relief with his "regarding Selbourne." She could not want Cabot's offer. Though as he stood there observing her, she thought only of whirling through the waltz, she did not want his offer. An offer would mean only the worst for him.

Abruptly he bowed and continued toward the library. Once Meg heard her father's greeting, she rose from the piano bench and quickly crossed the room to shut the doors. Let Cabot believe her such a dedicated instrumentalist that she did not wish another interruption. Let him think her rude. She could not bear that he should stop again.

For the next half an hour Meg dedicated herself to her practice, all the while listening for more than the music. When the footsteps returned they paused briefly at the closed double doors. But Meg bravely continued, until Cabot did as well.

When at last she heard him depart, she placed her hands to her cheeks. He must not make plans—he must not risk so much. And her palms touched tears.

Chapter Six

Their party to Vauxhall was a merry one. They traveled in two carriages, to accommodate Sir Eustace and his chair, and though they were only seven they managed to sound like a circus.

Aunt Pru must have suspected how it would be, for she had cried off at the last minute, claiming that though she did not yet have a megrim she was destined to have one soon. Sir Eustace had teased her about wanting to have her house to herself again, and much too early in the season. Aunt Pru had shushed him and sent the party off with a picnic hamper of delights from her chef—in case, she told Sir Eustace, the ham at Vauxhall proved too thin for him.

On arrival, Lucy insisted that they promenade as much of the central square as possible in the evening light, though why she should have been so adamant when she and Amanda seemed most intent on gossiping was a major mystery. Their group stayed to hear part of the summer's first concert in the concert hall, then ambled on to the busy colonnades to find the supper box Sir Eustace had reserved. There they reposed themselves away from the crowds, to sip punch and await the darkness, for the main event was to be Lucy's introduction to Vauxhall's vaunted illuminations.

"Do you think there will be fireworks as well, Papa?" she asked.

"So they tell me, Lucinda—if it does not rain. You must speak to someone else about *that* possibility." Sir Eustace's attention settled on Amanda. "I saw your parents, Miss Burke, in a box just down the way as we came up. It was kind of them to lend us your company this evening."

The girl mumbled an acknowledgement and hurriedly sipped some punch as Sir Eustace's gaze narrowed on her impatiently.

"We have enough room here to entertain two more of Lucy's friends this evening," Bertie remarked. "Is that your intention, father?"

"My intention, Bertram, is to please myself this evening, since I am out so rarely. With the permission of my family I hope to entertain some of *my* friends tonight."

"Then we could have done with fewer chairs!" Bertie claimed, whereupon Sir Eustace threatened to let him walk home.

Meg was delighted to see her father in such good spirits. She thought he looked better than he had in weeks, and she had hopes that the melancholy that had troubled him since his accident would recur less frequently. This evening she had hopes for herself as well, for after the unexpected sight of Cabot she had had difficulty dispelling a dark mood of her own.

The music from the concert hall drifted languidly across the square. Within the shelter of the supper box the ladies did not need their wraps. For mid-May, it was warm. Louisa and Ferrell returned from a brief visit with friends to join the rest of them for the meal—delicious cold ham and chicken, delicate shrimp rolls from Aunt Pru's chef and a lavish selection of breads, rolls, jellies, fruits and pastries. Meg made a point of nibbling whenever her father looked her way. But thankfully he seemed to have decided to let her be. She sat quietly, like Amanda, and listened happily to the music.

As he finished his meal, Sir Eustace looked to Louisa.

"Well, Mrs. Ferrell, have you something to tell your family?"

Louisa, who had always been a very composed young lady, turned bright red.

"Papa!" she cried. She had not called him 'papa' for years—"How did you know?"

"Louisa my dear, you are the image of your mother, who gave me four children. *Quod erat demonstrandum. That* is how I know!"

Ferrell laughed and moved to kiss his astonished wife on the cheek. Drawing a startled breath, Meg leaned toward her sister.

"Louisa . . . dearest," she said. "What wonderful news . . ."

Bertie and Lucy were a few seconds slower to comprehend, but Lucy was soon babbling with delight about *her* niece or nephew, and all the activities she planned for the new arrival.

"The babe is not to be a playmate for you, Lucy," Sir Eustace drawled. "You and Miss Burke must amuse each other for a while yet."

Bertie, having thumped Ferrell heavily and repeatedly on the back, surrendered him to Meg.

"Thomas . . ." Meg kissed him on the cheek. "You knew last week, didn't you? At Almack's—when Louisa did not dance?"

He nodded.

"I must be thankful you and Sir Eustace do not sit with the opposition, Meg. 'Twould be impossible to divert you."

"What of Aunt Pru?" Louisa asked. "We'd wanted to wait until we were all in company."

"Your aunt is knitting woollies this minute," Sir Eustace said. "She thought it best she begin preparations at once."

"Oh lord," Bertie groaned. "I think I shall have to take myself back to Selbourne, father. 'Twill be impossible to discuss anything else from now until"—he paused, and looked to Louisa—"when?"

Again she blushed.

"October," she said.

"Selbourne it is then, father," Bertie said. "I shall help Cabot's crew finish the terracing."

"That would be a salutary way to occupy your time, Bertram," Sir Eustace remarked. "Though we would miss your company." He paused. "Speaking of Mr. Cabot—I note he is visiting in the boxes across the way." Meg's gaze immediately shot to the other side of the square. "He told me he would be attending this evening. I have invited him to join us later—if he is so inclined."

"But father," Meg protested at once. "Mr. Cabot is . . ."

"I must be permitted to invite whom I choose to my own party! Do you have any objection, Margaret, other than his occupation? His boots look clean enough this evening."

Her father, it seemed, would not easily forget what she had said to Cabot at Selbourne. But he did not understand. And Meg noticed Bertie's raised eyebrows and Lucy's puzzlement. No doubt they wondered how she could take any exception to Cabot, having waltzed with him as she had.

"No, sir," she said through dry lips. "I have no objection to Mr. Cabot."

Her father surveyed her pale face, then turned his attention again to their feast. Despite the resumption of excited conversation, Meg's anxiety returned. She seemed never to experience anything good or pleasant without a consequent oppression.

She abandoned any effort to eat, sipping punch alone as she scanned the boxes opposite. In the dusk the lights were coming on, in the magical display so associated with Vauxhall and so evocative of an imaginative, twinkling fairyland. At last her seeking gaze found Cabot's distinctive blond head—next to an equally distinctive red one.

"I feel sorry for her," Louisa said of the Comtesse d'Avigne, who appeared to be sitting nearly in Cabot's lap. "I cannot comprehend, Meg, what it must be like to marry without love. Aunt Pru said the comtesse was wed at seventeen. Her father gambled—as well as her husband, it seems—and practically sold her."

"I do not intend to marry at all," Meg said, noting the other occupants of the box. The only one she recognized was the petite girl Cabot had danced with at Almack's.

"You think that will please father?" Louisa asked.

"I . . . don't know," Meg said, turning to look at her sister's thoughtful face. "Perhaps you and Ferrell will have enough grandchildren to pacify him."

"He wants you happy, Margaret."

"I know, Louisa. But it is not something one can manufacture."

"It is something one might choose."

"And if my choice should only cause *un*happiness for others?" Meg whispered. "What then?"

Louisa hugged her and continued to sit by her side.

" 'Tis said the Comtesse d'Avigne has a wealthy protector," she went on, observing the box opposite, just as Meg was. "Someone close to the Regent himself, one of the Prince's intimates. The very company Cabot shares there tonight. The association is surprising, though I must say he seems remarkably well connected. Ferrell says he is earning quite a reputation for his work."

Meg dared not make the comment that came to mind, not after her father's reprimand. Though it did strike her that the Comtesse d'Avigne, who had married without love, need not have demonstrated quite so openly whatever sentiments she now felt. Or at least, not with Cabot.

As she watched him rise from his seat and turn toward the young brunet, Meg was aware that another gentleman approached the Lawrences' supper box. She recognized Malcolm Wembly at once, though she had not seen him in almost three years. His hair was now grayer—like her father's, and perhaps he was not quite as thin. But as he stepped into the box and smiled easily around at all of them, his smile was just the same. He turned to her father.

"Eustace, my boy Harry has written to me. He says I cannot go on as I have, and that I must apologize. Harry is quite right." Wembly extended his hand. "I apologize, Eustace.

And I humbly ask your forgiveness—for being less of a friend than I ought to have been."

Her father's eyes brightened suspiciously as he clasped Mr. Wembly's hand. Mr. Wembly turned to Louisa.

"I owe you an apology as well, my dear," he went on. "And Mr. Ferrell, you are a lucky man." He reached to shake Ferrell's hand, patted Bertram on the shoulder, then looked with open pleasure at Meg. "Ah, Meg! Are you riding, girl?"

"Yes, Uncle Malcolm. I have Paloma in town."

"You must join me some morning. I shall call 'round."

"I shall look forward to it."

"Hello, muffin." Mr. Wembly took a seat between Sir Eustace and Lucy and turned to Lucy's blond head. He had always called her 'muffin.' "Are you enjoying yourself in town?"

"Yes, Uncle Malcolm," Lucy said. "I am seeing absolutely everything."

"The only way to see everything, my dear, is to see it absolutely."

"Do not encourage her, Malcolm, by speaking nonsense yourself," Sir Eustace said, which set the two men to bantering.

Meg had been so focused on Mr. Wembly's arrival that she had failed to maintain her study of the opposite box. Now she realized with dismay that Cabot had answered her father's invitation, that he had indeed come across to visit, and that he had brought the petite brunet with him.

He was dressed again most beautifully, in an immaculate superfine coat, and as her father had so pointedly remarked earlier, his smart boots were spotless.

He stood at ease at the front of the box, with the girl at his side. She was no older than Lucy, tiny and pretty and, Meg guessed, exceedingly shy, for her gaze repeatedly sought the ground.

"Well, Cabot," Sir Eustace said. "Good evening to you."

"Good evening to you, sir." He bowed.

"Malcolm Wembly, may I present to you Mr. Charles Cabot, who rides Arcturus."

"Ah—do you, sir?" It was all the introduction Cabot needed. Mr. Wembly was out of his seat and vigorously shaking his hand. "That is very good, very good indeed. Splendid. You must come see me at Havingsham Hall soon. I move back this summer."

"Thank you, Mr. Wembly." Cabot's gaze sought Meg's. Something about his smile suggested that he remembered her comment—about attaching the Hall for his landscaping projects. He placed a hand behind his companion's slight shoulders and gently urged her closer to the box.

"Mademoiselle d'Avigne," he said, "it is my pleasure to introduce to you Sir Eustace Lawrence of Selbourne and his family—Mr. Bertram Lawrence, Mrs. Ferrell, Mr. Ferrell, Miss Lawrence, Miss Lucinda Lawrence and here her friend, Miss Burke. Mr. Wembly is Sir Eustace's neighbor."

Lady Candace curtsied very prettily, claimed in heavily accented English to be delighted to make their acquaintance, then turned to Lucy and asked if she and her friend Miss Burke might care to take a stroll with them to explore the gardens.

As Lucy readily agreed, Sir Eustace suggested, "Why don't all of you go? 'Tis a sight to be seen, and we've very little left of our supper on which to gnaw. Yes, move along there, Bertram, Ferrell. Malcolm and I wish to have some discussion." As Meg hesitated and retained her seat her father's eyebrows rose. "Do go with them, Margaret."

"I would . . . rather stay, father."

"Why so skittish, girl? 'Tis a large party." Meg glanced at Cabot, who lingered behind the rest of the group— waiting for her. She thought his expression impatient, even a little angry. Her disinclination must have seemed rude.

As she rose to join him and the others she was embarrassed to have been so obviously tossed out by her parent, who was already lighting a pipe with his friend. And she remembered too vividly how just that morning she had betrayed herself to Cabot.

She did not take his arm, but walked beside him, just two steps behind Bertram and the three younger girls. Lucy, as seemed to be increasingly the case, held forth with her usual breathless discourse.

"I am so glad Mr. Wembly has made up with Papa," she said. "Just think, how terrible to have one's very best friend not speaking to one at all! And for so many years, too! Of course, Harry has had much to do with this, I can tell, though he said nothing to *me* about writing his father. I really do wish he'd stayed in town. Then he needn't have written his father at all, but could have arranged the meeting himself, and had supper with us tonight and be walking with us now. Instead, Mr. Harris Wembly must rush back to university for his studies. To be quizzed on his Latin. There is nothing as important in the world as Mr. Harris Wembly's examinations!"

"Lucy," Bertram interposed, "it is the end of the term. Poor Harry . . ."

"Poor Harry! Poor Harry who can only criticize me, saying I am not—not *circumspect* with Lord Knowles—though Trevor is so very pleasant, and dances divinely, and says he should like nothing more than to spend every day with me! And then for Harry to tell me he will not be able to come to my ball! I have a ball the end of next week, Candace," she diverted enthusiastically. "You must come. My aunt Pru has helped plan everything to be just so and Charles"— Lucy looked over her shoulder—"will come—as he promised?" Cabot nodded. "But Mr. Harris Wembly makes no promises, when they mean everything!"

"For goodness' sake, Luce! You cannot expect him to sacrifice a term's work for a ball," Bertram said sharply.

"Yes, Miss Lucy," Cabot agreed. "He will be with you all the sooner if he completes his examinations."

"But *you* are coming, Charles. And heaven knows *you* are always running off on some quest or other!"

"I have considerably more control of my time, Miss Lucy."

"Oh, all of you will find excuses for him!" she said, and dragging a compliant Amanda ahead with her, left Bertram escorting only Candace d'Avigne.

"What the devil just happened?" he asked.

"*Elle est amoureuse*," Candace said shyly.

"Eh?"

"Lucy is in love, Lawrence," Cabot told him.

"*Lucy?*"

"Do not say anything to her Bertie, please," Meg urged.

"Say anything? How could I? 'Tis impossible to get a word in edgewise . . ." He leaned to catch something Candace said to him. As the two walked ahead, Meg looked about at the lanterns high in the trees.

"It is a pretty place," she ventured. "I had forgotten."

" 'Twas well planned. Though now considerably overgrown. Do you know its plan, Miss Lawrence?" Cabot asked. Meg shook her head. She meant to keep her brother and Miss d'Avigne in view, but Cabot seemed in no hurry. "You remember I set Selbourne's improvements on a radial plan. Vauxhall was laid out as a parallelogram." He reached casually, unself-consciously, to pull a dead branch from a tangle at their side and quickly scratched the shape on the side of the path. "The walks cross so—and here is the central square. Should the paths not meet at right angles—you have reached an outer edge." He tapped the four of them. "So you need never," he said looking down at her, "be lost in Vauxhall—again."

In the sparkling lamplight, wrapped by the darkness, Meg thought she should not at all mind being lost—were she to have his company. But that 'again' recalled her to her circumstances. Cabot traced her reluctance to walk out this evening to a fear of the gardens, or of some repetition of the past.

"I have never been lost in Vauxhall," she corrected him, and heard his indrawn breath.

"My mistake, Miss Lawrence," he said shortly. "I presumed." As he moved ahead, Meg tried to match his lengthening stride.

"Lady Candace is very amiable," Meg said, once they spotted Bertie and his companion ahead.

"Yes. But she has had an unsettled life. I feel for her."

"Her mother is lovely."

"The Comtesse d'Avigne is her stepmama." He was starting to sound as brisk as his pace. He kept his gaze forward.

"The comtesse has a most . . . engaging manner."

"It is her way. She likes company."

"Yours—clearly."

At once Cabot halted and bent close to look into her eyes. In the dim light at this particular passage, his gaze looked black.

"What is it you wish to say, Miss Lawrence? That I have been indiscreet? That my behavior has lacked *circumspection?*"

Meg swallowed and looked away. Her brother and Candace had passed beyond the next lantern. The path was empty. The dense press of foliage about them seemed as abandoned and remote as a jungle.

"You and the Comtesse—"

"Have a history. From many years ago. My past is not sterling, Miss Lawrence, but I cannot apologize for having been young. I endeavor to improve myself."

"Her manner . . ."

"Is acceptable in certain circles." He sighed. "Miss Lawrence, if you wish to debate right and wrong, you must consult Sir Eustace. I cannot condemn, since I myself have been wrong, and will be again. Shortly, no doubt." His gaze searched her face. "The comtesse's manners are not mine. You make clear they are not yours. It is because they are not yours that Lord Sutcliffe makes you suffer."

The bold reminder instantly brought tears to her eyes. As her lips trembled, Meg noticed his attention to them. His frown fled.

"Miss . . . Miss Margaret," he urged softly. "Please . . ." His head lowered. He meant to kiss her. But he straightened abruptly as excited calls carried from the path ahead. They heard footsteps running back along the walk, then Bertie, Lucy, and Candace, closely followed by the Ferrells, moved into the lamplight.

"Meg, Charles—Mandy has gone missing!" Lucy declared. Her voice shook. "I just stopped to speak one minute with Mr. Gillen and his party, and when I turned back, Mandy was gone!"

"She did not pass us," Ferrell said.

"And there is only one crossing," Bertie added. "She must have gone toward town. 'Twas the only route crowded with company."

"Sutcliffe . . ." Meg ventured.

"Sutcliffe would not trouble Amanda," Louisa said firmly.

"In the dark—her hair—it is my color . . ."

"She hasn't your form, Meggie," Bertie said frankly, as only a brother could.

Cabot cleared his throat.

"The earl and Mulmgren were on the other side of the square," he said. "He could not have come around us so quickly." And Meg glanced at him, astonished that he should be so aware of Sutcliffe's whereabouts.

"Let us return the ladies to Sir Eustace," Ferrell suggested. "Then begin a search."

They walked quickly and silently back to the colonnaded square. Even Lucy stayed quiet, perhaps because Candace d'Avigne kindly held her hand and whispered encouragement. Meg frowned as they reached their supper box. Her father and Mr. Wembly were still comfortably smoking and talking; the orchestra had begun another set of Handel's music. Yet the evening's earlier ease was lost.

"Father, Amanda has gone missing," Bertie said shortly. "We must start a search."

"Nonsense," Sir Eustace pronounced. "She's run off with her true love, Sir Freddy Dymthorpe, baronet and nincompoop. Burke's been expecting it for some time."

"Freddy?" Lucy gulped. "She's never said a word!"

"How could she, Lucinda, when you steal all of them for yourself? If you must ignore your friends," he said sternly, "they are like to ignore you."

Mr. Wembly patted the empty chair next to him.

"Come sit next to me, muffin. I am sure this is a shock to you, as Amanda is your very best friend, is she not?"

"Yes sir," Lucy sniffed. "She certainly *was* . . ."

"Father, I think we should still go after them," Bertie said, with a glance at Meg. "They shouldn't just be let to run off . . ."

"Why ever not, if they're both willing? Barely brain enough for one between them. They shall scrape along nicely. The only reason to stop them is to prevent them from having children."

"Father . . ." Louisa objected. She and Ferrell had preceded Meg back into the box.

"Why should I spoil my evening, Louisa," Sir Eustace asked, "for a girl who has never troubled to put two words together for me? In contrast, my Lucinda makes a great deal of noise," he paused to remark Lucy's soft sniffling, "but she has never lacked for wits."

As though conscious that her father, in his way, had just complimented her, Lucy fell quiet.

Meg noticed that Bertie and Candace d'Avigne had followed her in to take seats in the box. Cabot positioned himself close to its front, to her side, and continued to stand.

"You must pardon our inattention, Lady Candace," Sir Eustace turned to say to the girl. "We have had some excitement."

"*Oui*," Candace agreed. "*Une fuite . . .*"

"Eh?" Bertie asked.

"An elopement, Bertie," Meg supplied. When she noticed Cabot was watching her too closely she worried her lower lip, only to realize how unwise that was. "Father," she asked quickly, "why are you not surprised?"

"You young people, Margaret, must learn to give your elders credit for greater skills in observation than you ever warrant. 'Twas apparent at this winter's assemblies that Miss Burke and Dymthorpe were partial to each other. All the usual clues were there: silly smiles, arguments over nothing, loss of appetite, standin' too close—" His gaze settled idly on Cabot, who moved two steps away from her. "Lady Dymthorpe and the Burkes agreed it would be an acceptable match. They had the settlements drawn up and the license ready before the Burkes even started for town. That batty old vicar in Dymthorpe's parish will do the honors tomorrow. I would not choose the method for my own daughters," he added mildly, "but all were agreed this is like to be the greatest thrill in Miss Burke's young life. She may never realize it wasn't an elopement."

Bertie nevertheless popped down along the colonnade to inform the Burkes that their dove had indeed flown; he returned with the news that Amanda's parents were on the verge of an unruffled departure. The Burkes assured Lucy they would have Amanda write immediately she was wed.

The warm night had presaged a fine drizzle. When the fireworks were called off, Lucy, happy with the attentions of Mr. Wembly and her new friend Candace, had no time for disappointment.

Cabot, who had obviously determined to squire Candace d'Avigne no matter the tedium, continued to stand at the side of the box. Though he did not speak to Meg, he managed to make clear that there was quite a bit to be said. They had had an argument. He had nearly kissed her. There were reasons for constraint. But, despite his polite responses to Bertie and the others, Meg thought he seemed distracted, as though he awaited a summons.

She understood that alertness, and the alteration from his usual ease, when the Earl of Sutcliffe appeared suddenly at the front of their box.

Their laughter ceased. Sutcliffe stood before them in all his false civility, his mouth set in that characteristic, slanted suggestion of a smile, the drizzle misting his hair and his shoulders. His gaze, with its usual boldness, settled on Meg at once; when he looked at her so she felt quite naked. She sensed that Cabot shifted his weight away from the wall beside her, as though he would spring at him. Meg had to glance down at her hands in her lap—to make certain they did not reach out to restrain him.

"Sir Eustace—how are you?"

"As you see, Sutcliffe." Her father tapped the arms of his chair. "You do not lack for gall."

"You were a horseman." Sutcliffe shrugged. "You had an

accident. Horses are unpredictable creatures." Mr. Wembly started to rise in protest, but Sir Eustace pulled him back.

"May I join you?" Sutcliffe's gaze again sought Meg. "It is, after all, a public garden. And it is raining." He smiled, as though that alone were enough to explain his intrusion.

"This is a private box," her father said, even as Sutcliffe stepped closer. "We are a family party."

Sutcliffe's smile slipped into a sneer. He glanced at Candace d'Avigne.

"Not all, I think," he corrected sharply. *"Bon soir, mademoiselle. Comment allez-vous?"*

"Très bien, merci, monsieur le comte," she said respectfully, but she cast an uncertain look about her.

Sutcliffe's gaze measured Cabot before settling again on Meg.

"Miss Lawrence, will you walk out with me? I shall find us an umbrella."

"No, my lord. As you see, I am at home here."

Sutcliffe threw a hand in Cabot's direction.

"You just walked out with *him*. You waltzed with *him*. Yet who is *he*?" When she stayed silent he turned a contemptuous look on Cabot. *"Vous êtes malotru. Sans honneur."*

As Candace d'Avigne gasped, Lucy, who was seated closest to Sutcliffe's taunting face, jumped up to slap him.

Meg heard her heart beat. Sutcliffe touched his cheek as Lucy turned wildly to Cabot.

"I'm . . . sorry, Charles." Her face was ashen. "I remember . . . what you said to me last week, but it was too . . . too much! I could not wait! I—"

"Lucy . . ." Sir Eustace cautioned as Mr. Wembly quickly drew Lucy back down to her seat. "*Please!*"

Meg's focus did not leave Sutcliffe's face as he dismissed quaking Lucy and fixed his venomous attention on Cabot's still form.

"Yes, *Charles*," he stressed. His tone froze. "For what does eager Miss Lucy wait?" He did not expect an answer. He did not receive one. With a last, long look at Meg, Sutcliffe turned into the damp and left them.

Chapter Seven

Hyde Park, blanketed by dawn-light fog, was curiously welcoming. After several days refining the plans for Abbey Clare, Chas appreciated being outdoors, the scent of the moist morning air, the sound of his horse's breathing.

He reached down to pat Incendio's neck. The huge black gelding was David's. The horse had helped see his cousin through many years on the Peninsula. A sturdier, less temperamental blueblood was probably not to be found, certainly not among the men who had celebrated David's return last night.

Chas had been spared a headache, but he knew so little sleep would take its toll later in the day. Last night's revelry was not the sort of indulgence to which he should be yielding just now, not with the business with Sutcliffe brewing. But for the duration of the evening it had been a relief not to feel the strain, to laugh with Myles and David and a host of friends, to know that Sutcliffe and Mulmgren and their minions could not, would not, invade the tavern and the raucous masculine company.

A condemned man, Chas reflected grimly, was supposed to be granted just such as that—a pleasure in the nature of a last request.

As Incendio champed at the bit Chas let him out. The ground was soft but firm, perfect for a run. The gelding must have found the green English sod a surprisingly springy surface after Spain's stony soil. They raced along higher ground above the lake before pulling up to the north of Kensington gardens.

He thought of Sir Eustace Lawrence, and of the tragedy for such a man never to ride again. Sir Eustace's crippling had to have been the last thing Sutcliffe would have wanted, for with it, he had permanently earned Meg's enmity. But the earl still bore the responsibility for that infamous evening's most lasting reminder. And his acts since had been unforgivable.

Chas knew that he had been lucky at Vauxhall. He had planned to attend only as a courtesy to Vanessa and her charge, but once Sir Eustace had invited him to stop in, the temptation had been irresistible. Candace d'Avigne had been his excuse for venturing over to the Lawrences. And then, as usual, he had been lost. Had Sutcliffe challenged him there, as Chas knew he very nearly had, Chas would not have been ready. He needed a few more days—to set his affairs in order, to finish the plans for Clare—rough as they were—and to visit Wimbledon Common, the likeliest venue.

Lucy's bravery, if that was what it had been, had almost forced him, where Sutcliffe had been unable to force him, to something he had been carefully avoiding. The contest would have to be with pistols. With pistols Chas suspected he had a chance. And Sutcliffe would only agree to pistols if Chas chose them.

He had been shooting now every day for weeks. He had been shooting at Clare's. He had no fear for his accuracy, only for the circumstances. There was so very little he could plan. He thought he might survive the confrontation, but Meg would never approve the method. She was like to think him a murderer, given his dedication. Still, the line would be crossed only when Sutcliffe challenged him.

He and Incendio trotted along under the plane trees. The waltz was in his head again, not as he had danced to it at Almack's but as he had heard it that brief moment at her aunt's—in simple, haunting reminder, played by Meg at the piano, with her lustrous hair streaming over her shoulders and down her back.

He noticed Lawrence's horse first, the gray with a crooked blaze and a tendency to drop his head. Then he distinguished Bertie himself and the neighbor, Mr. Wembly. Meg was behind them, accompanied by an unknown Wembly—but clearly a Wembly.

Chas abruptly halted his horse.

"Cabot!" Bertram called as the group neared him. "Well met!"

"Good morning, Mr. Cabot," Mr. Wembly said. "Who've you got there?"

Chas patted Incendio's neck as he turned the horse about to join their party.

"This is a Spanish boy, Mr. Wembly. Incendio. He's been with my cousin, Lor—that is, Major Trent, on the

Peninsula the past few years. Now, I fear, he finds the park tame."

"Oh, no doubt!" Mr. Wembly agreed. "Where is your cousin?"

"He just returned yesterday. He is . . . recovering."

"Not injured, I hope?"

"Thankfully, not at all. Though we have had"—he glanced at Meg—"a celebration."

Bertie laughed.

"I can imagine!" He turned to the stranger. "Walter, this is Charles Cabot. Cabot, Walter Wembly—Harry's brother."

The two of them nodded to one another. Walter was older than Harry, broader and sterner, but just as darkly handsome—curse him.

"Walter's just become a Fellow of the Royal College of Physicians," Malcolm Wembly said proudly. Chas thought Meg's sister, Louisa, had attracted a particular kind of ambitious gentleman. And it struck him as sufficient that the Wemblys should now have the inside running with Lucy. They did not need any more rein.

He neatly drew Incendio behind and to Meg's side.

"Did you take the colors yourself, Mr. Cabot?" Walter Wembly asked across her. Chas was distractingly aware of Meg's tidy blue velvet riding habit.

"No, Dr. Wembly. Though as a boy it was my dearest wish. I believed myself destined to be a master of artillery. But I was precluded."

"Precluded?" Meg asked, her gaze meeting his for the first time. He was so struck by the perfection of her face, framed by the feather in her pert little black hat, that he could not at first respond.

"I promised two elderly ladies that I would not do so while they lived, Miss Lawrence. They have demonstrated extraordinary longevity. Unfortunately," and he frowned as he again patted Incendio's neck, "so did General Bonaparte."

"Have you horses of your own, Mr. Cabot?"

This time Chas decided Walter Wembly's question had not been entirely friendly.

"I do, Doctor. But not here in town. They are out at Brookslea."

"Brookslea? In Hampshire?" his father asked. "Braughton's Brookslea?"

" 'Tis Cabot's Brookslea now, Uncle Malcolm," Bertie supplied.

Chas did not much care for the friendly term 'uncle'.

"Is it, b'gad!" Mr. Wembly enthused. " 'Tis a superior property."

Chas could imagine Hayden's drawling remark on the gentry's preoccupation with realty. But with Meg Lawrence's gaze reading his own he was very much aware that he had just played the game himself. He could not now make a show of flaunting conventions.

"I thank you," he said politely, and glanced at Meg again. "How is Miss Lucy?" he asked. "After the other night . . ."

"I believe she was in shock, Cabot," Bertie volunteered. "But after you left with Miss d'Avigne, we hurried her home to Aunt Pru, who has been most solicitous with her 'little lamb'." Bertie snorted. " 'Little lamb'! Perhaps we should have let Lucy fly at Bonaparte!"

Chas smiled.

"Lucy thanks you for the chocolates," Meg told him. "They were consumed with much enthusiasm."

Chas nodded and kept the smile, though he was not at ease. He thought Meg Lawrence's gaze concerned; she may simply have noticed that he looked peaked—that his smile was forced. But he did not want pity from her, not when Walter Wembly was looking so very smug. It amazed Chas that he could manage to deal rationally and purposefully with a danger like Sutcliffe, but find the inestimable Dr. Wembly insufferable.

"Where will you set up your practice, Doctor?" he asked. "Here in town?"

"I believe I will return soon to Berkshire, Mr. Cabot. The consulting physician in Buxley is close to retirement. It is an opportunity." He glanced at Meg, in a manner that indicated his consideration of other opportunities as well.

"Mr. Cabot has expressed an interest in further work in the county himself," Meg said sweetly. "He was much taken with the prospect of Havingsham Hall from that high point above our lake—you will remember, Walter."

Walter. The interloper was looking at her too fondly.

"Perhaps Mr. Cabot, you would consider giving us your opinion of Havingsham Hall," Mr. Wembly proposed. "After all, if Walter settles 'twould be a good time to make some improvements."

"I didn't know you were ready to settle, Walter," Bertie said.

"Well, I . . ."—Walter glanced at Meg—"just recently thought the notion was not to be dismissed."

Did he, by God! Chas' irritation conveyed itself to

Incendio, who started to prance. Chas felt the first of the sun's rays upon his face and coat as though he were touched by fire. He had no intention of sacrificing what he might for the Walter Wemblys of the world.

His gaze sought Meg's face, luminous in the fresh light. She was teasing him about Havingsham Hall. The hint of a smile drew his attention to her lips. He realized he had let Sutcliffe's claims influence him—that he had begun to think of her as inviolable, untouched and untouchable. And at once he knew he must kiss those teasing lips, before he departed the earth.

"Your mare looks tired this morning," he suggested smoothly, his gaze hooded.

"Paloma?" she scoffed. "Paloma is never tired!"

Chas tilted his chin briefly toward the high ground off the path, around the other side of the lake. He raised one eyebrow in silent challenge. She understood him immediately. It was her weakness, a dare she could not resist. Had Chas lived as confined a life he would have been equally susceptible. On her Paloma Meg believed herself invincible.

Chas drew Incendio into an eager, expectant circle, then kneed him into a run. The mare's hooves pounded right behind them. Chas was gambling—that the center of the park would still be empty, or that he would find a suitable spot that was. He, and not Paloma, would determine the finish line.

Over the rise from the Wemblys and up and down another, between two giant chestnuts and shy of the lake's far end, Chas slowed and pulled up, just as Meg's mare started to pass them. The girl was indeed lightning in the saddle.

He called halt. As both horses blew steam and tossed their heads, Chas brought Incendio to her offside.

"Miss Margaret Lawrence," he charged. "You need not peddle my services to the Wemblys."

"Shouldn't you like Havingsham Hall?" She smiled as she patted Paloma's neck; it delighted Chas to see her smile. But he was resolved.

"'Twould depend on what you forfeited for such an honor."

"Oh—if I were to attach Walter, as you proposed, you might devise a park for Havingsham. On a triangular plan, perhaps. That of an isosceles triangle? In time, Cabot's geometry might cover the countryside . . ." She was so taken with her own cleverness she did not notice when he moved Incendio closer behind her. In one deft movement he relieved her of her reins, then plucked her bodily from the saddle and pulled her with an iron arm across in front of him. Her lips parted in a startled "O" before he swiftly claimed them.

That she should yield to him with equal swiftness surprised him. Her mouth was so lushly welcoming that he did not break the kiss as he'd intended, instead releasing both horses to pull her up close in his arms, clear of the pommel. Incendio, who had been used to much, stayed blessedly still. But as the kiss deepened, as Chas was tempted to more, as Meg's hands inched up his chest, Chas knew he had to stop.

He drew back, looking into the dazed dark depths of her eyes, then reluctantly lowered her to the ground. Incendio had not moved. One of Meg's hands rested against the gelding's black shoulder, as though for support.

"So much for your sauce," Chas breathed. He wanted to haul her right up to him again.

"You have . . . practiced that," she said faintly.

"Never," he assured her softly, the word unsteady. " 'Twas entirely impulse. An impulse . . . I might hope to repeat?" The entreaty in his own voice confounded him.

"You hope in vain, sir." She attempted to order her hair. He willed her to leave it be, the image of its dark length down her back recurring in his mind.

"I thought so. Then I cannot regret my impulse, Miss Lawrence. 'Twill have to serve."

She searched his face for a second, as though to understand his resignation. Then her trembling fingers straightened her hat and habit. She was shaken by this. She was charming.

He loved her.

Noting the others' approach he brought Incendio closer, to shield her.

"Her hoof," he suggested quickly, "a stone . . ." And Meg knelt to take up Paloma's right front hoof.

"What has happened?" Bertie called, coming up, with the Wemblys close behind.

"Miss Lawrence won the race, but her Paloma may have drawn a stone." Chas looked down at Meg. "I hope it is nothing serious, Miss Lawrence?"

Her glance up at him was accusing and something else— wounded.

"Not serious at all," she said, managing to wound him in turn. To mask his confusion, he wheeled Incendio, and started away.

"I must be off. Until later, Lawrence. Mr. Wembly." He nodded to Walter. The good doctor would claim Meg only over *his* dead body. And with that ironic thought he at last felt his headache begin.

"Louisa—may I speak with you?"

Her sister looked up from her own dining table, which was serving—only for that afternoon—as a repository of every conceivable favor, prize, and decoration. Lucy's ball, just two days away, now consumed the Ferrell's home as well as Lady Billings's, and seemed to require ballooning space and undivided attention from every member of the family. Meg had just left the company of Lucy and Aunt Pru in the Ferrells' drawing room, where they reviewed some three hundred acceptances in anticipation of the need for great quantities of soup.

As she closed the dining room door, Meg could still hear Lucy's excited voice upstairs. The resulting silence was a relief.

Louisa pulled a chair out beside her.

"Come," she said. "Help me decide between the blue ribbons and the green." She tapped two seemingly identical strips of fabric.

"Lucy will prefer the blue," Meg said wearily, glancing only briefly at the samples. She paced to the window instead of taking the proffered chair. "Blue for anything."

"I knew you would decide," Louisa said, putting the ribbons aside, "and so you have just saved us half an hour's debate."

Meg's fingers caressed the edge of one of the drapes at the front windows.

"Aunt Pru's house has been scoured so thoroughly, and everything so ordered and readied, it scarcely seems livable." Meg spoke to the window. " 'Tis like trying to reside in a museum."

Louisa laughed.

"Do not despair, Meg. All this will be over some time in the wee hours of Friday morning—and then we may relax and think freely again. Until Lucy's wedding!"

Meg looked toward her.

"I am glad you can believe so, Louisa, given how much *you* now have for which to prepare."

Louisa smiled slyly.

"I have promised Ferrell not to turn his library into a nursery until August at the earliest. By then he hopes to have been invited up north shooting."

Meg shook her head.

"He is as excited as you are. He will not desert you."

"We shall see. I expect that he may occasionally seek relief by joining all of you at Selbourne this summer."

Meg turned again to the window. She planned to tell her father she wished to return to Selbourne as soon as possible with Bertie—even as early as next week. The remainder of the season held no further charms for her.

As her gaze focused on a man lounging against a lamppost on the street opposite, Meg abandoned the window. She now assumed every stranger owed allegiance to Lord Sutcliffe. She could not even think in privacy.

She turned to examine, on the dining room wall, a drawing she had rendered the year before, for Louisa's wedding. It showed a view of Selbourne from Cabot's knoll.

"You shall have to make another for us, Meg. Now that Mr. Cabot has rearranged things."

Rearranged things! Indeed he had. Meg glanced to

Louisa, who was observing her patiently, and wondered if her astute sister had purposely introduced Cabot's name.

"Louisa, how did you know—how did you know it was to be Ferrell and not Walter Wembly?"

Louisa raised her eyebrows, as though the outcome of that decision still vexed her.

"Because Ferrell told me so!"

"But you and Walter—you had an understanding—at least, at the time it had been so settled. You must have believed yourself in love with Walter?"

"Well yes, Meg, at nineteen I did. As you say, it had been settled for so many years that I think both of us believed it a given. I had known Walter all my life—to continue to spend the rest of it with him seemed comfortable and proper. Would I have been happy with him?" Louisa shrugged. "Perhaps. But after meeting Ferrell I knew I could never be as happy with Walter."

"Why?"

"Well, because . . . because I share so much more with Ferrell. Because I knew from the first that I could not bear to be parted from him. Walter would be gone months at a time and I never truly missed him; when Ferrell was away a week I thought I should die."

"But if you once believed yourself in love with Walter, why shouldn't you think that your love for Ferrell would also pass with—with time, or yet another man?"

"Meg, you do sound so much like father sometimes, in your quizzing!" Louisa again patted the chair next to her. "Do come sit down so I do not feel I am in the dock."

Meg at last moved to the chair and sat down.

"Walter now talks as if—*implies* that he might fix his

interest on me," Meg said. "Should I believe him fickle? Does it mean he never loved *you*? That love will only thrive where it is returned?"

"This is not about Walter," Louisa said firmly, her gaze steady on Meg's. "It is Cabot, isn't it?" When Meg nodded, Louisa smiled. "There is no mistaking it. 'Tis apparent to everyone. Even Lord Sutcliffe, unfortunately."

Again Meg felt that chill—that Sutcliffe, whom she cared nothing about, should have intruded so thoroughly upon her life.

"He must not know."

"Who?" Louisa asked. "Cabot? Of course he must know! You must tell him."

"I . . . Louisa . . . I must ask you—Did you kiss Walter?"

"Walter?" Louisa looked surprised. "Meg—have you kissed *Walter*?"

"No, oh no. I meant, did you kiss Walter before you kissed Ferrell?"

"Dearest sister, you would make me out a wanton. But yes, I did. And now no doubt you wish to know whether that is why I decided for Ferrell . . ." As Meg anxiously watched her face she said, "My *heart* had already chosen Ferrell, Meg. And when we kissed—I wanted more."

It was very simply said. But Meg could not imagine anything more devastating than a kiss.

"Have you kissed Cabot, Meg?" Louisa asked softly.

Meg nodded as she looked down at her lap.

"And did you not find it pleasant? Would you not like to kiss again?"

Pleasant? Meg's face must have registered how shatteringly *pleasant* that kiss in the park had been.

"Why, Meg, you look stricken. I'd have thought Cabot . . . Well, of course you've scarcely had opportunity . . . Perhaps you might try again? It is, after all, just a kiss." She placed a solicitous hand over Meg's tightly clasped fingers.

Just a kiss? Again? What had Cabot done to her?

"I think . . ." Meg managed hoarsely, "it is something I had best not repeat until I am wed."

Louisa's brow instantly cleared.

"I think you need not trouble to kiss Walter." She smiled. "You must have Cabot."

"He will not offer."

"Oh, I think he will. You must indicate your feelings."

"I cannot—I do not want him to offer. He would challenge Sutcliffe."

Louisa's expression became thoughtful as she looked down at the items on the table.

"He will not challenge Sutcliffe," she said slowly.

"But you must remember Douglas! Louisa, you see what this would mean. I cannot—I cannot have him . . ."

Louisa's arm came around her shoulders.

"Hush. Do you not see he has been careful not to challenge Sutcliffe? That he declined to do so the other night at Vauxhall? Sutcliffe wanted a challenge! Cabot did not oblige him."

"Lord Sutcliffe will find some other way . . . some other way to harm him. Oh, I see—I see from your face. I have been slow. You think to assure me—when there is no assurance to be had. You mean that *Sutcliffe* will challenge *Cabot*."

"Meg . . ."

"I tell you I *know* that man. He has plagued me now for years. He will not stop. I feel . . . I feel a trap closing.

Every day it grows tighter. How he hates Cabot! You said yourself that Sutcliffe can see how I feel. Yes, Louisa, and you said 'unfortunately' so. It . . . it becomes intolerable." She rose from her seat and paced to the window.

"It is outside of enough—to have my own words thrown back at me in such a manner, Meg. I really do believe you were intended for the Bar. I cannot say it is pleasing to know one is attended to so closely, if it means I reveal myself to be a fool."

"You are the opposite of a fool, Louisa. But you still believe there is some goodness in Lord Sutcliffe, whereas I know there is not."

"And here I have always thought I was so very practical—and you so romantic," Louisa said wryly. "You must tell me, then, what you intend to do."

"I plan to return to Selbourne with Bertie, right after this ball. Sutcliffe will have difficulty reaching me there. And I . . . shall not see Cabot again."

"Well," Louisa said, "apart from the fact that I shouldn't think it likely Mr. Cabot will be satisfied with such an arrangement, and apart from the fact that your plan sounds too much like the plot of one of Aunt Pru's Minerva novels . . ." As Meg wheeled to her, Louisa held up a hand. "Please, Meg, since you already know me for a fool, permit me at least to play at wisdom!

"Unless you hurt him in some dreadful and dishonest manner," she went on, "which does not sound at all like you, Cabot will not let you go quietly back to Selbourne. If he believes you return his sentiments he will seek to make a path clear for both of you. But if you choose to hurt him instead . . ." Again she silenced Meg.

"If you hurt him deeply, Meg, and you do return to Selbourne, he will not spend the rest of his days pining for you as you will for him. Men want their homes, dearest, just as women want theirs. They want to be comfortable. They want, in varying degrees it is true, to have children. How long do you think Cabot would wait for you to change your mind? For five months? Five years? Until Sutcliffe dies? Cabot is an active man. With time, even Meg Lawrence will become only a memory. Whatever his heart's desire, he will wonder why he is not living his life. Some other woman will make him comfortable, will give him a home and children—and eventually he will love *her* for doing so. And then how will you feel?"

Meg could not see clearly. The houses on the other side of the street looked set to collapse into a watery canal. She knew that every word Louisa said was true, but she could not, she could not . . .

"I would still . . . have him alive," she choked out.

Louisa rose quickly and moved to her.

"Little Meggie," she said softly, hugging her. "I'm sorry to have been so hard. I have not been the sister you needed." She kissed her on the cheek. "You are so lovely, Meg. The men must fight over you. All you can do is choose. And not be afraid."

"I am not afraid . . . for myself."

"But Cabot is an excellent man. You must tell him of your fears, Meg, and trust where you love. All will come right."

On Thursday morning, Meg received a note from Monsieur LeBecque:

Dear lady, I beg your forbearance. I have need of you to sit for me for one period more. In all else the portrait is finished, as I promised. Will you not return this morning, for no more than one hour? I await your convenience. LeBecque.

Meg frowned. LeBecque had assured them yesterday that he would need them no more. But there was no help for it—he was a master, a meticulous man—he was doing precisely as they wished. If her nose were not just so LeBecque would never release the painting from his studio.

With resignation Meg penned a response, saying yes, she would come *tout de suite*. Only after she had sent the messenger back did she have a moment's qualm. She had no company. Lucy and Aunt Pru had gone out to address last minute errands before the night's ball; Bertie had kept a regular appointment at Jackson's salon. But LeBecque had said no more than an hour, and he had always been most accurate.

Meg arranged for her father's carriage, and left a note for Bertie, letting him know where she had gone. She looked in on her father in the library. But as it was necessary to preserve the secret of the portrait she could not reveal her destination.

"Father, I must pop over to the dressmakers for just a bit. My chemisette is not quite right, and I must have it in sarcenet rather than crape for tonight."

"Margaret, you have just used two words I have never before heard in my life. But if you must do whatever it is you must do . . ."

"I must do it." She kissed the top of his head. "I know you are tired of this, father, but Lucy is in alt. You could not have made her happier."

"We shall see. We shall see. And you, my Meg, are you going to explain to me the flowers in the front hall?"

"You have a daughter who has just been presented," Meg teased. "Her ball is tonight. She has received flowers every day for weeks."

"Do not patronize me, miss! You know I am not referring to Lucy's flowers."

Meg checked. She had not thought her father had noticed.

"The bowl of violets was from Mr. Cabot, father."

"For you?"

"Yes, for me—as an apology."

"And for what would Mr. Cabot need to apologize?"

"For trying to best me on Paloma. The other morning in the park. With the Wemblys. Bertie told you about our race."

"Ah!" Her father's gaze was still too sharp. "Perhaps he will not be so bold as to challenge you in future."

"I hope not, father. Now I really must be off."

"You are taking the grooms?" He frowned as he asked.

"And Annie. With Joe Coachman that makes four. Do not worry, father. I am smothered in protectors!" She rushed away, sparing a glance at the bowl of violets on her way through the hall. They had arrived yesterday—modest, fragrant, charming, and so expensively past their season she had wondered that they were even to be had. Cabot's card had accompanied them, with no message. She had wanted them in her room, but had not dared to remove them, lest Lucy note their absence. She must remember to spirit them upstairs before the evening's event.

"It don't seem like Mr. LeBecque would have to call you back this way," Annie remarked as they settled into the coach. "He's been so particler 'bout his time. I've watched him paint all these weeks. Yesterday—he was finished, just as he said."

"Annie, he is an artist. He must have changed his mind."

"That boy he has that helps him mix paints said Mr. LeBecque was as pleased with this portrait as he's ever been. He would not want to change it. No—someit is wrong."

"Yes, and that something is probably my nose. And I shall be heartily glad of it, that someone should say to me: 'Your nose is not quite right, and so we shall let you be.'"

Annie looked at her very hard.

"You won't think that, Miss Meg, when you want to please a man."

"Oh, Annie!" she said, but as she gazed out at the passing streets she did bother to wonder whether Cabot liked her nose.

They reached LeBecque's and left Joe Coachman with the carriage. Meg walked on up to the spacious atelier with Annie and the two grooms, all of whom had visited before. The studio, redolent of turpentine and linseed oil and awash in the open light available along the river, had come to be almost a second home over the previous five weeks.

"Monsieur LeBecque!" Meg called gaily as she passed through his outer door. LeBecque was inevitably elsewhere when they arrived, tending his large canvasses or busily mixing and testing paints in the back room. "I have come . . ."

She halted abruptly as Lord Sutcliffe turned from studying

the finished portrait of the three Lawrence sisters. LeBecque hovered anxiously at the side of the canvas.

"I am sorry, dear lady," he said quickly, wringing his hands. "He says he must speak with you, that I must send the note, or he will destroy this work. He promises that he means you no harm—that you must meet—for the tryst, yes? I cannot have my work destroyed! You understand, Miss Margaret?"

Meg heard his explanation as a mere echo, she was so alert to Sutcliffe's presence. But she must have heard more than she imagined—LeBecque had been threatened, as anyone who ever dealt with the Earl of Sutcliffe was threatened. LeBecque had wished to save the portrait—the gift for her father, the father this man had crippled.

A *tryst*? Her instant fury was something she knew she had to control.

"All is well, monsieur," she said, forcing her voice to calmness. "You did exactly right. But you should know this is not a rendezvous," she said pointedly. "I would never so abuse your hospitality. Pray do not surrender your studio. Please continue with your work. There is nothing Lord Sutcliffe might say to me that cannot be said to an audience." As LeBecque sighed and ceased wringing his hands, Meg turned to Annie and the grooms. "You will stay, please?"

"Aye," Annie said, and shot a furious look at Sutcliffe, before directing the grooms to two different spots in the room.

Sutcliffe observed their maneuvers with an insolent lack of concern.

"You see, Miss Meg, that I am alone here." He opened his arms to the room, as though to prove himself defenseless. "I do not need an army to plead my cause. Your party is more than enough protection."

"It is revealing—that you believe I should need *any*."

"A man alone is no match for your defenders. What harm can I do you?" He smiled one of his curiously humorless smiles.

"I am quite certain this building is watched, my lord, that what I do not see here inside is quite vigilant outside. That has been the case for several years. You wage a silent, relentless war, Lord Sutcliffe."

"My heart has not been silent. My heart has waited to be heard."

"You have no heart."

His eyes flashed before he turned away from her to review the portrait again.

"LeBecque is indeed a master," he said easily. "I have already complimented him. The painting is remarkable. Destined for the Royal Academy. But no match," he spun again to look at her, "for the original. You are beyond beautiful, Margaret. You grow more so hourly."

"I have learned to trust that you review me hourly. You have clearly followed my movements here these past weeks, else you could not have planned this so well."

"I have been made desperate. You have made me so. You make me survive a year at a time without sight of you."

"I have never given you reason to hope for anything from me, my lord."

"Ah—but you promise! Everything about you is promise. It is inconceivable that you should be unaware. You must know what you do. I love you, Meg. I must have you."

She drew a sharp breath and looked at the painting.

"I am not something to be collected." She turned away from him and started to walk toward the door.

"If you leave now, I swear I shall destroy this portrait," he said coldly.

"I see." She turned back to him in contempt. "You speak of love and destruction in the same breath. I begin to understand you."

"That at least is something, Meg. We are matched in passion, you and I."

"What passion would that be? You kill a pure-hearted boy, cripple my father, invade my sister's house! You spy upon me at my home—at Selbourne! What I feel for you is the opposite of love. Is *hatred* what you wish from me?"

"I tell you again, Meg—I will have your love."

Meg shook her head. His suit was in the nature of a threat.

"You have rank and an ancient name, my lord. Power and wealth beyond most men's comprehension! And I hear you have a son, a boy to carry all forward. I must wonder, if you were to have me as well, just how long your interest might last. The evidence would indicate—not long."

"The rest is not enough. Only *you* are enough. I shall have no peace without you."

Meg thought she must have made an error in suggesting, even conditionally, the possibility that he might ever have her. Something had lit in his gaze when she had mentioned the smallest chance, even as example. He was a hunter, for whom the pursuit was all; the mere thought of attainment set him on his course.

"Meg . . ." He broke abruptly, and started to move toward her. "I tell you I love you."

"You cannot love," she said simply. "It is not in you." She again turned away from him, but this time he crossed to her quickly and gripped her arm. She still remembered that hard grip from years before, when she had been seized and tossed into his carriage.

Annie and the grooms started toward her, but Meg shook her head. She forced herself to stay still.

"Do you not know, that men love—what they most desire?" he asked low, as though he would coax her. When she did not respond his voice hardened. "I shall prove it is in me. I shall prove I love you. There is nothing I would not do for you."

"The only way you could prove anything, Lord Sutcliffe, would be to release me this instant, and release me forever. Leave me and my family alone."

"No!" Sutcliffe's grip tightened. "Why must I do so, when *he* is permitted to hold you? To dance with you? Why should you grant *him* such favors?"

"You are mad," Meg said. Her arm was beginning to throb. "There is no one."

"Oh, I agree—he is *no one*! A mongrel out of Braughton, descended from half the bawdy houses on the Continent. Yet you care for this no one—*Cabot*!"

"Mr. Cabot is employed by my father. He is nothing to me."

"You may dissemble all you wish, my dear. For your sake I hope that is true. But it does not matter. I have seen that you mean much to *him*! That is all I need know—to remove him forever from your company."

"Murder is your solution to all problems, my lord, is it not? It is all you hold in your heart."

"I tell you, Meg, that you could keep me from it. You need only come to me."

"Are you such a stranger to decency then, that you bargain with lives?"

"You have made me so." His hold on her arm eased. Instead his hand moved as though to caress her, but she quickly drew away from him.

"You have already bargained one life away—to the devil. You have bargained your own."

"I am not yet so entirely forsaken, Meg. You might save me, if you choose."

"And why should I choose—to do you such a favor? You killed Douglas Kenney. You have killed other men who had nothing whatever to do with me."

"It could not be helped . . ."

"Could not be helped! It is murder!"

Sutcliffe's smile was coldly tolerant.

"I have dueled, Meg. It is not a crime. Sir Eustace himself could not portray it so." He viewed her thoughtfully. "I wonder—if Douglas had killed *me*—would you have married him? Or would you have recoiled from a murderer?"

"That is a most exaggerated *if*, my lord. You arranged every detail, every circumstance, to make it an impossibility. Douglas had no chance with you."

"Still—I think you may not understand yourself." He considered her. She noticed, for the first time, that his eyes were an icy, soulless gray. And she noticed when that pale gaze sharpened with calculation. "Meg . . ." He moved as though to touch her once more, but restrained himself. "You will come to me," he said confidently, and very softly, as though his own assurance now intrigued him. "I believe you will choose to do so. You will do so to spare him. To spare him from death, or from murder. It is all the same."

"You speak nonsense."

"Do I? I promise you, that unless you act, there will be a meeting. And there is always a risk. Much as one hates to accept it, there are . . . accidents. You object so particularly to my own record. I wonder how you would justify *his* taking of a life—even mine. You are your father's daughter, Meg. You and your family share the morality of your origins"—his voice condescended—"of the so quaint and comfortable county parish. Such virtue has kept you from me. But now, my dear, it will bring you to me." He had the gall to touch her chin with one finger. "Yes, I think so. You see, Miss Meg, had you been my daughter—or my sister— I would have eliminated a Lord Sutcliffe long before now. It is to my benefit—at last—that your family is so very *good*." His smile was satisfied.

"Your scheming trips you up, Lord Sutcliffe. It is a wonder you need converse with me at all—you converse so admirably with yourself."

"That kind of conversation is not what I have in mind for you, Meg." He looked at her frankly. "You shall learn to love me."

His look made her think of Cabot's kiss, but in an entirely different way. For Meg at once felt an unlooked-for power. Sutcliffe had told her she promised. It was possible he might be worked upon.

"If I come to you," she said slowly, and watched his gaze grow darkly penetrating. "If I come to you—would you not take that as proof—that I cared too much for *him*?"

"It would not last," he said with supreme confidence. He

stepped even closer to her. "I would soon have you forget him."

"I think you might surprise yourself, my lord. And find that you no longer want what you would win."

"I will always want you, Meg. Have I not impressed you with my constancy?"

She bit back a retort. Obsession was a peculiar constancy. But she must continue to 'promise.'

"If I should come to you . . . ," she said again, and the light eyes darkened even more. She feared she had gone too far—he looked as though he might grab her right there. He was a man maddened by his passions; it must have taken effort for him to discourse with her this long. ". . . what assurance would I have—that you would harm no one?"

"No one, again," he remarked with a cynical lift of a brow. "You would have the assurance that I'd have obtained what I wanted. I would want nothing more." He noticed her dubious gaze. "You will come to me, Meg," he repeated firmly. "I shall make it easy for you. You must send word to me at Grosvernor Square. I will collect you immediately. Mind you"—again he placed a finger under her chin, but this time he raised her face for his inspection—"I shall not wait long. Mr. Cabot might press me."

"My sister's ball is tonight—as you no doubt know."

Sutcliffe smiled.

"Little Lucy did not invite me."

"My sister is braver than I."

"It does not take bravery to deny me, Meg. It takes bravery to invite me in—as you, at last, dare to do."

She had the horrifying feeling he meant to kiss her, and stepped back abruptly. His look was sardonic.

"Yes, I think I shall have to teach you to love. And we must find you a new maid," Meg glanced over at Annie, "since I believe this one does not share your aversion to murder."

Annie was indeed glowering by the door.

"She is from the North, my lord. Not a comfortable county parish."

"She will be returning there shortly," he said with annoyance.

Meg silently applauded his displeasure.

"If you do not hear from me," she said, moving toward Annie and escape, "'twill be because I do not choose to join you."

He bowed to her, a courtesy that under the circumstances seemed a mockery. He had effectively just robbed her of any choice.

"If you do hear from me, Miss Meg, 'twill be because Mr. Cabot chooses to join his maker." And she knew his gaze was on her as she turned to leave.

Chapter Eight

Dressing for Lucy's ball was such an extended, tortuous process, at least as overseen by a valet as fastidious as Dietz, his uncle's man, that Chas was tempted to send last minute regrets. According to Dietz, a gentleman must wear so much in evidence of his standing and good taste that Chas was convinced he could evidence neither. He consented to the elaborately styled cravat, to the ostentatious buckles on his shoes, and to the impressively high, stiff shirt points. But he balked at having his hair powdered. He told Dietz in no uncertain terms, and in the only language Dietz understood, that he refused to appear looking like a character from Fasching carnival.

Dietz, who had to be nearing ninety, could manage offended pride and servile abasement simultaneously. Chas considered it an opportune moment to suggest that Dietz remove himself permanently to Brookslea, where he would have a large staff to terrorize, instead of one transient, obstinate master. How that would work, Chas hadn't a clue, since Dietz spoke neither English nor French. But Dietz took the proposed removal as a sign of promotion, and retreated to a pleased and dignified silence. As Chas finished with his finery he could only stare resignedly at his reflection in the mirror.

He thought tonight might be the last time he saw her.

Of all the eventualities for which he had prepared over the previous weeks, that was the one for which he had not prepared—for which he was perhaps incapable of preparing. The finality of the thought affected him as nothing else had.

Yet there was no other recourse. Had there been, Sir Eustace would have thought of it and acted before now. All remedies at law were closed to them. All society's penalties for uncivil behavior had been exercised. And Chas knew he could not continue as he wished while Meg was effectively in Sutcliffe's power. The earl was quite literally squeezing the life out of her.

The hour was close. Chas had been to Wimbledon just that morning, to walk the ground, to see if there were any possible advantage to be had.

Sutcliffe might challenge him at any moment now, but at least the challenge would not come tonight. There was little likelihood the earl would approach Lady Billings's home, with hundreds of guests attending, and all the protection Sir Eustace and Bertram would have arranged.

Chas sighed as he touched his cravat. He wanted to concentrate on the task at hand, on meeting Sutcliffe, and not on the outcome. Even then, like some troubling refrain, all he could contemplate was his desire to see Meg, to hold Meg, to more than hold Meg.

"What a lovesick puppy you are," he muttered to himself, only to quickly dismiss Dietz's inquiring "*Bitte?*" In his present state, Chas had to believe himself fortunate to have a man who did not speak English.

He had been asked to arrive at Lady Billings's a bit early, just why he could not imagine. Perhaps Lucy had requested his presence so that she might regale him with some extensive description of a recent revel. Ordinarily, he would not have objected. But tonight . . . tonight would be difficult enough, having to be surrounded by so many, when so much was at stake.

Dietz, quietly observing Chas's prolonged attention to his dress, probably assumed his master was courting. Well, so he was. Courting an invitation, courting disaster. As he headed out the door, Chas took some comfort in knowing he met with the elderly Austrian's approval. However much one might resent them, the proprieties had been closely observed. Such attentions had never mattered much before, but now, with the lady involved . . .

Out of doors, the late May night was lovely, warm, still and clear. As the hired carriage deposited him at Meg's aunt's home, Chas took a moment to survey the street. The lamps were lit; a few people were out walking, but no vehicles waited. A man standing by the garden gate to the side touched his hat when Chas nodded.

The strong scent of lilacs graced the air.

Once in the hall, Chas scarcely recognized the place. All the wide doors between the front rooms had been opened to create an airy, broad gallery, from the garden, past the piano and orchestra at one end, through the hall and into a morning room and further dining room. The table had been removed to make space. He could hear servants clattering dishes in a supper room in back. Scores of lanterns flared, reflecting brightly in the many mirrored walls.

As the butler left to announce him to Sir Eustace, Chas glanced toward the piano. The evening's small orchestra was just setting up. He wondered if there would be a waltz—and then wondered if he would dare. The memory of Meg at the piano rose to haunt him yet again.

To distract himself he moved to the display of flowers on a long console table. The offerings were extravagant, elegant and colorful. But one simpler arrangement of white roses and blue ribbons drew his inspection. He fingered the card, noticed the unmistakable name Wembly—and frowning, immediately released it.

" 'Tis an 'H,' " Sir Eustace said as he propelled his chair forward, "for Harry."

Chas glanced at him, then scanned the rest of the flowers.

"Which are your favorites, Cabot?" Sir Eustace asked.

"I do not see them, sir."

"There are, as you know, two young ladies residing at this establishment. Lucinda's are here tonight, of course," he gestured broadly to the table, "but I believe Margaret has taken all her flowers upstairs."

Chas had to rally. His initial relief had been too quickly doused by the reference to "all" of Margaret's flowers.

"It promises to be quite a crush this evening, Sir Eustace." He tried a smile. "Miss Lucy has gathered a raft of admirers."

"I must inform you, Cabot, that Lucinda has thrown you over several times in as many weeks."

"So I hear. I regret to say—I had expected it."

"You are not heartbroken?"

"Not on her account, sir."

Sir Eustace's smile was warm. He tapped the top of his cravat.

"I note your magnificent cravat is rather askew, Mr. Cabot," he said, and indicated the mirror further along the wall. Cabot stepped over to it with a frustrated sigh. In his discomfort with Dietz's noose he must have unthinkingly loosened the devilish thing on the carriage ride over. The damage was not severe, though, and he was able to right it and secure the repair by relocating his cravat pin. As he fixed his linen he could not help but notice the portrait reflected from the wall behind him—of Meg as a young girl, with her sisters and mother. He turned to consider it.

"For some years I had it out at Selbourne," Sir Eustace told him as he too viewed the portrait. "Until I could no longer bear it. Perhaps," he mused, "I am ready to have it back."

" 'Tis a fine portrait, Sir Eustace. Of a fine-looking family."

"My wife was a most handsome woman—and beautiful to me. Louisa is much like her. Lucinda is a very pretty, lively girl. But Margaret . . . Margaret is something more." He gestured at the big-eyed child. "Even then I had to wonder where she had sprung from."

"Did you, sir?" Cabot looked from the portrait to Sir Eustace. " 'Tis no mystery. She is very like you."

"I am not near so comely," he scoffed.

Chas smiled, but glanced thoughtfully again at the portrait.

"She is the same in her essence—in her confidence. In her strength in her family. In you, sir."

Sir Eustace's eyes glistened as he looked at him.

"She causes a good deal of trouble," he said gruffly, as though he would mask his sentiment with irritation. Chas viewed the empty hall.

"I seem to have arrived excessively early. I misunderstood—and thought perhaps that Miss Lucy had some last minute directive or mission for me."

"No, Cabot. I sent for you." As Chas glanced at Sir Eustace in surprise, he added, "I wished to have a few minutes alone with you. Unfortunately, one of Lady Billings's ancients can no longer read time. Ferrell has detained him in the library for me, whilst we are demoted to the hall. I hope you do not mind?"

"Not at all."

"Cabot," he began, then hesitated. "Cabot—I am well aware that events now move—much too quickly—toward an inevitable conclusion. Though I know you intend only the best, I would counsel you not to do what you are set to do."

The direct words temporarily robbed Chas of response.

"You—ask me not to do this?"

"Yes."

"But sir— Pardon me, Sir Eustace. I can do what you cannot."

"Unquestionably. But that is not reason enough to do it. I would never have asked so much of you."

"I know that, sir. I ask it of myself. In similar circumstances I believe you would have done as much."

Sir Eustace looked down as he slapped both arms of his chair.

"Perhaps," he said. "We shall never know. I cannot ask it

of Bertram, who has proposed it He has his strengths, but in such a confrontation . . ."

"He must be kept from this," Chas stressed. "He has come too close on more than one occasion. He may yet present a problem."

"I am sending him to Selbourne—with Margaret—on Saturday." Cabot nodded, but Sir Eustace said, "There is another difficulty," adding pointedly, "Margaret. She will not let you."

"She will not know."

"And after?"

A sharp, metallic crash echoed throughout the house. Someone had dropped an item in back. The sound and the resulting excited chatter drifting from the supper room broke some of the tension Chas had felt as they talked.

His course was plotted. He could not let Sir Eustace sway him.

"I do not permit myself to think of after," he said frankly.

"She is like to believe it murder. I fear that is my own influence."

"It is a good influence, sir. Do you think I intend to present myself to her—*after*—and say 'Miss Lawrence, I have killed a man. Will you have me?' " Despite his effort at composure, Chas knew the words sounded bitter. Sir Eustace simply watched him. "I would not ask her. Whatever choices she might be free to make *after*—that is unlikely to be one of them."

"My boy, I believe you do yourself a disservice." The older man's gaze briefly sought the scarcely distinguishable mourning band on Chas's coat sleeve. "I understand you have interests on the Continent?" When Chas reluctantly nodded, he persisted, "You could not take her there?"

Chas dared not dwell on what the question tacitly assumed.

"I could, sir—if she would go. But such a removal would only delay the inevitable, as you term it. Sutcliffe also has interests on the Continent; I understand he comfortably located himself there until just a year ago. I would have to anticipate pursuit, sooner or later. 'Tis better to attempt to free her *now*, before . . . before she . . ."

"Cabot, I believe she already *has*. But she must tell you herself."

Chas sighed, to ease the oppression in his chest.

"You mean to hold out your daughter as a prize, Sir Eustace. As though the hope of attainment might alter my path."

"I mean to give you reason to stay alive, my boy."

"I cannot be alive, sir, if she is trapped."

As though on signal, the orchestra began to tune up. Bertram, still adjusting his cuffs, came running down the stairs with a loud "'allo, Cabot!" and the butler flung wide the front doors to the evening air and the sound of carriages.

Again Chas caught the heady fragrance of blooming lilacs. Even as he shook Bertie's hand, he realized he felt drained by the conversation with Sir Eustace. All that had been accomplished was some weakening of his will; it lightened his heart to know that Sir Eustace would consent to his taking Meg away. But he knew such an escape could never be safely executed, or last for long . . .

A commotion at the top of the stairs announced the presence of Louisa and Meg, aiding their aunt as she slowly made her way down the stairs. Chas could not take his gaze from Meg in a striking, low-cut gown of some fine white gauzy stuff. Indeed, as he watched her descend, he fought the urge to do precisely as her father proposed—and spirit her away across the Channel that night.

"Ladies," Sir Eustace acknowledged. "Pru, may I present to you Mr. Charles Cabot. Cabot, my sister-in-law, Lady Billings."

Chas made his best bow and purposely kept his gaze from Meg.

"I am most pleased to make your acquaintance, Mr. Cabot."

"I am honored to meet you, Lady Billings. I had the good fortune to speak with your husband many years ago. At the Royal Society. He gave a lecture on early Etruscan architecture."

Lady Billings's features softened.

"It was a subject most dear to him. You have a good memory, sir."

"'Twas an affecting lecture, my lady." Chas smiled. Old Lord Billings had in fact been a most learned gentleman, if a bit given to circumlocution.

"You are an architect, Mr. Cabot?"

"I trained as one."

"I noticed that you are properly trained in the waltz as well," Lady Billings remarked.

"I thank you, my lady. Will you do me the honor this evening?"

She looked shocked.

"Do not gape so, Pru," Sir Eustace said. "I suggest you take advantage of the offer. 'Tis unlikely to come again."

Lady Billings shot a sharp look at Sir Eustace, but her smile at Chas was wide.

"We are not set up for the waltz here this evening, sir. But I do hope you will be so good as to partner my nieces again."

"With pleasure." Cabot bowed once more and let his gaze slip to Meg. From where he was standing he could see her portrait as a child just beyond her right shoulder. The effect was enchanting—like seeing a fairy creature come to life. A very womanly fairy creature.

"What happened to the chemisette, Margaret?" her father asked idly, and all of Meg's luminous skin turned a delectable blush rose. Chas wondered what her father could mean. The gown was alluring but far from immodest—in fact he thought it perfect.

"Charles!" Lucy shrieked from the top of the stairs, proceeding to race down at a pace hardly slower than Bertie's had been. "I hope you are prepared to dance and dance and dance. I'm so excited I can scarcely stand. We shall have hours and hours of music, and Aunt Pru's chef is the very best in town—isn't he, Papa? Oh look! Everyone is here!"

If Chas had nurtured any hope that the incident at Vauxhall had subdued Lucy in the slightest, that hope had just been firmly dashed. As eager guests flooded into the hall, Lucy and her family moved to greet them. Chas stayed back and observed the growing throng. He had best lose himself in it as soon as possible; under the circumstances there was too much poignancy in being accepted so readily within the intimate circle of the family.

He eyed the arrivals. Candace d'Avigne had ventured out with two friends rather than her stepmama, which was a relief. As he moved to pay his respects, Chas noticed the advent of the Wemblys, father and both sons. He was surprised and pleased that Harry had managed to attend, though it astonished Chas that Lucy, after all her complaints, did not appear to share that pleasure. Poor Harry looked exhausted.

Walter, on the other hand, looked far from exhausted.

Chas wisely removed himself from the Wemblys' vicinity. He guessed there were several hundred people in attendance. In the course of the first hour, he danced with a number of sweetly interchangeable debutantes, all the while keeping most of his attention and all of his thoughts on Meg. Tonight she did not lack for partners, a fact to which he had a mixed reaction. When she moved to another part of the house, he moved as well, even as the crush of guests impeded pursuit. The evening was not as he would have pictured one of his final ones on earth—he would have imagined a night of revelry with his cousins, or one of quiet reflection walking the grounds at Brookslea. But as he again sought a glimpse of Meg's dark locks he knew he could not have been more satisfied.

"You are staring," Hayden said to his side.

"I do not care."

"She will know."

"By now—she should." He turned to look at Hayden, who was examining his cravat and collar through a quizzing glass.

"Dietz?" he asked.

Chas nodded, as well as he could in the stiff contraption.

"You have possibilities, Chas," Hayden said dryly.

"Unlikely to be explored. I have just suggested Dietz remove himself to Brookslea. I refuse to be ruled by my valet."

Hayden sighed.

"There are worse things."

They parted to do their duty as bachelors, Hayden with Lucy, and Chas with Lady Billings. The dance was a quadrille, which Lady Billings navigated with a great deal of panache. Chas complimented her in its aftermath.

"You are not the only one, young man, who can cut a dash on the dance floor," she suggested roguishly.

"We must do this again, Lady Billings."

"Perhaps at your wedding?"

"Oh, long before that I hope." As he bowed he knew he had disappointed her. But she was doomed to that in any event. He would not be offering for her niece.

He presented himself to Louisa, standing nearby, for the next dance, which was enjoyable enough until he espied Meg partnered with Walter Wembly for the same. Despite his best efforts, Chas could not command his gaze.

Louisa noticed.

"He is not near as good a dancer, Mr. Cabot," she told him.

"He is a much better physician."

"It is lucky then—that my sister has always been in excellent health."

He had to laugh.

"You must pardon my aunt, Mr. Cabot," Louisa added. "She is elderly—and has her hopes."

"It is not a bad thing for any of us to have hopes, Mrs. Ferrell."

"Except for you?"

As they moved apart in the steps he did not respond. But his curiosity warred with his good sense. If anyone were likely to have Meg's confidence, it was Louisa. When they came back around again, he asked,

"Should I hope, Mrs. Ferrell?"

"Yes."

The single word struck him silent. Sir Eustace and Louisa seemed to be in accord, and intent on shaking his resolve.

"Lucy is being very bad about Harry," Louisa remarked. Indeed, the youngest Miss Lawrence had rebuffed Harry's invitations to dance at least three times that Chas had noted. "Might you say something to her, Mr. Cabot? She values your opinion."

"Having thrown me over several times, she now considers me her sage advisor, does she?" They smiled at each other as they took their leave.

Chas sought out the belle of the ball, who had just finished with Lord Knowles. After one look at her face, Chas speculated that Knowles's famed loquacity had eclipsed even chatty Lucy—even at her own ball.

"I think I must have your cousin Lord Hayden, after all, Charles," Lucy mused, as though an offer were outstanding. "His address is so perfect! He is always most attentive and complimentary, and he does not talk . . . quite so much as some. He does dress divinely, doesn't he? Is he very, very wealthy?"

"Very, Miss Lucy. Which is why it does him no harm to spend much of his time gambling."

She frowned.

"And is your uncle, the duke, in good health? I know it must be a dreadful thing in a family, to have so much of one's standing depend on the standing of another. One would never *wish* for unfortunate events of course, but they do happen. Though on its own a marquisate is a very high station, isn't it?"

"My uncle is hale and hearty, Miss Lucy, and likely to live another thirty years or more."

Again the girl frowned.

"Does your cousin have any particular interests or hobbies? Perhaps he is a sportsman, or a scholar, or a patron of the arts?"

"He is exceedingly fond of port, which will no doubt give him the gout."

"Oh, but surely he is too young?"

"He is two years older than I, Miss Lucy, and I have already noticed some gray in those distinctive gold locks. He is likely to be completely gray within the year." As Lucy bit her lower lip, Chas said, "Mr. Harris Wembly did manage to attend tonight, Miss Lucy. Are you not pleased?"

Lucy roused herself from her blue study.

"If he were going to come he should have told me so, instead of pretending otherwise, and having me so anxious and upset. I have scarce been able to concentrate on all the arrangements for the ball, I have been so troubled by Mr. Wembly's excuses and delays."

"Perhaps he did not know until the last minute."

Lucy's little nose tilted dramatically.

"Some things should come first," she said.

"Yes," Chas agreed on a sigh, and let her continue uninterrupted as she eagerly relayed plans to visit Astley's circus. He had tried. At least he had countered some of her interest in Hayden.

He joined Hayden and Bertie in observing the ensuing country dance.

"I believe I have done you a service, Hayden," Chas said. "You are a graying, gouty gambler."

Hayden's eyebrows rose.

"I promise to return the favor. Perhaps with Miss Meg?"

"You needn't trouble. She is avoiding me easily enough without your reinforcement." Indeed, as he remarked it Chas realized that Meg had never once tended in his direction. At once he felt unjustifiably angry, particularly when he noticed that Walter Wembly was partnering her in this dance—his second.

"What—should you like to dance with Meggie, Cabot?" Bertie's gaze was openly inquiring. Chas reflected that it was in its own way refreshing—that Lawrence, so taken with town's distractions, was capable of being so utterly oblivious. "I shall nab you the supper dance—the second in the next set."

"Thank you, Lawrence."

As the dance came to a close, Ferrell and a morose Harry drifted over to their quiet group.

"Harry is being cut," Ferrell informed them.

"I cannot make her out," Harry said. "I have done just as she wished. I slaved to take my exams early. I could not possibly have done more." He drew a deep breath. "I shall probably be plucked. Yet she promises only . . . to drive me mad." He watched Lucy step lightly through the last measures of the dance. "Thank God for my work."

"Amen, Mr. Wembly," they agreed, in surprising chorus. They exploded in laughter. They were still in good humor when Meg brought a subdued Lucy over to Harry.

"I hesitate to interrupt your entertainment, Lord Hayden. Gentlemen." Meg curtsied to them all. "Mr. Wembly, my sister has discovered an error."

"Yes, Mr. Wembly," Lucy said, looking to the floor. "This dance is free—should you desire it."

"I do indeed, Miss Lucy," Harry said with alacrity. He bowed to Meg before offering Lucy his arm. "Thank you, Miss Meg," he said gratefully.

As the young couple moved to the floor, Bertie asked Meg, "How did you fetch her?"

"I told her—that if she did not dance with Harry at her ball, she would regret it the rest of her days." Meg's gaze was on Lucy and Harry.

"And that was sufficient inducement, Miss Lawrence?" Hayden asked.

Meg turned to smile at him.

"Does a lifelong regret not strike you as severe enough penance, my lord?"

As Hayden answered with silence, Bertie said, "This is our dance I think, Meggie," and led his sister away.

Hayden observed them through his quizzing glass.

"You must marry her, Chas," he said at last, "and soon. Else I fear I shall be forced to it." He dropped the glass and turned to him. "And that you know you would regret." He walked off toward the other room, leaving Chas to reflect that his cousin might be preferable to Dr. Wembly—but not by much.

He waited. The music was good, though the few instruments with the piano sounded thin compared to Almack's orchestra. The tune just barely bested the hum of conversation. The rooms had warmed with the lights and the activity of the dancers; the cool garden beckoned. But Chas would have his dance. He watched Meg with her brother. For some reason Sutcliffe came to mind—for the first time since the dancing had begun.

Chas tried to dispel the thought but could not. The image was of the music continuing, of the evening still bright and lively, of Meg still dancing—with Lawrence, with Hayden, with Knowles and Demarest and Wembly. But he himself watched as though through a veil, as though he had passed on.

"What is it, Cabot?" Ferrell asked him. He had been standing to the side in companionable silence.

"A shadow across my grave, I should imagine, Ferrell."

Ferrell contemplated Lady Billings's grand ballroom, with its high ceilings, glowing sconces and chandeliers, and decorative swags.

"He isn't here tonight, Cabot," he said perceptively. Then he grinned. "Nevertheless, would you care for something to drink? Negus—or something stronger?"

Chas thanked him but declined. The dance was coming to a close. As Ferrell wandered away Chas kept his gaze on

Meg. He was determined that she should not elude him again.

When the music stopped he moved quickly to intercept her. Bertie had just placed her hand upon his sleeve when Meg withdrew it.

"I believe I shall take a rest now, Mr. Cabot. I am feeling fatigued."

"But you cannot . . ." He stopped himself from pleading. She did not look fatigued. "Of course, Miss Lawrence. As you wish."

He stood with her. She could not very well dance with anyone else after such an excuse. He stood close enough to note how exercise had dampened the fine wisps of curls against her forehead. As she fanned her face he had the overwhelming desire to kiss her delectable neck. When he noticed her foot tapping to the beat of the music, Chas knew he had had enough.

"Did you receive my violets, Miss Lawrence?"

The fanning briefly paused.

"I did, thank you."

He turned fully to her.

"But you are determined to do to me . . . what your sister did to Harry?"

"It is not the same," she insisted, again fanning vigorously as she kept her attention on the dancers.

"You must know—it is worse." That drew her gaze. His own was steady; he reminded her silently of their shared kiss in the park. It was best she know that he thought her unfair. As her fanning lapsed altogether he pulled her into the remainder of the dance.

They had to skirt the set. He deftly maneuvered her past

the orchestra, toward a door to the garden. And when the music stopped he slipped her quickly outside into the night air, just as everyone else headed to supper.

"Mr. Cabot . . ."

He placed a finger against her lips, and coaxed her further, away from the circle of light at the door, down the steps and on beyond a line of clipped pear trees. The scent of lilacs again filled the air, and the leaves on the pear trees rustled. The shadows of the trees and of the high garden walls crossed the light from the ballroom.

"Do you not hear it?" he asked softly, drawing her closer. He had had her in his arms before—she belonged there always. "Do you not hear the waltz?" He turned with her as though to music, holding her as he had at Almack's, even, perhaps, a bit tighter—because there was no one to see— and she did not protest. He recognized helplessly that he was above all things a lover.

He led her silently through a series of slow, gliding turns, his arm hard against her waist. Her face was pale in the darkness, her eyes large and beautiful. When they closed, he leaned to kiss her.

His lips, the wonderful warm lips she had missed, had just touched hers again when Meg heard something quite different from the muted rustling of leaves. It sounded distinctly intrusive—a soft scraping against brick; it sounded as though someone were climbing down the garden wall to their side.

Instantly Cabot put her from him and moved to the wall, listening intently as he eyed its height. There was no gate to the alley beyond. He returned to grasp her hand and pull her none too gently toward the ballroom.

"You must stay inside," he commanded as he ran her up the steps. His voice was now anything but coaxing. "I have been incalculably foolish."

Meg was deposited, blinking dazedly, in the suddenly harsh lights of the ballroom, where only the musicians still lingered away from supper. As Cabot strode quickly ahead of her, she trailed in his wake, conscious of the first flush of embarrassment. If Cabot were to tell father, or Bertie, they would know she had been out in the garden with him—alone . . .

Cabot did not go to the supper room but out through the library behind the dancing gallery. The library's tall glass doors fronted both the garden and the mews; none of the doors was open. Cabot unlocked one in back and straddled a low iron rail to jump easily down to the lane. Meg knew the back route well, since she and Bertie had used it often as their exit for their early morning rides. From the safety of the library, she watched Cabot rapidly walk the length of the garden wall and beyond into darkness. Nothing was in sight—no people, no horses, no carts or carriages. Meg could not imagine how someone could possibly have gained the top of the wall without aid—and then disappear so quickly.

When Cabot reappeared down the alley, he entered at the kitchen door below.

Meg looked about the library, which had been used as a card room. Dealt hands still lay upon the tables, awaiting renewal of the games. The players must have recessed reluctantly for supper, though the sound of conversation and laughter from the dining room was continuous and cheerful, and clearly, Meg thought enviously, untroubled.

Cabot returned to her in the library and pointedly locked the glass door to the mews.

"Someone helped him up. There are no signs of hooks or ropes. Our visitor must have been atop the wall for some time. Since before the guard was posted at the kitchen door, at least—for he saw nothing. The guard says he heard only what he believed to be a cat. It is dark enough the sneak could have slipped quietly into the shadows and been off in mere seconds." He sighed heavily. "Curse me for a simpleton!" He brushed off his coat with impatience.

"You could not have known . . . ," Meg said.

"I should have guessed. Even with guards front and back I should not have taken you out there. I apologize, Miss Lawrence."

She watched his face, wondering if he apologized for everything. If so, she did not want him to.

"Come, let us say nothing of this." He placed a warm palm at her waist to direct her back toward the hall. "Nothing further can be done. It would only distress the rest of your family."

"You think he was—someone from Lord Sutcliffe?"

"I know he was." He stopped her there in the library and turned her to him. The playfulness of her waltzing partner had disappeared. All was tense expectancy and purpose. "Your father said you return to Selbourne Saturday?"

"Yes."

"That's for the best—for now. Sutcliffe can reach you too easily here in town."

Meg thought her face must betray her guilty secret, the meeting at Monsieur LeBecque's and the earl's dreadful offer. Cabot was looking at her too closely.

"He has not attempted to see you—since Vauxhall?"

Meg shook her head. Silence seemed less of a lie. And yet she wanted to tell him everything. The desire to unburden her heart was acute.

"When—will you return to Selbourne?" she asked, thinking her voice sounded pitiable.

"This fall."

Did that mean three months from now? Four months? Five?

"Not—before?" She stared intently at his gorgeous cravat.

"Before would certainly be preferable," he said softly, and when her gaze sought his eyes she thought she read a smile in them. "If I am not detained. You must trust that all will be well—Meg." He took her hand and raised it, palm up, to his lips. Even through her glove she felt the warmth of that kiss; her fingers curled inward. With his other hand he lightly traced the line of her jaw, then caught a tendril of hair curling at her neck. When his lips lowered to hers it was as though to a decision. But his touch was scarcely more than a breath, as though he restrained himself. Meg knew with a pang that he would not have been so careful out in the garden.

The noise from the supper room increased. Cabot drew away from her and led her out into the gallery. A few guests were filtering back toward the ballroom. When he released her hand, Meg felt adrift, as though she were returning from a distant journey, though they had been away from the gathering for scarcely twenty minutes.

In the crowded supper room she moved toward Louisa and Ferrell, but her gaze still accompanied Cabot.

"Margaret!" Walter accosted her. "I've been looking for you! I thought we were to come into supper together."

"I—I'm sorry, Walter," she said. "I had no idea you were waiting." She watched Cabot find Lord Hayden, saw Hayden listen and nod, saw Cabot find her father. Her father glanced quickly at her. Meg made no effort to follow what Walter was saying—she was too thoroughly attuned to Cabot.

He was taking his leave. He was leaving now, even before supper was finished, even with more music to come and the lilacs still perfuming the warm night air. And why should he feel compelled to leave now? He had not told her. Because Sutcliffe would have him followed? Because Sutcliffe's men might at this moment be awaiting him at his rooms? Because Sutcliffe would challenge him, or have him murdered in the dark?

He was bowing to Aunt Pru, he was kissing Lucy's hand. He was walking, in all his formal elegance, toward the door.

Meg felt faint. She grasped the back of a dining chair and clung to it.

"Miss Margaret, you are very pale. You must take a seat." Walter was hovering. From the front hall, Cabot looked back at her, standing at the entrance to the supper room. She thought he frowned, as though he debated removing her from Dr. Wembly's attentions. But he turned away, and Walter blocked her view, and Louisa thrust a glass of punch into her hand, saying firmly,

"Drink this, Meggie."

At breakfast the next morning, the post brought a sealed note addressed to Miss Lawrence:

Charles Cabot is a dead man. Unless . . . ? Sutcliffe

Chapter Nine

"Whatever the reckoning may be, my dear," Sir Eustace said as he buttered a slice of toast, "I assure you your father will pay it."

Meg roused herself from her shock.

"It is not a bill, father." She looked up to meet his frown. "I am being taken to task—for being a dilatory correspondent."

"That doesn't sound like you, Meggie," Bertie said. "Who dares charge you with tardy replies?"

"Oh—she is . . . a friend of Aunt Bitty's. You do not know her." Meg folded the page and placed it carelessly to the side of her plate. She had not had supper last night; she had no appetite this morning. She thought she might never wish to eat again. But she reached for her teacup and forced herself to take a sip. She could think only of Cabot telling her last night, "You must trust that all will be well." He had, for the first time, called her Meg.

Sutcliffe wanted him dead.

As her hands shook she returned the cup and saucer to the table, and fell once more into silent despair. She had thought it difficult enough last night, moving numbly through the rest of the ball's festivities.

"Margaret?" her father asked.

"It is nothing, father. Just too much excitement, and too little sleep. I shall feel better directly."

"I should be surprised that you are here at all, given that Lucinda has not troubled to make an appearance."

"We had a very gay time last night. Lucy could not have been happier. But I believe she has a bit of a headache—as, unfortunately, do I."

"Too much punch," Bertie suggested, with a wink at his father.

"And you, Bertram, I believe you had too much punch as well," Sir Eustace said.

"No, father. Just enough." He laughed.

"There is no question it is a phenomenon, Bertram. A most unnatural one at that—that spirits do not appear to affect you."

"I am a lucky fellow, father."

"I will not debate you." Sir Eustace again turned his attention to her. "Margaret, I'm concerned. Will you be able to travel tomorrow to Selbourne as planned? Or shall I delay the caravan?"

"Do not delay—please. If I rest today I shall be fine this evening." She rose from her seat and removed her deadly missive from the table. "I must finish packing though."

"My dear—Walter asked to see me today. Have you any notion what that might be about?"

Meg drew a frustrated breath. Walter was much too precipitous; she had given him no encouragement. In the space of four days he had advanced from resuming an acquaintance to attempting to seal his future.

"Father—I—have given him no sign."

"Tsh, Meg—have you ever given anyone a sign? Do not worry. I shall deal gently with Walter. But I am just as glad you are heading back to Selbourne and will spare me another round of simpering suitors. 'Tis best you and Bertram spend your time helping Cabot tear up the lawns."

She felt his name, like a sorrow.

"Mr. Cabot said he would not return to Selbourne until autumn."

"Did he?" Her father was concentrating on his breakfast. "My mistake then. You and Bertram will have to tear up the lawns on your own." His gaze flashed to her. "Go get your rest, Margaret. I do not wish to see you again until dinner."

Meg moved to kiss his cheek before exiting the dining room. She was too distracted to engage him further. And she was tired of feeding him fabrications.

Weeping would have been a relief. But Sutcliffe expected an answer. She doubted he would give her the day; in fact, he might give her little more than the morning before seeking out Cabot.

Meg had known since the meeting at the studio that she would be compelled to go to Sutcliffe, but some small element of what must have been hope had kept her from actually planning. She had wanted to continue with her dream, with her family and Cabot safe and with nothing and no one to be confronted.

In her room she again read the note, then stared pensively

at her partially packed belongings. If she were to go to Sutcliffe, she might as well leave most of these things behind.

Her gaze settled on Cabot's bowl of violets. Annie had faithfully refreshed the water for them, but they would not last long. They were as ephemeral as spring itself. It was time for a new season, for yet another stage.

The threatened tears pricked her eyes.

She had had little sleep. Her mind had replayed the evening's encounters with Cabot—seeing him in the hall with her father. Having him remind her of their kiss in the park, his gaze alone had demanded that she recall it. Having him waltz silently with her and start, so very like a whisper, to kiss her again. Not once, but twice.

He had walked away because of Sutcliffe, and now she would walk away because of Sutcliffe.

Truly, the earl was a most powerful gentleman, to so intimately dictate the actions of two other people.

She should have been clever enough to do away with Sutcliffe years ago. She should, perhaps, have hired an assassin. Or set his home ablaze. Carefully arranged for his meals to be poisoned. Or stabbed him while dancing. All sounded worthy of the novels Louisa had mocked. And Meg could only imagine the horror of compelling Sir Eustace Lawrence to defend his daughter, a murderess.

She had tried fleeing and tired of it. Even with Aunt Bitty she had felt a prisoner. She had missed her family and she had not been free to begin one of her own. And if she were to escape now, Sutcliffe would still blame Cabot. With the long-sought prize lost Sutcliffe would persist in attacking the apparent cause.

Meg could see no option but to go to the earl. She had to

rely on him to keep his word, though she had little enough with which to bargain.

She moved to her writing desk and sat down to pen her response. Outside, clouds gathered; for the middle of the morning her room was unusually dark. She lit a candle, and carefully wrote:

I shall come to you at your pleasure, with the under-standing that you will keep your promise. Margaret Lawrence.

She folded and sealed the thin sheet, wrote its direction as

The Earl of Sutcliffe, Grosvenor Square

then rang for Annie.

Annie was surprised to see her already back from breakfast.

"They are still at table. Miss Lucy has just gone down. Did you not eat anything, Miss Meg?"

"I was not hungry. Annie, I must ask you to run an errand for me this morning. I know you have been busy with the packing, but this is more important and perhaps, perhaps it will not be necessary to complete the packing today at all."

Annie's brow furrowed.

"What would you be wanting, Miss Meg?"

"I would have you take a note to Lord Sutcliffe at Grosvenor Square."

"I will not!"

Meg sighed.

"Please, Annie—it is critical. And it must go at once."

"I tell you, Miss Meg, I will not! You should not be writin' to that devil! You should have naught to do with him!"

"Annie, you make too much of this . . ."

"I cannot make enough of it!"

"Oh, Annie . . ." Meg placed a palm to her forehead. She had pleaded a headache earlier; now it had become a reality. "What do you know of this after all? You are making it so much harder."

"I know enough! That you now think to do what you would not do before—and it's wrong as it ever was."

"I am wrong either way. But Annie, you were married once. You should understand that I . . . I love the man."

"Sutcliffe?"

"Oh, do not be absurd," Meg said wearily. After a moment's silence, Annie said,

"You should be holdin' yourself even more for him now then, Miss Meg. For I'm thinkin' he loves you, too."

"I . . . cannot know that."

"Glaikit!" Annie looked stern. " 'Tis foolishness! You say that because you want an excuse to decide without him havin' a say!"

"Decide what, Annie? How can you know?"

"I seen that milord with you. Like a cat with a mouse. " 'Taint no walk in the park he's wantin' of you, Miss Meg."

"Whatever he may want, he first needs a response from me. If he does not receive it, something very dreadful will happen. Do you understand me, Annie? I do not command you to go, but I ask it of you as a friend."

"Then as a friend I mustn't go. You should have no truck with the devil, Miss Meg."

"I cannot afford your scruples. *Someone* must go to Lord Sutcliffe, without father or Bertie hearing of it. If you will not oblige me, I must have Thwaite send one of the footmen. And you know how they talk. Perhaps I must go myself, now, and let *that* be response enough."

With her lips set grimly, Annie held out her hand for the letter. Meg did not find any compassion or resignation in the older woman's gaze, simply determination.

"Give it to me, then, Miss Meg, and I shall see it where you wish. But mind you, I know I do you no favor."

Meg thanked her and gave her some pocket money to pay for a hackney. Before departing for Grosvenor Square, Annie fetched her something for a headache, but Meg knew the response to Sutcliffe would be speedy.

The subsequent solitude should have been welcome, but she could do little but worry. Her packing remained unfinished; the few farewells she had intended to pen went unwritten. She tried to rest, but could not put Cabot from her mind.

He must have known how it would be—even as they had been alerted to the intruder in the garden last night. He must have known—that from that moment he was a marked man. His deliberate but hasty departure had been the result.

It started to rain. After so many days of fine weather the change seemed ominous. Seated at the escritoire in her third floor room, Meg could look out over rooftops at the darkening sky. But the sound was steady, soothing. With the page before her blank, Meg rested her head on her arms. Her tears dampened her sleeves.

She had tried to discourage Cabot. Yet from the first he

had acted—bringing her the gift of the tree, helping to trap Sutcliffe's spy, leading her into the waltz at Almack's, right under Sutcliffe's nose. She realized he had known even then what he was about. He had been most purposeful; he had designed all. Did he expect her to sit idly by while he went to his grave? She could not. Sutcliffe was far from trustworthy, but Meg did trust in the violence of his hatred. If Meg did nothing, Cabot was most assuredly a dead man.

She at last raised her head and dried her cheeks. Annie had been gone a very long time. It was past noon—the candle was guttering. Perhaps the rain had caused delays, or Annie awaited a return message with Sutcliffe's proposal. Sutcliffe's proposal! Well yes, Meg knew what that was. But the arrangements to implement his wishes were another matter.

Again she stared at the sheet of paper before her. At first she thought to leave some explanation for her father, but she decided he would comprehend everything. He knew her very well. Would her father believe his sacrifices had been in vain? They had not been. She was stronger now than she had been at seventeen, and she knew what it was to love. Sutcliffe would not break her.

Meg dipped the pen in the ink and began to write.

'Dear Mr. Cabot'—she paused. Surely she should call him Charles? But much as she thought it should signify, she knew it no longer could.

Dear Mr. Cabot,

You will think it strange that I write to you under the present circumstances, since you have done so much to attempt to prevent them. For your many efforts I thank

*you, and I know my father thanks you. What I do now
I should perhaps have undertaken a long time ago,
before so many I care for surrendered so much on my
behalf. I do not wish to add your name to my list of
regrets.*

*I believe I know what you intended. Such an en-
deavor speaks well of your nobility and great kindness to me and to my family. But I cannot ask it of
you, and I cannot accept it from you. I am forever in
your debt for believing me worth such a sacrifice. To
assume you would have acted out of anything more
than generosity can only be painful to me—I pray it is
not so. I shall always remember you as a man of good
heart and determination to do right. You have my
highest esteem. I pray that you will find in future the
happiness you deserve.*

*Mr. Cabot, will you allow me to apologize for the
many times I chose to misinterpret your words and actions? I thought I would have more time to make
amends. Please do forgive me. God bless you,*

Margaret Lawrence

She stared at the page for a long while before folding
and sealing it. As an expression of her feelings it was clear
enough; the letter would serve adequately as a thank-you.
She could not say what most needed saying—as she went
to one man she could not very well confess her sentiments
for another.

She wrote Cabot's name across the front. She rose and
stepped to her dressing table to find Cabot's violets, but

Annie, in watering them, had moved the card. Meg could not find it, but discovered that she had memorized the direction in any event. She scribbled it shakily.

Having noticed in her dressing mirror the evidence of her weeping, Meg turned to the washstand to rinse her face. She was patting herself dry when Annie returned.

Annie glanced at her face, then frowned.

"You've been cryin', Miss Meg."

"Which would not be surprising. Did you have difficulty finding the earl? Did he have a response?"

"No difficulty. But I had to wait for the response as he— he had to make various arrangements."

"I should have imagined he'd be well prepared," Meg said bitterly, "he has been that certain of me."

"Well," Annie said, "he had to make arrangements as to time an' all. I'm to fetch you to his coach this evening. He said—let me see—'out of concern for her sensibilities' he will send it to wait at the end of the alley."

"Lord Sutcliffe is most gracious," she said dryly. "I'd have thought he would prefer me to announce my departure to the neighbors. He sent no note?"

Annie shook her head.

"He just said you should bring only what you most need and cannot do without. And to dress for travel."

"Travel? Did he say where?"

"No, miss."

"And the time I am to meet the coach?"

"Five, Miss Meg. I am to go with you."

"Oh, Annie!" Meg reached to squeeze the maid's hand. "That at least is something. If you can bear it?"

"I will not leave you, Miss Meg. But I must pack a few things for myself. And I must also order you some tea, as you have had so little and we must not rely on dinner."

"Yes." Now that the plans had been set, Meg felt oddly resigned. "Was it—was it an imposing residence, Annie? He is said to have extraordinary collections, to have many fine things."

"I couldn't say, I'm sure. But you mayn't be there long— if at all."

"And was Lord Sutcliffe surprised?"

Annie appeared to mull that over.

"I don't rightly know what to tell you, Miss Meg. I was so angry at first, perhaps I did not notice as I ought. He said you should be certain you were eager to surrender your life. That does not sound like *surprised*, does it?"

Indeed, it did not. Meg's certainty wavered. The man's audacity seemed boundless—to place her in such straits, and then play the philosopher.

"Having gained his end with me he is now strangely keen to dissuade me. Did he say anything further about the attractive circumstances in which I shall find myself?"

"Well, let me see . . . I don't remember much he said because I was anxious to get back here to you as soon as I could. As you know I . . . I do not like the man . . ."

"To put it mildly, Annie!"

". . . and as I had to remember about the coach and time and all. But he did say he was 'eager to get on with the business' and he said you must 'come to him whole'—no, *wholly,* and that there would be no goin' back. I think he thought to remind you that you mayn't never return to your father, who would be unlikely to welcome you home."

Meg swallowed. This was hardly in the nature of wooing her to her future. Could the man have scruples after all? But no, she should not hope as much. "Come to him wholly" was clear enough. Meg sensed she would be measuring years before she felt whole again.

Annie had rung for tea and was carefully laying out Meg's best traveling dress. Given her earlier anger and obstinacy, Meg found Annie's calmness now difficult to fathom. But Annie had always had a practical nature, and they had little time in which to ready themselves for a momentous departure. Meg could only be grateful. She found reassurance in Annie's silence and in her promised company. However unsavory the future she would at least have that.

Once the tea tray arrived, Annie left to gather her own belongings. Meg settled herself to eat something. Part of her wanted to see her father, to explain. But he would prevent her from going—and she had to go. She hoped Annie was carefully masking her own preparations to leave.

The household's eagerness to carry tales was only too obvious upon Annie's return.

"Mrs. Ferrell came visiting, an' your father said you had to rest, so Miss Lucinda has gone out with her to make some calls. And Mr. Bertram has gone to see to the horses, to make certain they are ready to travel tomorrow." Annie ignored the catch in Meg's breath and carefully averted her gaze. "Mr. Wembly—that's the doctor, Mr. Walter—came to see your father. An' Giles, that's Lady Billings's under footman as you know, took them some refreshments an' believes Mr. Walter must have made an offer. Because Giles said Sir Eustace was saying as how he would have to consult

Miss Margaret on the state of her heart. Giles said, let's see . . . that Sir Eustace said that 'in all honesty I believe her inclinations lie elsewhere'. An' Doctor Wembly looked a bit like a sick sheep, or so Giles said, an' left soon after." Annie at last looked up at her. "Mayhap you should be consulting your heart, Miss Meg."

"I do not need to consult my heart, Annie. I know very well what it has to say to me. It would have me be foolish—and see harm come to Mr. Cabot. I cannot suffer so. I cannot see him lost in such a pointless manner. In a . . . a clash of honor. So I do not rely on my heart. It must be stored away."

"You think your honor pointless?" Annie asked hotly.

"Against a man's life? Yes I do."

Annie was shaking her head again.

"You are very young, Miss Meg. You do not understand men."

"That is unquestionably true, Annie. And now I am un-likely ever to understand them—since I go not to a man but to a devil."

Annie fell silent as they finished packing Meg's bag. Then she offered to take it downstairs to join hers by the kitchen steps. Annie had told the other servants that she was readying her own belongings for the journey to Sel-bourne the next morning. Annie would keep an eye out for the quiet period, before the kitchen's preparations for din-ner began, when they might slip out into the alley. She would collect Meg shortly.

Meg packed a few favorite books and personal items into a satchel. At the last minute she pulled several violets from the bowl Cabot had sent her, and pressed them between two sheets of vellum. They seemed little enough, to sustain a lifetime.

When Annie returned and said it was a good time to take their leave, Meg handed her the note for Cabot.

"I don't wish this to go from the house, Annie. Perhaps you know how it might be forwarded?"

"Is it to him, then?" Annie asked, reminding Meg that she knew very few of her letters.

"Yes."

Annie took the note and slipped it into a pocket in her skirts.

"There's a boy who runs errands for the houses around here. I'll give it to him. Are you ready now, Miss Meg? Your father is resting, an' everyone else is still out. But we must be quiet."

Meg nodded and followed Annie down the several flights of stairs to the kitchen door in back. Annie had thoughtfully found two umbrellas and placed them at the ready. Though the rain had stopped, it threatened to return. When they opened the door Meg realized the evening had turned chilly as well. She was grateful for the light wool traveling cloak that Annie had recommended.

She silently voiced a farewell to her family as she followed Annie out into the damp. She silently voiced a farewell to Cabot as they walked past the high garden wall he had surveyed only the previous night. The whole world looked gray. At the mews entrance she could see a large black coach and four dark horses. Two men sat above with the coachman, while another, mounted separately behind, held the reins for an additional saddle horse.

Meg had insisted on carrying her own bag the few hundred

feet down the alley. As she and Annie made their way, one of the men from atop the carriage jumped to the ground to come toward them.

For a second Meg's breath caught, for he was tall, like Cabot, and something in his bearing, even in a high-collared greatcoat, reminded her of him. But as he neared them, Meg noticed his black hair beneath an obscuring wide-brimmed hat. As he reached to relieve them of their bags, she also noticed the flash of bright blue eyes. It wasn't Cabot he resembled, but someone else . . .

"Miss?" He had stowed the bags and now offered a hand to help her up into the coach. Again Meg felt the scrutiny of those keen eyes. She looked around for Annie, only to find that her maid had already scrambled atop to the box. Annie's desertion surprised and hurt her.

Meg refused to look toward Sutcliffe's cloaked form in the opposite corner of the coach. As they started up, she settled as far away from him as possible and stared down the mews toward her aunt's garden wall.

"Are you pleased, my lord Sutcliffe?" she asked distantly.

"I am far from pleased. I am not *your* Lord Sutcliffe. But as you are determined to shame yourself, I shall serve as well as the next man."

Chapter Ten

Meg met Cabot's gaze. In the dimness she could not read his expression. But she did not have to.

She turned to the window and closed her eyes. She permitted herself a few seconds of relief—even of joy. Then the anxiety and restraint returned.

"How did you know?"

"Annie," he bit out. "At least she has some sense. Thank God for her."

When Meg glanced back at him she saw that Cabot had resumed his observation of the wet streets behind them. He must despise her.

"This coach," she said, nervously stroking the upholstered leather seat, "is it . . ."

"Hayden's," he supplied shortly.

"And that man—the footman, or . . ."

"My cousin David. Major Trent, Lord David. I apologize if he was rude. He's been foxed for six days running."

191

"Oh no, he was not rude at all. I thought I recog—"

"We are all armed, Miss Lawrence. Hayden rides with the coachman and Annie, and an outrider with David postern."

"Why are you armed?"

"Should Sutcliffe pursue you. Lady Billings's home may have been watched today as well. In fact, that is likely."

Meg fell silent for a moment. Even as the earl had awaited her answer he had probably spied upon her.

"How did Annie find you?" she asked.

Cabot pulled a card from his waistcoat pocket and tossed it across to her.

"From the violets I sent you as an apology. For presuming so much against your *innocence*."

"I did nothing with Lord Sutcliffe."

"Except promise him everything. I read the note you sent with Annie. You volunteered, Margaret Lawrence. After so much from so many. After your father!" He did not give her a chance to respond. She would have told him that he meant even more. "When did you decide? After you saw him at the studio? Annie told me of your meeting."

"I decided this morning—not before." She turned again to the window. "I had no choice."

"No choice?" His voice, his presence in the confines of the coach, affected her alarmingly. She wanted only to sit with him, to have him pretend to love her once more. Yet his anger fed her hesitance.

When she glanced at him again his dark gaze was fixed on her.

"How could you?" he asked. There was such disdain in the question that she did not know what to say. "What did he promise you? Your note said you would go to him with the understanding that he would keep his promise. What did he promise you?"

Meg looked down at her clasped hands. It hardly mattered now. If Sutcliffe had not heard from her all day, if his spies had witnessed this venture, it was all for naught.

"Whatever his promise," Cabot concluded at her silence, "he was most unlikely to have kept it. You may be assured of that." As she looked to him again he said, "I see you keep confidence with Sutcliffe—when it never occurred to you to come in confidence to me."

"Given how understanding you have been, that is hardly surprising."

"Understanding? My dear Miss Lawrence, how can I be *understanding* when I've been given no explanation? Last night you might have said anything to me, and I'd have shown you as much understanding as you could desire. As I recall, I even asked if Sutcliffe had attempted to see you. You did not tell me the truth. You had no faith in me. You do not trust me." He turned grimly to the window again.

"I do trust you. I trust you in every way but . . . but one." She did not trust him to get the better of Sutcliffe. In all else she would trust him with her life. "He killed Douglas," she said aloud.

"Douglas was a brave boy. I am not a *boy*. And increasingly, I feel myself a match for Lord Sutcliffe—in everything base."

The claim gave her pause, though she did not believe it.

"Where are you taking me?" she asked faintly.

"To be wed, Miss Lawrence. Most opportunely. Since I am at this moment compromising you."

"I cannot . . ."

"If you could contemplate going wholly and forever to Sutcliffe, you can certainly resign yourself to ten minutes of vows with me. It will be most proper and aboveboard, I guarantee it. I have a special license, through Clare, who happens to be a great friend of the Archbishop."

"Sutcliffe . . ."

"Must face disappointment," he retorted. "I am determined that your life shall be your own."

"By *marrying* me?"

He appeared to shrug.

"As a method, 'tis nothing—a construct."

"Nothing," she repeated. "A construct? Like one of the landscape impositions you so disdain, a picturesque grotto, perhaps? Or more aptly a folly! I think more highly of marriage than you do, sir."

"Oh, I agree—the Countess of Sutcliffe sounds very high indeed."

"I had thought," she choked out, "more highly of *you*."

"And I of you. So, Miss Lawrence, we are at *pointe non plus*."

She was crying, but in the darkness she knew he could not see. She dared not raise a hand to her face. She could not believe they could reproach each other so.

"By marrying me, you will have choice," he said, though he spoke to the dark window. The carriage lights had not been lit. "You will have choice beyond anything you could otherwise have envisaged. And you will have the protection of Braughton—and of Hayden. You need not spend a moment more thinking of Sutcliffe—not one second. Unless you choose to. And you will have Brookslea . . ." For a moment he fell silent. He was relaying his reasoning, as calmly as possible. Meg knew she should have been grateful, but she could not be grateful for such coldness.

"Once wed, you may choose to do as you please. You will be a young and wealthy wife. You may follow the path of the Comtesse d'Avigne, whom you so admire. Perhaps you will soon be a young and wealthy widow. Then no one, not even Miss Lawrence of Selbourne, can censure you."

"You mean to fight him."

"I do."

Meg slid toward him across the seat.

"Do not." She reached to touch his broadcloth cloak. "Let us go away from here. Now—tonight! He will not follow the both of us. We might go anywhere—the Continent, the West Indies . . ."

"I have wandered too much," he said. He stared at her gloved hand on his cloak. "And it is not what you choose."

"But it is what I choose! I choose it now, freely, before we are wed, before you confront him—while there is still choice!" She edged closer to him, so that her skirts brushed one of his boots, and spread her fingers upon his knee. "Will you not take me away?"

She was close enough now to see his face more clearly. Given the passion of her plea his expression was frustratingly blank. And his dark eyes were hooded.

"Mere minutes ago you were fleeing to Sutcliffe."

"I know. But you do not understand. I did that because . . . because . . ."

"Yes? Because you simply tired of telling him no? Because you wish to be a countess? Because you preferred his bonbons to my violets? *Dieu m'en garde!*"

"Oh please . . . stop . . ." Meg covered her face with her hands.

In the silence she tried to steady her breathing, then Cabot asked again, "What did he promise you?" This time his voice broke. "What could it possibly have been?"

"He promised to spare you. He promised me your life."

In the instant quiet, Meg heard the rain begin in earnest on the carriage roof. The horses were slowing, the coachman called to them as the wheels stopped. Cabot moved closer, directly across from her, and gently pulled her hands from her cheeks. They sat knee to knee as she looked up into his eyes.

When Lord Hayden opened the door, both of them glanced to the side.

"Wait!" Cabot said, and his hold on her hands tightened.

"We were followed, Chas," Hayden said. Rain dripped from the brim of his hat. "Two men. One's remained here across the road. There's little time."

Cabot sighed and released her hands. He stepped out into the damp. Meg rose to follow him. Instead of simply taking her hand he clasped her at the waist and swung her completely clear of the puddled street. One arm remained possessively about her. Meg watched Annie and Major Trent entering a stone house set back amid some trees.

Hayden handed Cabot an umbrella, which he carried as he walked her to the front of the house. Inside, in the modest hallway, he pulled her urgently to the side.

"One minute," he told Hayden. "Just one minute."

Hayden shook his head, but turned into a parlor, where Meg could see Annie, the major, and two gentlemen in collars. Then Cabot blocked her view. He stood so close she caught the scent of his cloak's damp wool.

"Sutcliffe bargained my life for your compliance?"

Meg nodded as she held his gaze.

"He would not have kept his promise," he said. "Even had he tried, which I sincerely doubt, I would not have let him keep it. Not at that price." He took one of her hands, and raised it to his lips. Even through her glove his kiss was warm. Meg's other hand sought his chest. She wanted simply to cling to him.

"It seems to be my habit," he added softly, "to misuse what little time I have with you. Forgive me, Meg. But we must do this now. At once."

"Why?"

"Because it is the only way to protect you. Because it draws another line that Sutcliffe might hesitate to cross— whether I am to hand or not. Marriage works to the advantage of both of us, and distinctly to his detriment."

"How does it work—to your advantage?"

Cabot smiled down at her.

"When I meet him—he shall know it."

"You must meet him?"

"If he calls me out. And he will."

"I cannot bear it."

Again he kissed her hand.

"I shall survive it. You must expect me to. But now we must hurry." He turned to glance at the others, talking softly in the further room.

"Is it . . . is it real?" Meg asked, following his gaze. They were clergymen, but this was not a church.

Again he smiled.

"You must ask the rector here. I believe he is properly ordained. If not, I shall happily repeat myself."

Meg drew breath.

"You must know . . ."

"Chas," Hayden said sharply from the doorway. There was little of the aloof marquis in his manner at the moment.

"Yes." Cabot again slid an arm about her waist. Meg reached up to remove her bonnet as they walked into the parlor. She focused only on the arm at her waist and the kindly features of the rector.

"Are we ready, then?" he asked.

Even as Meg nodded he began to speak. Meg heard something less than words—something like a soothing incantation. She heard the rain spattering against the windows; she was aware that Annie stood at her side. She heard what sounded like ten names for Cabot before she was asked to say "I do." She knew he raised her hand and pulled off her glove. He slid a ring on to her finger. It was heavy and unfamiliar. She glanced at it briefly before Cabot kissed her even more briefly, just to the side of her lips. Then Annie took her bonnet from her numb hands.

"Miss Meg," she said. "Please remove your cloak. I must change with you."

Meg obeyed, fumbling with the clasp at her throat before shedding the soft blue wool. She exchanged it for Annie's gray homespun and chip straw bonnet. Meg hastily signed the license and register: Margaret Rowe Lawrence.

Cabot led her back into the hall, but took her toward the rear of the small house. He kept that reassuring arm about her waist.

"You'll be going to my grandmother's, with one of her men—Alphonse, just here." He nodded to a sturdy gentleman outside, mounted on an equally sturdy brown horse.

Alphonse held the reins for another saddled giant. *"Grand-mère* expects you. She lives some miles away. You must hurry."

"But I thought we would be . . . That I would be going with you."

"Not just now. We must lead Sutcliffe from you. And I must know you are safe."

"When will you come for me?"

At that he paused, long enough for her to lose heart.

"Perhaps tomorrow. I shall send word if I'm delayed."

Her vision was blurring.

"Shall I now call you Chas—as your cousin does?"

The question seemed to hurt him. He sighed deeply as he tilted her chin with his free hand. This time his mouth met hers, fully and hungrily. She knew why he had not kissed her before. When he raised his head, she opened her eyes. She knew her gaze accused him. He could not leave her now; he should not leave her now. Not after this.

But he turned from her. As he strode back into the hall he signaled his cousin David, who moved with alacrity to take Meg out to the waiting horseman. The major gave her a hand to help her mount.

"Do not worry, miss—ma'am," he amended with a smile. Touching his hat he returned quickly to the tiny stone house. And Meg followed Alphonse in the rain.

"So that was Meg Lawrence," David said. "And I thought I had sobered up."

The silent group in the carriage eyed him tolerantly.

"It makes no difference," Hayden advised him languidly. "She is as she is."

Chas closed his eyes as he leaned his head back against the upholstery. There was much to be endured, yet he felt he had done enough. He would not soon forget the way she had looked at him. He had needed all his discipline to leave her.

Hayden knocked twice on the carriage roof, and received one knock in return.

"We are pursued," he said. "Still one rider."

Chas looked at Annie, sitting to his side in Meg's blue cloak.

"Annie, we are returning you to Sir Eustace and Lady Billings. You must stay there tonight. We want Lord Sutcliffe to believe your mistress is at home with her family." He pulled a note from his waistcoat. "Please deliver this to Sir Eustace. It explains all—that I have married Meg and that she stays tonight with the Dowager Duchess of Braughton. Did Alphonse collect her things?"

When David nodded from the seat opposite, Chas again leant back. There had been much to plan today. He prayed Meg would safely reach his *grand-mère*, who had promised to send word to him at White's should Meg fail to arrive. If all went well, Chas would hear nothing. They hoped thus to limit the number of messengers who might be intercepted and quizzed.

"Sir—Mr. Cabot," Annie said. "Mr. Cabot, I don't rightly know what to do with this." She held out a letter addressed in a clear, elegant hand. "Miss Meg asked me to get it to you after she'd gone, once she'd gone to *him*. I guess it'd be yours now anyways."

Chas accepted the note carefully, as though it were a talisman.

"Thank you, Annie." He kept it in his hand. Had she explained, in writing, what she had so reluctantly revealed in person? He doubted it.

His thumb passed repeatedly over the paper as they traveled in silence back to Lady Billings'. The rain had stopped, but the chill had grown. It would be a cold night and, Chas realized, a cold morning.

Before Annie moved to leave the carriage, Chas stopped her.

"Annie, I must ask you not to speak of this to the household."

"I won't, sir."

"And if you would, find Mr. Bertram and send him out to us, or send someone to tell us where he is to be found."

"Very good, sir."

Hayden helped her out of the carriage, showing her the courtesies he would have shown were she indeed Meg, such that the footman's mouth was agape as Annie swept up the steps to the door.

Chas had the carriage lanterns lit as they waited for word of Bertram. He broke open Meg's letter and quickly read it.

"Sir." A footman knocked at the side of the carriage. "I am to tell you Mr. Bertram is dining out with a friend. Do you wish to send a message to him?"

"Ask him to meet Lord Hayden's party at White's as soon as he is able. That is all."

The footman bowed. As the carriage started up Charles glanced at Meg's letter again. 'I thought I would have more time to make amends.' He leaned his head back against the seat once more, and looked across at his cousins. They were observing him with matching, blue-eyed concern.

"I've been unmanned," he noted ruefully, slowly folding Meg's note and pocketing it.

"I should think you would be the opposite," Hayden drawled.

"In the poetic sense only, Hayden." He glanced out the window. "If there were more time . . ."

"Second thoughts, Chas?" he asked.

"No—there was no other course." Chas glanced briefly at him. "This would have happened one way or another." Again he sought the view outside. "Although this business of ricocheting about in a carriage all evening leaves much to be desired. I could do with a good night's sleep."

"Did she explain—why she went to him?"

"A small mistake in judgment. She thought Sutcliffe could be trusted." Hayden looked his disbelief as Chas wearily passed a hand across his forehead. "All she had to do was *nothing*," he added on a sigh.

"An impossibility, Chas—for a woman."

"When did you become such an authority on the ladies, Hayden? Come to think of it—you were alert to Lucy and Harry early on as well."

"I've simply been observin'," Hayden said. He glanced at his brother, who had spoken only the once. "Haven't you recovered yet?"

"I shall never recover," David said. "To find my angel— only to have her appropriated by my *cousin*—and my little cousin at that!"

"'Tis all in the family," Hayden said lightly.

"I am not so little anymore, David," Chas said. "In fact, I believe I have a good inch on you."

David's glance dismissed the possibility.

"I think I shall have to beat you, Chas."

"You are welcome to try. Given my present condition, Hayden would probably grant you the odds." They had at last pulled up in St. James's. "Speaking of which, what are the odds running now?"

"Eight to one—Sutcliffe's favor," Hayden said promptly, following him out of the carriage.

"And have you made your wager?"

Hayden smiled.

"I cannot reveal my methods."

"You are the devil, Hayden."

"Not quite. Though I know you expect to encounter him here tonight." They shared a meaning look, then Hayden led the way into his club.

It was still early, but the inclement weather had brought many indoors. Despite the crowd, the Marquis of Hayden commanded his usual corner table. They were soon out of their wet cloaks and hats, supplied with wine and some approximation of dinner, and once joined by Hayden's friend Demarest, played privately and contentedly at whist. The normality of the pursuit restored Chas to some semblance of balance. He did notice that a bemused David appeared to be looking everywhere other than at his cards.

"You would be doin' us a favor, major," Hayden said mildly, "were you to pay more attention to your hand."

"I can see nothing before me but an angel's face."

Hayden glanced to Chas, who was trying to concentrate on the game, then looked back in frustration to his brother.

"Either play or leave," he said coldly. "But stop bawling."

The reprimand brought David up short. Chas suspected his cousin was still not quite to rights, a situation that owed less to meeting Meg than to a week of celebrating.

"I would be glad of your company, David, if you can forgive me," Chas told him. "She might soon enough be available."

David looked stricken. Mumbling an apology, he rose and surrendered his cards to an eagerly waiting George Gillen.

"I shall just take a turn," David said, and Chas occasionally glimpsed his regimentals as he circulated the rooms.

Chas knew he was not playing well; he was too aware of the other activity in the club. Any unusual noise set him on edge. But at least no message had come from his *grand-mère*; Meg had reached her house in safety.

"Dash it all, Hayden!" Gillen complained as he and Hayden took yet another trick. "Why are we playin' for pennies?"

"Because that is my mood this evening, Gillen," Hayden said affably. "I find no particular virtue in the amounts. D'you wish to withdraw?"

"Oh, no, no. Not at all. Just wondered."

They were attracting an audience, solely because of their dedication. Anyone coming upon them would have thought that the stakes were very high indeed.

Eventually David returned, to all appearances having dipped too deep. As he leaned to whisper something to his brother, Hayden pulled away from him in distaste.

"You are a disgrace, major!"

"Pardon," he mumbled, and carefully sought a seat behind Hayden and Chas. Given the earnest concentration at the whist table and among its onlookers, Bertram's cheerful arrival, accompanied by his round-faced sparring partner, was strangely disruptive.

"Allo, Cabot! Lord Hayden." He bowed to Hayden. "Allo, Gillen, milord Demarest. This is m'friend Chick Hugh, the pride of pugilists! So what's a-foot?"

"Lawrence, meet m'brother." Hayden casually tilted his head toward David's slouching form. David rose unsteadily.

"My pleasure, my lord," Bertie said, bowing smartly.

David waved that away.

"You're *her* brother, then?" he asked.

Bertie laughed.

"I've three sisters, milord. Which d'you mean?"

"Lawrence," Chas interrupted. His own voice sounded odd to him, as he had been silent for some time. "Come sit next to me a minute. Perhaps you might advise me on my hand."

As his stocky friend Chick Hugh readily excused himself to seek a game of hazard, Bertie settled next to Chas.

"You wanted to see me?" Bertie asked.

Chas nodded. His hand was so negligible that it scarcely mattered what he played.

"Lawrence," he said very low. "I am honor bound to tell you—I have just married Meg."

Bertie tried a smile.

"You're shammin' it! Why, she was just at home this afternoon!"

"I am serious. Hayden and David stood up for me this evening. I'm afraid—it was not entirely her choice."

"Not her choice!" Bertie's smile fled. As he started to rise from his chair, Chas tugged him down. "Why you— you're no better than Sutcliffe!"

The conversations immediately around their table ceased. Chas leaned closer to Bertie, in an effort to keep their voices low.

"That is undoubtedly true. Though I meant her no harm, I may have done considerable—unintentionally."

"I cannot believe this of you, Cabot! I have treated you—*we* have treated you . . ."

"Better than I deserve. I am fully conscious of it, Lawrence. It will not matter, I know, but I did it to protect her."

"I can protect my own sister!"

"You could not marry her," he said simply. "It will help her."

"You take too much on yourself, Cabot! Why, I've never thought her partial to you at all! If anything, Walter—"

Chas' chin rose.

"It is done," he said. "She may correct the situation tomorrow if she wishes. I shall not be presuming upon the connection."

"Presuming upon the connection! I should say not!" Bertie leapt to his feet. "Cabot, I demand satisfaction! M'-sister's honor!"

"You shall have to wait in line, Lawrence," Hayden suggested smoothly. "My brother here wants at 'im, and I judge there are more to come. Now do sit down like a good fellow. You are my guest, and I should not like to be tossed out with you at the moment. Here, play my hand," he rose from the table. "I must have a quick word with Leigh-Maitland. He has just got to town."

Bertie, looking flustered, allowed Hayden to draw him unwillingly around behind Chas to the empty seat. He glanced at the hand of cards, then his eyebrows shot high. "I say, Hayden. Are you sure you want . . ."

"Play the hand, Lawrence. Well done." And Hayden slipped quickly into the crowd.

Chas picked up his new cards. Hayden had been masterful—and lucky. But the problem simmered. Bertie's glances were resentful. And there was worse to come.

"Chas," David said softly behind him. Chas had thought his cousin befuddled. "He is here."

Chapter Eleven

Chas had grown accustomed to Sutcliffe's foul temper. As he looked up from his cards he might have predicted with accuracy that look of scarcely suppressed rage.

"Mr. Bertram Lawrence," Sutcliffe commanded, moving to the edge of the table, "I think it time you properly present your friend."

Bertie glanced up at him, but did not abandon his cards.

"I wouldn't present my worst enemy to you, Sutcliffe. In any event, I'd need a mirror for that—and none's to hand."

Sutcliffe sneered, but there was little else he could do. As Meg's brother, Bertie had a peculiar immunity; he would have to push Sutcliffe very far indeed to bring harm upon himself. That possibility was likely enough, but always, *always*, Sutcliffe thought first of his objective—Meg.

Chas forced himself to take a breath, then retired his cards and stood up.

"You know me, Lord Sutcliffe," he said evenly. "We are on practical terms. You have spied upon me for weeks."

"And why should I not spy—when you dare go where you are not welcome. When you dare trespass against a lady!"

"That she is still a lady—owes nothing to you."

Sutcliffe's indrawn breath was savage.

"*Cur!*"

In the instant silence Chas heard only the fire, crackling in the hearth. Behind him, David's chair scraped back as he rose.

"Sir . . . Lord Sutcliffe," he said. "You have the honor of addressing Charles Rainer Cabot, Der Graf von Wintersee."

Sutcliffe's sneer deepened.

"*Do* I?" He swiftly surveyed David's braid. "Boney slaughtered the rest of the poxy Austrian family, did he, Major?" As Chas placed a restraining hand against David's chest Sutcliffe added contemptuously, "You are quite a novelty, Cabot. A titled heir who plays the *cit.*"

"I have my *métier.* My interests."

"Your interests, yes—in dirt!"

"At least *I* do not wallow in it." Cabot made much of rubbing one hand thoughtfully against his chin. "*Wie sagt Mann? . . . ein Schwein.*"

Sutcliffe's eyes fairly blazed.

"You insult me!"

"It is gratifying to be understood."

The earl slapped his card on to the table between them.

"This can no longer be deemed *mal à propos*, Monsieur Le Comte. I shall be pleased to extinguish your despicable line—now that we are *equals.*"

"Equality with you, Sutcliffe," and he bowed, "is not something to which I would ever aspire."

"Unfortunately for you, Cabot, equality—of a kind—is a state for which you must fervently pray, lest you find yourself deceased. Now sir," he hissed, "choose your means."

"Pistols."

"And your second?"

Chas paused. Standing at Sutcliffe's shoulder, the disconcerting Baron Mulmgren regarded him with chilly satisfaction.

"I stand his second," Hayden said, his voice carrying clearly from behind Mulmgren. Both Sutcliffe and Mulmgren had to swivel about to view him.

Sutcliffe's gaze narrowed.

"I have no quarrel with you, Hayden. You needn't involve yourself."

"Oh, but I think I must. Chas bein' family an' all." It was a pointed little reminder—that Sutcliffe challenged the house of Braughton as well. Though Chas had not doubted it, he felt an instant pride.

"Lord Mulmgren speaks for me," Sutcliffe said abruptly. And with a curt nod to Hayden, he turned and left.

Chas watched Hayden and Mulmgren remove to a far corner of the room. Given Sutcliffe's history, Mulmgren must have served this function for him many times before; indeed, Chas suspected the baron welcomed the role. Sour Mulmgren actually looked animated. Hayden was less seasoned, but Chas was confident his cousin knew his preferences— and the protocol—as well as anyone.

Chas swept Sutcliffe's card dismissively from the table and sat down to play. But Bertram was staring at him as though he had never seen him before, and Demarest and Gillen were clearly more interested in watching their idol Hayden across the way than in renewing the game.

"You must think me very stupid, Cabot," Bertie whispered. "I beg your pardon."

"You could not have known."

"I should have. By all rights, *I* should be the one—"

"No. I've rights as well now, Lawrence."

Bertie swallowed, then nodded.

"Meggie—does she know?"

"Unfortunately, yes."

"She is safe?"

"She is at home." Chas glanced around the room. He could say no more here at White's, where Sutcliffe might have unknown allies. He turned to look at David, who was also watching his brother in conversation. Chas noted that David's gaze was too vividly alert—for someone supposedly in his cups.

"You missed your calling, major," Chas told him very low. "You should be treading the boards with Kean." And David dared to wink at him.

Hayden returned after less than five minutes. Mulmgren was already slinking out the door.

"We are set," Hayden said, gesturing easily with an elegant hand. "Lord David, I believe I should see you home. Demarest, Gillen—keep the table, should you desire it. Lawrence—you're welcome to stay as well. I note your cheery friend Mr. Hugh is in thrall to hazard. And Chas?" Hayden looked at him through lowered lids. "What is your pleasure?"

Meg, he thought for one wild instant. But he rose from the table.

"Sleep, I think, Hayden."

The others ignored Hayden's invitation to stay, standing at once to file out, stopping only to collect cloaks before spilling somberly into the cold night. Once they were outside and alone, Hayden spoke abruptly,

"Tomorrow. Seven A.M. On the common. We shall have to leave town before dawn. Demarest, Gillen, if you breathe a word of this to anyone I shall personally see you outcast."

"Good thing Knowles ain't here," Gillen mumbled.

"But I must say something to Ferrell," Bertram protested. "Father mustn't know, but m'brother Ferrell—"

Hayden looked to Chas, who nodded.

"All right," Hayden conceded. "Seven of us. No more."

Chas drew a breath of the damp night air.

"I thank you gentlemen," he said. "Tomorrow then." And he turned to leave with his cousins.

Meg had been received at the duchess' kitchen. The large manservant, Alphonse, had shielded Meg bodily, seemingly on all sides, as they walked the few feet from their horses to the house. Meg was quickly relieved of the wet cloak and bonnet and whisked upstairs to a bedroom, where a bright fire blazed.

The duchess, she was told, had adhered to her usual Friday night appointment, so that no signal should be sent that anything was amiss. Her Grace would join Meg later. Some tea would be brought up.

Meg prowled the room for some time, examining the

paintings, books and ornaments, looking for any evidence of Cabot, of which she disappointingly found none. She read for a while, but as the hour grew late, she found it increasingly difficult to concentrate. She opened her journal and carefully unwrapped the pressed violets.

She fell asleep there in the chair by the fire, because she was next aware of gentle fingers on her arm and a soft voice saying,

"Ma belle . . . ma belle . . . Meg."

Meg looked up at a petite, silvery lady in shimmering gray silk. She leaned upon an ivory-tipped cane. As Meg started to rise, the duchess placed a hand on her shoulder.

"No. Do not stir yourself." Her voice was sweet and calming. "I shall join you here." She signaled a waiting maid, who curtsied and left the room.

As the duchess took the chair opposite her own, Meg realized the fire had been stoked, and that someone also had covered her with a blanket.

"I apologize, your Grace. I did not mean to sleep."

"You must not apologize. I am returning much too late—it is after ten. I should not have come in, but I wished to see that you were here, and safe." She leaned forward from her chair and gently cradled Meg's hands. *"Ma belle,* it must have hurt him to leave you this night."

Hurt him? As Meg glanced down, the duchess patted her hands and sat back.

"They are from Brookslea," she said, gesturing to Meg's pressed violets on the table beside her. "They are the favorites of Charles—for his favorite, yes?"

"Your Grace . . ."

"Non, non. You must call me *Grand-mère,* as do my

grandsons. Or if you choose, Thérèse, as do my friends—
for I know we shall be friends."

"Thérèse. You must know that your grandson . . . that we
are not really married."

The duchess smiled.

"I think you will find that Charles is most determined
on it."

"But Charles . . ."

"You call him Charles, then?"

"I . . . hardly know what to call him." She again looked
down and toyed with her new ring. The duchess noticed.

"It is very old," she said. "It was his father's—given to
my daughter, his mother." She observed Meg's frown.
"You did not wish to marry?"

"I did not expect it."

"Ah, Meg. I see that you are the daughter of Sir Eustace
Lawrence, barrister!" She smiled. "What did you wish for,
then?"

"I wished—for him to love me."

"But you have your wish, Meg. You are all to Charles.
He could not love you more."

Meg sat up straighter in the well-plumped chair.

"Where is he then?"

"Ah! He hurts you, when he would never want to. So, I
must tell you something more of Charles—and of men."
She turned to the maid, who had returned with a tray bearing steaming cups of broth and a basket of rolls. "I hope
you do not mind, Meg. My physician tells me that I must
have these small meals at the odd hours. You will join me?"

Meg nodded, and accepted some broth. Her appetite was

returning, or the broth was exceptionally good. It tasted delicious.

"Now—" the duchess said, "I know only that Charles is with his cousins tonight. I cannot say where. Not at just this hour. Perhaps at White's club. They may stay there very late. But then they will return to Myles's house. That is Hayden's, *ma belle*," she added at Meg's quick frown. "This house is not too far from here. But please, do not think to go running to him."

"Am I . . . a prisoner here then, Thérèse?"

"No, no. If you wish to leave, you may. I hope you will not wish to leave. You may return to your father, you may go even to Sutcliffe, I cannot stop you. But thoughts of Charles should stop you. Because you may endanger yourself, and you will certainly endanger Charles. He means to duel. If you go to Sutcliffe, Charles will find it *très difficile*, and Sutcliffe will find it easier."

"You have known of his plans—all this time?"

The duchess shook her head.

"No, Meg—my Charles has told me very little, when he used to tell me all. But I am most pleased. *Enchanté!*" She smiled.

"But—this duel! He told me he had pledged to you not to go to war, yet you condone a duel?"

"Ah, *ma belle* . . . Of course I fear for him. *Mon petit* Charles! But he is a man. He would not choose this path if he did not believe it right and trust himself capable. You are part of him now—of his honor. He must have you safe. I pray Charles also will be safe. He does this for you, Meg, because he loves you."

"I did not want him to do this."

"Of course you did not. But you think it is wrong?"

"It . . . repels me. It is not . . . It is not that I think Sut-cliffe is good. What he did to my father cannot be forgotten, will never be forgotten. He *deserves* to suffer, perhaps to die. I have thought of murdering him myself, *Grand-mère*! But it must not be on *his* . . . on Cabot's conscience. What a terrible gift for me to give to him! Do you understand?"

"I understand very well—that you have both tried to give each other much, and that you have not yet had the pleasure of discovering this for yourselves." She looked kindly at Meg, who had set her cup of broth aside and pulled the soft blanket comfortingly up to her chin. "This concern for the conscience—is a good concern. But I think honor is more. I have known men who believed that they could surrender honor for love, or for money, or perhaps for conscience. But they are broken. They are never the same. You must com-prehend, Meg. Charles is a serious man. The only thing he will fear is that you will not forgive him."

"Forgive him?"

"For forcing you to this—to marriage. And for pushing Sutcliffe to this."

"Sutcliffe pushes himself. He is—obsessed."

"*L'idée fixe. Oui.* It is a madness. And yet he is not mad. I cannot comprehend. His desire to possess is great. It is most unlike Charles. With Charles, the wish to *give* is much greater than the wish to *take*. He will cherish you. His love— is a man's love."

"But surely this . . . our marriage . . . must prevent a duel?"

"Ah! *Je regrette—non.* The marriage protects you. And kept you from a most unfortunate choice. Had you gone to

Sutcliffe, you would have ruined yourself—you would have killed Charles. Does he know that you love him, *ma belle*? I think he would not believe you could love him and give yourself to Sutcliffe."

"I . . . have explained to him."

"*Bon.*" Again she smiled. "You are a surprise to him, Meg. You were not to *act*, you see. He did not plan it. And how Charles plans! Since he was a boy. At twelve years, he lost his father, who fought Bonaparte. Then his grandfather, a noble from Milan, died imprisoned in France. Again by Bonaparte! Everything of the family Cabot is destroyed. Soon his mother, my daughter, is taken by the typhus." The duchess looked to the fire. "He was only fourteen when he came to stay at last with us at Braughton, and my dear husband passed within the year." She shook her head. "So much of home—to slip so quickly from him! I think this is why he builds, why he must arrange the earth. The trees and streams must go here just so, where he would place them, *oui*?" She smiled. "But some things he does not touch. They please him. *C'est intéressante, n'est-ce pas*? That he has also this understanding. There must be certain freedom." She roused herself from contemplating the fire.

"But now *you* are his home, Meg. The Englishman fights for his home—his castle, yes? Charles is stubborn. He chose this course, I think, soon after meeting you. He has known from the first.

"The dueling—it is terrible," the duchess admitted. "But is it not better than the family disputes, the feuds that last for generations? Your brother was, he is *still*, much at risk. My own brother dueled twice. For those in a certain position . . . of a certain standing, it is a form of law. No one will touch the Earl of Sutcliffe in your father's courts. They have not done so, have they, *ma belle*? They have not because of his station. Yet he cannot be permitted to continue."

"Charles . . . would not leave England with me," Meg said.

"Never! This is not right. Why should you leave your home?"

"If Charles does not . . . if he should not survive, Sutcliffe will take me anyway."

"No, no, Meg. If such should occur, and it will not, my son Braughton would see Sutcliffe banished forever! Do you understand? You are now of the house, of the family. But Charles," she said firmly, "will succeed."

Meg wanted that assurance. But she could not trust it. And despite the warm fire and the hot broth, she felt a chill.

"You are very certain of the outcome, *Grand-mère*."

"*Bien sûr!* I know Charles," she said with a smile.

"Yes. But I fear that I know Sutcliffe." Meg again looked to the fire. "How long do you think we must wait?"

"I expect to hear from one of my grandsons in the morning. They are very close. They will see to each other. You have met Myles, yes? But David, his brother, I think you do not know."

"I met him today. The major. Lord David."

The duchess nodded.

"My happy David . . . I have seen him only once these five years! He laughs still, but he is sad. He has lost so many friends. All he knows is war. Now my son Braughton hopes to employ him—to marry the neighbor's girl! I think I must do something . . ." She tapped one fragile finger against the arm of her chair. "Braughton toys with marriage. It is for him a tool!"

"Cabot—Charles said just this evening that marriage was nothing—a construct."

"Did he say so? He thought to sway you with such nonsense? No, I think he tries to tell you how you may perceive it—if you wish to end it. He must have been angry when he said this. He did not mean it. I hope you will not wish to end it, *ma chérie*."

"I do not wish to end it."

"No, I did not think so. You must convince Charles."

I cannot convince him of anything, Meg thought desperately, *when he is not here.*

"Yes, I am most pleased with Charles," the duchess said, again tapping a finger as she looked to the fire. "But Myles! *Mon Dieu!*"

"Why should Lord Hayden disappoint you? He is—much esteemed."

"Esteemed? Yes, most clever, most amusing—all the fashion! But where is the purpose—the passion? He is close to Charles, to David, but all else is nothing. His father—my son, requires much from him—and receives what he expects. But it is all duty, duty. I fear Myles will wed someone very grand, very cold, to please his father!" She shook her head. "*Quel désastre!* But now he is tired of his *Grand-mère. Que dois je faire?*

Meg felt for the duchess, but thought the day's wedding should not be upheld as a model.

"*Ma belle* Meg, I have been thoughtless. I have indulged myself with talk—with an old woman's complaints—when you are tired. I must let you sleep." With the support of her cane, she moved to rise from her seat. Meg pushed her blanket aside and rose to help. She took the elderly woman's left arm.

"It has been a pleasure, *Grand-mère*. You must not think you have tired me."

As she leaned fully on her cane, the duchess withdrew her arm from Meg's grasp and reached to caress her cheek.

"*Ma chérie*, you are most gracious, and so tall! Like Charles. Like his cousins. But now everyone in life is tall to me!"

"You appear to be in excellent health, *Grand-mère*," Meg said.

"Ah! You tell the tall tales—also like my grandsons! Well, it is better to hear this 'gammon' as Myles would say." Again she shook her head. "His language—it is incomprehensible! And your Charles insists he will not speak French with me. He says that I must be the English duchess! He is so stern. Meg, *ma chérie*, I hope you will speak French with me. I am old. I would find it most agreeable."

"As you wish, *Grand-mère*," she said.

"*Tu es charmante,* Meg. You will see—your Charles adores you. He will make you most happy. And he will be a fine father." As Meg blushed, the duchess touched her on the cheek. "Now you must dream of him. We shall hear from him in the morning." And Meg's face was still warm as the duchess departed.

Chapter Twelve

Chas attempted to hold the dream—of Meg at Brook-slea, in her blue riding habit, walking toward him across the lawn. But she slipped further and further away, though he wished her closer, and he heard voices—his cousins, speaking low and urgently. As the carriage lurched, Chas realized where he was, and that the tense conversation about him had nothing to do with the morning's mission.

It was still dark. He kept his eyes closed and stayed propped against the squabs, nestled into his comfortable corner. He wanted to remain as calm and quiet as possible. But he was also, quite frankly, curious.

"I don't remember a girl," David was saying. "Just great noisy bands of boys. Always missing teeth and scuttling about the countryside in dirt and patches. Look at one of 'em the wrong way and you'd risk reprisals—painful ones to boot. Or some brand of vexation."

"The girl's the youngest. With four—no, five brothers."

221

"Egad. Do you recall her looks? Missing teeth, perhaps?"

"All the Caswells look alike. Skinny little dab of a thing. Hair rather—oh, mouse, I suppose. I don't recall any missin' teeth, though there must have been at one time, of course. From all accounts she turned out well enough."

"Well enough," David echoed. "Then what's wrong with her?"

"Wrong with her? I shouldn't think anythin's wrong with her—ceptin' she has five brothers. One was in the Horse Guards, by the by."

David snorted dismissively.

"Didn't she take?" he asked.

"Not out yet. Been shunted off to schools for years."

"How old?"

"Just eighteen."

"Hang it, Myles—I'm no nursemaid. Why's father doing this?"

"He's not *done* anythin' yet. Merely suggested . . ."

"In the manner of a command."

"Good heavens, David. You may choose whomever you wish. Unlike some of us. And you will have the satisfaction of knowing you are chosen for yourself, and little else."

"Do not sound so forlorn, Myles. You are well aware that half the females in the country would still find you adorable even if you weren't Hayden."

"Adorable? You flatter me. And—poor boy—you are appallingly naïve. I shall have to educate you."

"*You*? Educate *me*?"

"Well—'tis true you've spent untold hours in too many pestilent pits. But I'd wager they are nothing to the *ton* in season for tramplin' a man's spirits. I swear some ladies are so fond of the married state they're recirculatin'!"

David smothered a laugh.

"Perhaps the word has passed. That anything in a skirt worth looking at, the Marquis of Hayden *has* looked at."

"You make me out a regular *roué*."

"Aren't you?"

"My dear David—have you been listenin' to *Grandmère*?"

For a moment there was silence, then David asked,

"What's father's obligation to Caswell anyway? Why doesn't he foist the brat on you? You'd be the logical choice as you . . . Ah!—I see. How convenient for you, Myles. I've been your dupe once more. Why, you're worse than father with your scheming! Look here, I haven't sold out yet, devil it. I've a mind to head back without even stopping at home. I'd rather be a pawn for Wellington than father."

There was another pause.

"That would be cruel, David. They have missed you. And as for my schemin' I understand the overture came from Caswell. 'Twasn't my idea at all."

"Caswell! I don't recall ever harming the man! Perhaps a token apple from his orchards now and then . . . Begad! I've no interest in the unfortunate girl or anyone else. Why couldn't you have taken my part in this?"

"I thought it might be in your interest. From what Caswell implied . . . well, everyone wants you happy again."

"Happy? I *am* happy. To be home—and let be! The problem with you, Myles, is that you've no idea how simple 'happy' can be. Some day you'll find you don't always know best. Then I shall *happily* laugh myself hoarse!"

"Your laugh is one of your rare charms, David. 'Tis a pity, then, that I shan't be hearin' it."

"Why, you arrogant popinjay. I ought to plant you a facer."

"Fightin's not always the best solution—"

"What a philosophy to claim here this morning!"

Again there was a pause.

"I note you do have some brawn on me, major. At least, we shall hope 'tis muscle, not fat. But you forget I still hold the record at Jackson's for rounds."

"That does seem like you, Myles—simply wearing down the rest of us." There was a muffled laugh. "Though I still believe Chas could whip you—if he chose."

"Chas no doubt could. But, you see, he hasn't your intemperate thirst for blood. And then, there is that undeniable advantage I have always had over you."

"Advantage? Hah! I can't think what that might be."

"Naturally not. The advantage bein' brains."

David scoffed.

"Do you ever reflect on accidents of birth, Myles?"

"All the time, *Major-Lord-David.*"

When David retreated to superb gutter French, Chas thought it wise to yawn and open his eyes. David was staring out the window into the dark, his open flask in his hand. In the muted glow of the carriage lights, Hayden's expression was grim.

"I had forgotten how truly comfortable your carriage is, Hayden. I could not sleep much of last night—but I do sleep here."

" 'Tis the springs," Hayden claimed, yawning affectedly himself. "Sometimes the only sleep I get these days is transportin' myself from one do to another."

David proffered his flask.

"Will you have some, Chas?" As Chas shook his head, David smiled. " 'Tis just coffee."

"You've been most mysteriously sly of late, major," Chas said, accepting the flask. "To what purpose?"

"I cannot tell you. But 'twill serve—I hope."

The landscape outside had perceptibly lightened. As the carriage swayed gently, Chas settled back again into his corner, only to feel Hayden's assessing attention.

"You must not think of her," he said pointedly.

"I can think of no one else." At Hayden's exasperated glance, he added, "You needn't worry. I've no intention of thinking at all this morning—only of acting."

"I cannot stress enough how dangerous this is, Chas. Sutcliffe has only the most rudimentary of principles . . ."

"True," Chas sighed. "Though I confess I cannot help but have some sympathy for the man."

"You are joking."

"No. He is risking his life. For something that is, for him, unattainable. Perhaps for me as well. In that we are alike."

"He does not love her."

"Certainly not in the way you or I would understand. But for him?" He shrugged. "Unfortunately, he cannot worship from afar. He must possess. And I cannot let him. But, yes, I sympathize, Hayden. I love Meg myself—how can I not sympathize?"

"He is a different animal, Chas. Something quite apart. I

226 Sherry Lynn Ferguson

wish you would not sympathize. He does not deserve the compliment. Consider the company he keeps. Mulmgren is not among those with hearts."

Chas considered Hayden's set profile in the gray light.

"Granted the man is unsettling. I don't believe I've ever seen as ugly a smile. But why do you dislike him so?"

"Dislike? That's not the word." Hayden looked down as he fussed with a cuff. Then his glance shot to David. "Mulmgren is not sound."

"Sound?" Chas also looked to David. "We know Sutcliffe and Mulmgren are unpredictable and extreme in their interests. But what have you heard?"

"There have been incidents," David said. "On the Continent. Relayed by those whom I have no reason to question. Mulmgren in particular is reputed to be immoral."

"That might cover a host of defects."

"He is reported to like pain, Chas," he said abruptly. "In others."

Chas felt the shock of that to his heart. The thought of Meg in the power of such a man filled him with revulsion. His cousins could not have devised a more direct means of strengthening his purpose.

At last the woods cleared for a corner of the heath. They were first on the scene, giving Chas another opportunity to get his bearings. Yet as he exited the carriage, he turned to Hayden.

"No matter what happens—you will get to Meg immediately?"

"Immediately, Chas," he said easily, his gaze moving to watch the carriage pulling in behind them. Lawrence and Ferrell had brought the surgeon. Thankfully, Lord Demarest and George Gillen, in remarkable deference to Hayden's wishes, had stayed behind in town.

"You didn't tell me, Chas," Hayden said, observing the others as they arrived. "Apart from bein' out of the city proper—why here?"

"You forget I am a landscaper." Chas surveyed the tranquil grassy clearing he had chosen. "If you can, you must see that I have the north side." He indicated that direction. "It gives me an advantage."

"How so?"

"*Trompe l'oeil*, cousin. Even that small deception might aid me." He took his leave, to stretch his legs before Sutcliffe arrived.

The whole exercise had assumed an air of unreality, particularly here, in such an idyllic spot. The scent of fresh earth lingered after the previous day's rain, which had also cleansed and heightened the varied tones and textures of leaves. Moisture darkened the trunks of the watchful oaks. A few birds were starting to sing. Soon, very soon, the sun would seek them out in their coverts, warming them after the night's chill.

Chas flexed his fingers, then tucked his hands into the pockets of his coat. He should have remembered his gloves, but no matter—he would have had to remove them soon enough. And Hayden had told him not to think of Meg, though she was everything.

As he heard carriage wheels approaching, he turned and walked back. It struck him that apart from the surgeon, who had sensibly remained warmly inside Lawrence's carriage, his party consisted entirely of family—his own, and Meg's. That recognition was unexpectedly fortifying.

A pale Bertie merely nodded to him. But Ferrell beckoned Chas over to one side, even as Sutcliffe's carriage halted. They watched Sutcliffe and Mulmgren descend and turn to speak to someone, probably his surgeon, inside.

Chas smiled tightly at his new brother-in-law.

"It was good of you to come this morning, Ferrell, though perhaps—impolitic?"

Ferrell smiled back.

"If Pitt could duel in '98—and Castlereagh and Canning just five years ago—mere attendance is unlikely to redound on *me*. But I feel I must say something impolitic." He glanced at Sutcliffe. "Any decent man might think to spare him, Cabot. But I advise you against it. I have known Sutcliffe and the Lawrences some time. So I urge you, do not reserve your shot. Do not be so much the gentleman. Do not spare him. For he will have Margaret at any cost. And then he will kill Bertram in the blink of an eye."

Chas drew a slow breath.

"The back rooms of Commons must be bloodier than I'd imagined," he said.

"My dear brother—you have no idea."

At Hayden's call, Chas turned. The mist was rising off the high grass at the edge of the woods. The first flushed pink of dawn had abandoned the clouds to filter softly into the clearing. Pointless as it would be, they were bound to make one last attempt to negotiate. He returned to Hayden, who had reviewed the rules with Mulmgren.

"I must again relay your conditions, Chas."

"I have only the one—that he must cease to pursue Meg. That he must leave her be."

Hayden walked over to speak with Mulmgren, who

laughed shortly and sharply, then spoke with Sutcliffe. Sutcliffe responded with a shake of his head.

Hayden turned abruptly and returned.

"He accepts no conditions from you, Chas. Your very existence is an affront to him. He wants you dead."

Chas swallowed—it would have been difficult not to—and grimly accompanied Hayden to the center of the field. Even knowing how much the man hated him, even knowing that he returned the sentiment, Chas had to admire Sutcliffe's poise. With proximity it was even more remarkable—no flush of color to his cheeks, no bead of sweat on his brow—no sign of anything approaching a nerve. He was clearly a proficient.

And yet there was something there all the same, for though etiquette demanded that they not speak directly, Sutcliffe troubled to do so.

"I pay you last respects, Cabot."

"Will you not yield, my lord?"

"I will have her."

"You are not her choice."

"Because of *you*."

Chas shook his head.

"You were never her choice—and never will be."

Sutcliffe's eyes narrowed. That simple fact was, for him, the severest insult.

As Hayden touched his arm and paced with him to his position, Chas could feel Sutcliffe's unforgiving gaze. That gaze did not waver as Hayden repeated their final instructions.

"Coat," he said at last, and Chas shed his coat. The cold morning air was bracing. Then Hayden handed him the primed and loaded pistol—a beautiful instrument, silver-mounted and deadly. "He is exercised," Hayden observed.

"Yes. Surprisingly. I think I would prefer him more so."

"Leave it be, Chas," he said sharply. "If you press, he will dispense with honor." He glanced at the pistol, grasped backward and by the muzzle in Chas's left hand. "The pistol is fine. I examined it closely. You have every reason to best him. But do not forget . . ."

A shout from behind them drew their attention again to their adversaries. Mulmgren was signaling Hayden to return.

"What is it?" Chas muttered impatiently. "What the devil is it?"

"Calm," Hayden cautioned, and strolled back to join Mulmgren, who was confronting an obviously discomposed Major Trent. Chas heard Hayden's exasperated "David!" and saw David fumble to remove his sidearm, which he relinquished to Hayden. Still carrying Chas' coat over one arm, Hayden dangled the offending weapon loosely from his free hand as he regained Chas's side.

"Sorry Chas," David called out, with abashed good spirits. "Part of the kit, don't you know. Forgot all about it."

"Half-wit," Hayden muttered under his breath as Sutcliffe and Mulmgren sneered. "Sutcliffe objected to the major's sidearm. Within his rights of course . . ." He frowned as he stood there burdened with a coat and a pistol, his gaze on Sutcliffe.

Chas could tell that something was amiss.

"I know you, Hayden. Something troubles you."

But Hayden grinned broadly.

"Just realizin'—that I never said good-bye to the man."

"*Mon Dieu,* if it is only that . . ."

"Groundskeeper!" Sutcliffe challenged. Even from twenty paces his tone rankled. The pother over David's pistol had emboldened him and his callous companion. "I hope you have chosen a fine plot on which to lie."

"I have, my lord," Chas countered easily. "I shall lie with my new countess, Margaret, née Lawrence."

Sutcliffe's shoulders tensed as though he would strike. But he clearly comprehended the truth, and Chas exulted in acknowledging it. He had nurtured the news for just such a moment, and Sutcliffe had called it upon himself. But the earl recovered quickly—more quickly than Chas would have.

"That will only ever be in name alone, Cabot," he bit out, and turned to speak to Mulmgren.

Hayden leaned toward Chas.

"You must wait 'til I say 'present,'" he counseled, his voice low and even. "You must not risk firing beforehand."

"I have listened to you, Myles. I am ready."

"*Bonne chance* then, Chas."

Hayden stepped back and away from him, and Mulmgren moved from Sutcliffe's side. Chas could feel a first, warming ray of sunlight grace his left sleeve as he grasped the butt of the pistol in his right hand and brought it around. As Hayden called "present" he turned fully to face Sutcliffe and raised his pistol. But Sutcliffe was already firing.

Chas flinched and staggered at the sudden, sharp burn along his left shoulder. His pistol arm fell, and he glanced down numbly at his linen, aware that it was bright crimson where it should have been white. But he could see. He was standing. It would not affect his aim. And Sutcliffe had fired too early.

Hayden moved closer.

"Chas! You must stop—you've been injured . . ."

"No," he grated. "We had terms for firing—at pleasure, were they not?"

"I cannot permit you to proceed."

"You have discharged your duty, Myles. Now stand clear."

For some reason the faint morning sunlight felt particularly hot and penetrating. Sutcliffe stood before him, relaxed, exposed. He boldly tossed his pistol to the ground.

"You should be dead, Cabot," he called gaily, as though it were all a joke. He was very certain—or very brave.

"And so," Chas countered darkly, raising his pistol again, "should you."

He had never drawn a truer line. He knew that even as he forced himself to look lower than Sutcliffe's evil grin, even as pain from his shoulder radiated across his chest—where he held his breath. *Do not spare him.* In one quick, fluid motion he cocked the hammer and fired. But he did not see the result of his shot. Two reports, almost upon each other, cracked hard after his. A powerful blow to his left side spun him around and dropped him to his knees.

He gasped, then blinked, and in the sudden dimness saw Hayden standing now to the right. His left arm was raised, and David's pistol smoked in the cold air. Chas tried to say something to Myles, something about Meg, but his lips formed only a meaningless moan. Then the morning went black.

Meg and the duchess, trying not to think or talk about the only subject worthy of either activity, sat at breakfast. Their conversation became increasingly limited, for even an exchange on the weather held all manner of import. It was not raining, yes, but it was unexpectedly cold. Meg could not help but wonder if such a thing mattered when one dueled.

She crumbled the rest of her toast into a small heap on her plate. She had been married all of fifteen hours.

"*Ma belle*, Meg . . . the clock will move no faster for your attentions."

"I am sorry, *Grand-mère*—it does seem we should have received some message by now."

"We will hear something very soon. Perhaps they believe they might disturb us. I am not the habitual early riser. My grandsons know this."

Meg tried to smile at that effort to reassure her. But the comment only reminded her that the duchess had also slept poorly.

"I see I am too severe," the duchess admitted. "We should not avoid what is dearest to our hearts." She opened a locket to reveal miniatures of her grandsons in younger days. Cabot was handsome even at sixteen, when his portrait had been rendered.

They were speaking low over the tiny, framed paintings when the sound of footsteps in the hall had them turning eagerly to the door. But Lord Hayden's look was solemn. As Meg started to rise, Hayden extended a staying hand. An awful, sinking sensation made her grateful for her seat.

"Chas lives," he said quickly, his gaze meeting hers. "But he has been injured—gravely. *Grand-mère*," he glanced at his grandmother. " 'Tis likely to be a very close thing." He looked again to Meg as the duchess reached for her hand.

"Where is he, Myles?" his *grand-mère* asked, while Meg sat for a second in gratitude—or weakness.

"David and Lawrence are with him at Dr. McCaffrey's—the home of one of our surgeon's associates. At Putney. 'Twas nearby, and we determined it best that he not be moved far." Again his gaze met Meg's. "He took two shots."

"Two?" she asked faintly. "How is that possible? Sutcliffe . . ."

"Is dead." He spoke with curt satisfaction. "Mr. Ferrell came back with me to town. I left him at your aunt's, to advise your father. I believe the sly old—I believe Sir Eustace is anxious to see you. But Miss Meg, I would ask two favors of you."

"I shall go to Cabot at once," she said, rising unsteadily to her feet.

Hayden actually smiled at her.

"That is not one of them. In fact, I would ask that you stay here, where you might be protected. And—if necessary—remove to Braughton with *Grand-mère*. 'Twas Chas' wish," he added at her frown.

"No doubt that was his wish, my lord. Before. But surely it no longer signifies."

"To the contrary. The circumstances were such that I have reason to believe you may still be in danger—of being taken, or harmed in some way."

"How so, my lord?" Meg asked. Her need to reach Cabot was most alien to her, but undeniable. "The earl's resources can be nothing without his direction. And you have told me he is dead."

"Others have acted in his stead. I am not assured that is the end of it."

"But I cannot simply stay here!"

"It is one favor I would ask of you."

"Meg, *ma chérie*," the duchess said, rising to intervene. "Charles is in good hands."

"What is your second request?" Meg asked stiffly.

"That you admit no knowledge of this . . . *contretemps*. Sir Eustace, and others, should not be aware of the details. 'Tis best for all concerned."

"That should not be difficult, my lord. Since you deliberately withhold knowledge of this '*contretemps*,' as you term it." Her gaze challenged his. "Am I also to pretend that I have no knowledge of my husband's injuries? Or even, perhaps, to dispute that he is my husband at all?"

"No one hearing you, my lady, could have any doubt." Hayden gracefully nodded to her. Meg was so astonished that she stayed silent.

"Your father will come to you here," he added. "And your brother intends to return to town this evening. David will look after Chas. My brother—Major Trent—is unfortunately well used to the needs of the wounded, Miss Meg. Chas will have everything he ought."

"Not everything, Myles," his *grand-mère* corrected, and Meg was surprised to note the merest break in Hayden's composure. "You will be returning to him?"

"After I . . . complete a task here in town. But yes. Soon, *Grand-mère*."

"Then you must at least take notes from us."

Hayden's gaze again sought Meg's face.

"He is not conscious, *Grand-mère*."

Meg abruptly sat back down at the table and clasped her hands. For a moment she pictured the worst, wondering how she could continue. Then she looked again to Hayden.

"Would you now make me as much of a prisoner as Lord

Sutcliffe ever did, my lord? Given the situation, your—your driblets of information are a type of torture."

"Yes, Myles," the duchess agreed. "You must tell us all. Is Charles . . . whole? What does the surgeon say? You play the game with our hearts!"

Hayden's lips firmed.

"He is whole, but unconscious," he relayed stiffly. "The surgeon expects him to pass through several days of fever, to flirt with wakefulness, then to recover—or fail to. Chas took a shot through his left shoulder, and another—much more severe—to his left side. The ball broke a rib but seems to have spared his organs. He has lost considerable blood. If he recovers, 'twill take him many weeks to be as he was." Hayden surveyed their white faces, nodded briefly and sharply, then turned as though to depart. But sounds of a commotion in the front hall halted him.

At her father's impatient "Good heavens, man, give me some room . . ." Meg rose and moved stiffly toward the hall. She could see the duchess' man, sturdy Alphonse, attempting to make way for her father's chair. She glanced once at her father's face, but feared his swift perception. Instead she moved to clasp his hand at the side of his chair, and kept her composure by focusing on Ferrell's calm features. As their group entered the breakfast room, the duchess looked most intrigued.

"Your Grace," Meg managed, "I beg your pardon. May I present my family? My father, Sir Eustace Lawrence, and Mr. Ferrell, my sister's husband."

"It has been some time, Sir Eustace," the duchess said.

"Too long," her father agreed. "I apologize for the intrusion, Your Grace, Lord Hayden—but I should very much appreciate a moment alone with my daughter—if you would permit me?"

Hayden's glance cautioned Meg, but he obligingly drew Ferrell out of the room. The duchess patted Meg's arm.

"Meg is now also a daughter of this house, Sir Eustace," she told him warmly.

"So I understand. Though I have not yet had the opportunity to tender my blessing. You realize I am a most frustrated father."

"You must take whatever time you wish, then" she said, kindly yielding her breakfast room to the two of them.

"So, Margaret . . ." But Meg had already fallen to her knees before her father's chair and brought his hand to her suddenly tear-streaked face.

"Oh come, girl," he said gruffly. " 'Tis not so bad . . ."

"I cannot see him."

"Surely you're not so squeamish."

Meg shook her head.

"Lord Hayden will not let me go to him."

"Will not let you, eh? Well, we shall see. After all, you are his wife."

Meg summoned a small smile.

"You do not mind, father?"

"It's what you wanted, Margaret?"

"Yes."

"And if he is—after this—as I am?"

Meg drew a sharp breath.

"I shall thank God he is alive."

He patted her hand.

"You see it is not so bad. You love him, my dear?"

"Yes, father."

"Then, having been your champion, he deserves his reward. Like the knights of old." He smiled. "Lord Hayden is overly cautious in denying him your company. I suspect he discharges a promise to Cabot, which is commendable, but given the situation—misguided. He does not understand matters of the heart."

Meg shook her head.

"I think you are wrong there, father. He certainly understood Lucy and Harry before any of the rest of us. Even before Lucy."

"Did he? Perhaps there is hope for him then. Tell me, Margaret, are all these fools afraid of me?"

"I believe so, father." Her eyes were still tearing. "Lord Hayden will not relay the facts to me, for fear I shall tell *you*."

"What—do they fear I shall have them all clapped in irons? At my great age and state of decay, it is most flattering. Surely the cold as Christmas marquis is not afraid of me? He is untouchable."

"He fears for Cabot. And—that something might happen to me."

"Ah—yes! That I can see. Well, I shall have it all from Bertram soon enough. But in the meantime you must assure yourself that Cabot cannot be faulted in any way—for Ferrell told me he took two shots. Two shots is evidence enough, my dear, that Sutcliffe and his accomplice were intent on murder. Do you understand? They duel with single shots. Cabot could not have fired even before the signal and taken two shots himself. His honor cannot be impugned."

Meg swallowed and wiped her face with one palm.

"Sutcliffe is dead."

"Yes, Margaret. But by whose hand?"

Meg stared at him, at once aware that the morning's encounter had been more involved than she had first supposed.

"Now here is what we shall do, my Meg," her father said with satisfaction, drawing her attention back to her predicament. "Bertram promises to return this evening with Ferrell's carriage. If Lord Hayden consents to send you to Putney, you shall have Bertram to accompany you. And if Putney is prohibited, perhaps we shall still get you to Selbourne. For I know my Margaret. An imprisonment in town, even at the home of a duchess, will be quite beyond you. What say you?"

"I shall try," she said.

"Good. Then you have only to wait this day for Bertram. And if this does not work, I shall put you on Arcturus, who will fly you wherever you wish to go." At that Meg smiled. "Now dry your eyes," Sir Eustace passed her his handkerchief, "and let us see the others, sheepish lot that they are."

Meg kissed him before rising to open the door. The others, apparently having lingered in the hall, returned quickly to the breakfast room.

"My lord," Sir Eustace addressed Hayden. "My girl knows little of this morning's adventure. Will you not enlighten us?"

"'Twas a sportin' event, Sir Eustace," he claimed easily, "that went rather awry." Hayden's gaze sought Ferrell. "I believe Mr. Ferrell will confirm?"

"Indeed," Ferrell agreed. "More awry for some than for others."

Sir Eustace snorted inelegantly.

"You know I am a decrepit old cripple, with no power to harm any of you. Why will you not consider what I might do to aid you? What if Cabot should die?"

"In that unwelcome event," Hayden said, ignoring Meg's small gasp, "we would not need your aid, Sir Eustace."

"Ah—I see. The law cannot touch you and your kind. But you fear it might still grasp at Cabot. From what little I have heard, that is most unlikely."

Hayden acknowledged that with a tilt of his head.

"Nevertheless, Sir Eustace, it is best that you continue to remain—unapprised—for the nonce. I refuse to burden you with knowledge that can only weigh unnecessarily on your conscience. There remains a continuing threat from an unpredictable quarter."

"This is why you restrain Margaret? I am convinced Cabot would wish to see her."

"Undoubtedly." Hayden nodded to Meg. "But there may have been plans, to harm her—vengeful plans—should Sutcliffe not prevail."

"Umph! In all his cursed days, Sutcliffe only ever expected to prevail. So it must be that menace Mulmgren for whom you prepare." As Hayden's gaze narrowed, he added, "You think I would protect such a fellow?"

Hayden smiled tightly.

"I think you are as you are, sir," he said frankly. "Sir Eustace, I regret I cannot stay to chat. Some other time perhaps. *Grand-mère.*" He bowed to his grandmother, then abruptly took his leave.

"A clever man, that," Sir Eustace mused as he shook his head. "'Tis a shame."

"What is the shame, *monsieur*?" the duchess asked sharply.

"Why—that he is a marquis. Do you not agree, Ferrell?"

"I do indeed, sir."

"I hear of your independent views, Sir Eustace," the duchess said with a small smile. "I will surprise you, by agreeing with you." But Meg, eager to catch Lord Hayden, had swiftly abandoned the exchange.

"My lord," she called, stopping Hayden even as he was at the door. She could sense his reluctance to be detained. "My lord, I would go to him. Surely . . . surely you must understand?"

"'Tis not so entirely incomprehensible," he said. His tone was both wary and amused.

"Then—must I plead?"

"Miss Meg," he started with some impatience, but seemed to collect himself, "you are nearly a sister to me now, Miss Meg. So I hope you will trust in my frankness. As a practical matter, 'tis an impossibility. Doctor McCaffrey's house is small. He and his wife have given Chas their own boys' room and packed the youngsters on a sofa. My brother will sleep in a chair, or on the floor. There is no one else we might evict, not even a maid. And before you suggest it— yes I see it in your eye—Chas cannot be moved. I promise you," and she thought his voice softened, as though he would be kind, "David will care for him. And protect him."

"But perhaps I might stay in the village?"

"Then who would protect *you,* Miss Meg? In any case you would wish to be with Chas. I cannot order you, ma'am, if you are determined. But I do wish you would take my recommendation. If you cannot bear to stay in town here with *Grand-mère*, you must consider removing to Braughton. Or go home."

"Home? Do you mean to Brookslea?"

Hayden looked as though he might smile.

"I must tell that to Chas. He will rally instantly. But no—I meant to Selbourne, with your brother, as you had originally intended. I understand that was your plan only yesterday, so your preparations must be advanced. Is that not so?"

Meg nodded, while looking down.

"Chas asked me to keep you away," Hayden repeated. " 'Twas his wish."

At that she looked straight into those sharp blue eyes.

"I must know the nature of this threat my lord. You suggest that Mulmgren might attempt . . . to make further mischief. Will you not tell me why?"

"I will not be indiscreet, Miss Meg. You are your father's daughter."

"But I am not a barrister," she countered softly, holding his gaze. "And I am your cousin's wife."

She noticed when his gaze conceded the claim. His sigh was resigned.

"Chas does not yet know this," he said. "We have not told him. But David and I were convinced Sutcliffe and Mulmgren were not to be trusted. On the way to Wimbledon, as Chas was sleeping, we primed and loaded David's pistol. He was to act a bit foxed, but be prepared to shoot should anything untoward occur. Unfortunately—though my brother is a competent actor, Miss Meg—he could not disguise his sidearm, and Sutcliffe objected. I had to take it. We tried to dissemble, to feign an oversight, such that they would believe I had no thought to fire it. Mulmgren must have forgotten watchin' me deal left-handed at whist . . ." Hayden looked as though the inattention puzzled him. "Sutcliffe fired before times as, no doubt, you and Sir Eustace suspect. He hit Chas in the shoulder. When Chas took his turn at Sutcliffe, Mulmgren was raising his pistol. And he and I fired at the same time."

"Then you—did not fire at Sutcliffe?"

He shook his head.

"No. Chas's ball killed Sutcliffe. Unmistakably. I fired only to stop Mulmgren." He shrugged. " 'Tis always possible Chas's aim was off, that without Mulmgren's interference Chas would have missed. If so," and Hayden smiled coldly, "Sutcliffe managed to defeat himself."

"But Mulmgren?" Meg asked.

"I know I struck him, but I cannot know the extent. I should have done better." Meg suspected Hayden rarely came so close to an apology. "Naturally enough, Chas had all our attention—Mulmgren's shot knocked him to the ground. And Mulmgren's carriage quickly left the field. We rushed Chas to the doctor's and I returned here at once to see you. But now I must try to locate Mulmgren. I fear an injury will only encourage him. He is most unsound, Miss Meg. We have heard tell of practices on the Continent that would strike no one as civilized."

The comment caused her to shiver. And she knew it was in the nature of a warning. But she had every intention of avoiding Mulmgren.

"Cabot, is he . . ."

"As I described. And heavily dosed with laudanum. Were you to travel to see him, you would not even find him awake. Or if so, he would insist that you leave. He was most adamant. It is a great testament to his strength, Miss

Meg, that he would sacrifice your presence. Will you not draw some confidence from that?"

Meg swallowed.

"I shouldn't wish to create a greater difficulty, than you—and he—must confront already." She could feel his detachment, and strove to sway him. "I will wait, because you ask it, because *he* wishes it, though it is certainly not what I choose. But you should know—" She stopped, then said urgently, "My lord, I have lived with threats from Sutcliffe and Mulmgren for some time. You and the major should be aware that I believe Mulmgren will choose to come for me and for Bertie, whether we are here in town or out at Selbourne. I cannot explain why I think it. It is as though he has been trained to the scent. Like the vicious hound that he is. You see how he has acted so far. With his master dead, he will be ruthless in his spite. What you say convinces me—that Cabot would be in more danger were I to go to him."

Hayden frowned.

"If this is true, I am miscalculating."

Meg shook her head.

"'Tis but a feeling after all, an instinct. If you hunt for Mulmgren, he will be robbed of time to plan. And 'tis clear that the major is best capable of seeing to Cabot's needs—in this—difficult situation." It was hard for her to admit.

"Perhaps," Hayden said abruptly, "I must contrive something else."

"My lord, if Mulmgren is injured, he will not be pursuing us just yet. We shall let him believe us still in town, but Bertie and I will leave for Selbourne by dawn tomorrow. And then, should he try us—oh, woe unto him!" The strain of the past day, of being parted from Cabot, and in such uncertain circumstances, seemed strange reward for what he had accomplished. Her heart still wished to go to him.

"I shall tell Chas and David what you've told me," Hayden said. "Clearly you must take care, wherever you are. I shall be in touch with your brother. But be assured I shall make every effort to locate and keep Mulmgren on leash."

"I—I thank you, my lord." She could sense then his desire to leave; she was conscious of noises from the street beyond the door and the sound of conversation from the breakfast room behind them. But rather than permitting him to go, Meg held him back a moment longer. He was her last tie to his cousin, perhaps for some time, perhaps forever. She raised damp eyes to his direct gaze. "If you would—please tell him that I love him," she said simply. And the Marquis of Hayden bowed deeply as she turned back into the hall.

Chapter Thirteen

The late June day had been too hot. As a lowering sun baked every surface—soil, silk and skin, Meg sat in shaded stillness, contemplating Selbourne's stone and lofty chimneys, shimmering in the distant heat haze. Atop the knoll that she would now forever consider Cabot's, she remained motionless—like a small basking creature that had no thought to move again. Paloma, cropping the grass nearby, objected to the attentions of a fly with the toss of her head and mane and the metallic jingle of her bridle.

After a survey of the park with Meg, Bertie had ridden across to speak briefly with the Wemblys, who had opened up Havingsham Hall just the week before. But since returning home, Meg had been disinclined to pay calls on their neighbors. She had begged off visiting that afternoon, telling Bertie that she would not go socializing in her riding breeches. In truth she was embarrassed to have so little word of her new husband, which was what kindly

Mr. Wembly would solicit. And the subject of her precipitous marriage made Walter too obviously unhappy.

Mimicking Paloma, Meg plucked out a long blade of grass and nibbled one end.

At least on this Sunday Selbourne was blessedly quiet. The few workmen remaining for the summer had the day to themselves. Most of the major projects had been completed; the foreman had taken himself off to provide some guidance to Cabot's other commitments. But Cabot . . .

The latest note from Lord Hayden to Bertie had claimed Cabot was mending rapidly, daily. Through Hayden, Cabot had conveyed his concern for her, but she had nothing in his hand. She longed for a word, for the most meager acknowledgment. She feared Cabot had not believed her message—and each day of silence increased her fear to repeat it. Perhaps she had mistaken his commitment. Yet he had ventured all. He had *shown* her. Indeed, she felt she now owed him the greater effort at fond expression.

Hayden anticipated Cabot's removal to town shortly. For days Meg had lived in a state of readiness, prepared to travel swiftly at Hayden's notice. The rest of the world, she thought with some envy, had been descending on London, celebrating Bonaparte's abdication. Why should she not join the jubilant throng? Her father and Lucy had remained at Aunt Pru's, sampling the festivities of the peace, expecting her arrival any day. Meg had hoped she might hear that very morning, but no, nothing had come, except the sunlight and oppressive heat.

At least Lucy was happy these days, since her father and the Wemblys had consented to an understanding. In open adoration, Lucy was convinced "her" Harry would become a bishop—as indeed everyone else was convinced Harry would become a bishop. But first poor Harry had to finish his studies, and then, perhaps, next June . . .

Meg fingered Cabot's wedding ring. She would like to be a bride herself—someday. She had spent too many weeks thankful not to be a widow.

She and Bertie had seen nothing of Mulmgren or any other strangers, though men had been posted to watch regularly about Selbourne. They had wondered whether Hayden's shot had injured the baron more than supposed. Only once had Hayden referred to Mulmgren, claiming that he was known to be in town, but Hayden had made no further mention of Mulmgren's injury, nor of the necessity to find him.

Meg's gaze strayed idly toward the river. A coach moved along the road in the distance, and slowed at the end of Selbourne's drive. On any given Sunday people took outings along the river—they would often stop to view the splendid beeches beyond the gates. Just that morning at church, one of Bertie's acquaintances had commented that Selbourne was looking "prime", and hadn't they had a great deal done to the place? Bertie had enthused over Cabot, while Meg had stood glumly by.

Perhaps she would have to leave for Aunt Pru's that week; she could not bear to stay so distressingly safe here in the country.

She impatiently dismissed contemplation of the coach and its imagined, gawking occupants. Her attention focused closer to the knoll. There was movement in the trees at the bottom of the slope. Even as she watched, a horse and rider appeared from the shadows, and started to climb slowly up the path.

Meg had thought at first it was Bertie, taking the easier route uphill to join her. But closer consideration proved her wrong. Though the horse was dark, it was not Bertie's Sam. And the shape—she knew the shape of the rider.

She stiffened and glanced toward Paloma. Mulmgren must have spotted and recognized the mare from below. Meg doubted he could have seen her as well, not where she was sitting hidden in the shade. But he would know she was there.

At once she was on her feet, debating her route as she walked casually toward Paloma. She could not flee straight down toward Mulmgren, no matter the element of surprise, for she suspected he would be armed. And jumping the hedges toward the Wemblys would only risk leading Mulmgren straight to Bertie. Mulmgren would gleefully shoot her brother on sight.

That left the remaining choice, the only choice, which was to head down the wooded slope behind her toward the lake. This afternoon she was luckily riding astride. As Meg caught up the reins, she made an effort to appear unaware of Mulmgren's presence. Yet even in her tension she thought it ironic, that Mulmgren should trouble to follow Cabot's path to the knoll, when he might have come directly up to intercept her. Now she would not give him the chance.

Turning the mare she headed north at a walk, just to the point that she knew Mulmgren, still below grade, could no longer see her. Then she kneed Paloma to a startled charge directly downhill.

They did not follow Cabot's woodland trail, but crashed through the thickets of rhododendron and laurel. Meg was grateful for Paloma's trust, glad that the mare did not hesitate to career at such a breakneck pace, down a hazardous incline and through the obscuring foliage.

Meg hoped Mulmgren would be too late to note her path, or that he would hesitate to set upon the steep slope to reach her. If he tore along on the trail he would be behind her by a half a minute or so—and that, she reasoned, was all she would need.

She had almost reached the bottom of the hill when she heard Mulmgren's horse neigh furiously from above. Mulmgren must have attempted, unsuccessfully, to goad his mount down the direct descent. Even as Meg turned Paloma to the left, out of the woods and toward open ground and the house, the rapid drumming of hooves on the trail echoed behind her.

"Precious Paloma," Meg called to the mare, "You must trust me once more." And if it were possible Paloma ran faster.

Between the knoll and the long rise to the house, Cabot's team and the estate gardeners had worked for months on what Cabot termed the "terracing." Central to these efforts, and running at least half a mile in front of the knoll and the lawns at the perimeter of the house, the ha-ha had served as a sunken road for the heavy dredging carts during the expansion and improvements to the lake. The trench could now be crossed at either end on turf-topped bridges, but for most of its length it posed a barrier to man and beast alike. The ha-ha had been masterfully designed, for it served its purpose admirably—keeping the lawns from the less cultivated pasture of rough grasses near the lake and knoll without breaking the sweeping view from the house. Indeed, the trough was essential to the illusion of open space and distance Cabot had attained on the whole eastern side of the property.

Today she would rely on the ha-ha's most illusory width, for it did not appear much of an obstacle. Yet Paloma had wisely balked at jumping the completed channel. So too had mighty Arcturus. Meg intended that Mulmgren's horse should balk as well.

But she had to reach the other side without betraying the means. Meg glanced quickly back over her shoulder as they sped toward the lakeside turf bridge. Once across it, instead of heading straight for the house, Meg directed Paloma to the left, further along the ha-ha. Mulmgren was still in the woods behind them. If she could position Paloma before Mulmgren reached open ground and a clear view, he might be made to believe what Meg wished him to believe.

She brought Paloma to a sudden halt at the side of the trough, then carefully and quickly backed her almost to its edge. On this side, the ha-ha's wall was nearly vertical, reinforced with stones. Cabot had claimed that a man might ascend it, but that an animal certainly could not. Paloma tossed her head, nervous at being brought so close, and blindly, to the edge of the ha-ha. Meg looked behind her. She caught a flash of motion where the woods opened to the lake. Mulmgren was coming. Now he had only to be convinced that the ha-ha was breachable—that she had in fact just jumped it.

She applied the crop in a light fashion to Paloma's

flanks, causing the anxious mare to buck in irritation. Meg gathered the reins and drew her into a forced stumble, throwing off her balance just enough to simulate recovery from a landing. Then Meg deliberately set out to make Mulmgren believe she was not an experienced rider. Let him think any novice might take that deceptive ditch!

He was advancing apace. Meg glanced back as she kept Paloma to a slower gait and erratic path toward the house. At this distance she could see Mulmgren's dark clothes and barely distinguish his features. She had assumed that by now he must at least see the ha-ha, but he kept on. All the worse for him, she thought grimly, concentrating on clipping Paloma's stride. Mulmgren must think his prey attainable, else he might not make the attempt.

In a few more seconds he had certainly seen the barrier, for another brief glance over her shoulder convinced her that Mulmgren was urging his horse forward, readying for a jump. She thought he must have murder on his mind, to risk coming after her this close to the house. Even as she thought it she saw Bertie on his faithful Sam coming around from the road side of the knoll. On seeing them, Bertie abruptly kicked Sam from a walk to a run. Meg prayed Mulmgren would not notice her brother's arrival.

She heard a frantic neigh. Mulmgren's horse had slid to a terrified halt at the verge of the ha-ha. As she whirled Paloma about Meg saw Mulmgren propelled over his mount's head—to disappear from sight.

One strange and strangled cry broke from the bottom of the ha-ha.

She kept Paloma still, heaving from exertion, and waited—collecting her own breath, watching the spot where Mulmgren had been lost to view. She expected him to rise suddenly from the ground, phantom-like, brandishing his wicked pistol, but there was only stillness. Mulmgren's horse pranced nervously away as Bertie at last drew near.

Meg started to move back toward him, but Bertie held up his hand, signaling her to stay. He dismounted, stood for a few seconds at the top of the opposite slope, then slowly descended below her sight.

For a moment Meg heard nothing. She was once again conscious of the stifling heat, of her shirtwaist clinging to her damp back and of the curls falling in disarray about her shoulders. In the distance, rooks cawed to one another. Then a pistol shot broke the steamy stillness.

"Bertie!" Meg started forward. She was almost to the edge when she saw first Bertie's head, then his shoulders as he climbed up on her side. Again he held up a hand to keep her from approaching. As they neared each other, Meg noticed Bertie's white features.

"You don't . . . you don't want to see 'im, Meggie. The way he landed. He could not have lived—that way. Hayden's shot nicked him worse than we'd supposed, and his sword . . . he'd lost all his . . ." Bertie grimaced and swallowed hard. "I think he meant to kill you, for his pistol was ready. It's amazin' it didn't fire when he hit the ground, given the way he was, all twisted." He drew a deep breath and looked at her apologetically. "I shot him as I would any poor creature, Meggie. He was . . . he must have been in agony."

"Bertie," she choked out, sliding from the saddle to stand on shaky legs. She reached out to touch him on the sleeve. "You are too good. No wonder mother loved you so." She moved to hug him tight.

" 'Twill be difficult—telling father," he said sadly.

"Oh no, Bertie, it needn't be. Father would have done the same."

Bertie frowned, as though dubious.

"You're trembling, Meggie, and cold." He shrugged out of his open coat, to drape it loosely about her shoulders. "Are you . . . are you certain you are all right, then? He didn't harm you?"

"No, I saw him coming, and fled as fast as I could."

"You should've ridden in my direction."

"I . . . I didn't think."

"Well, we're free of him now, at any rate. Too bad for him he tried the ha-ha. Foolish to imagine he could jump it." Bertie shook his head. "Go on up to the stables, Meggie, if you please, and ask Nichols to send for the magistrate. And I shall need a hand getting Mulmgren . . . getting 'im fixed."

He helped her back up into the saddle and patted Paloma's glistening neck. His glance moved beyond her to the house.

"Well, of all things! Here's Hayden!"

And indeed the elegant Marquis of Hayden, trailed by an anxiously puffing groom, was striding rapidly down the long slope toward them. He had already come a surprising distance from the house.

Meg trotted Paloma closer. In his left hand Hayden held a pistol to the ground.

"My lord Hayden," she said breathlessly, starting to dismount, but he stopped her.

"You must go on up, Miss Meg. I shall help your brother. Mulmgren is dead?"

Meg nodded.

"You are a superlative horsewoman," he said, gently stroking Paloma's nose. His light gaze held admiration—and knowledge.

"You . . . saw?"

"I did." He actually smiled. "I must apologize, ma'am. I believed Mulmgren further behind us. I hope you trust that I would never have placed you in such jeopardy."

"You've come . . . you have . . ." She swallowed. "My lord, what news have you?"

"All is well, Miss Meg. Will you await me above? I must first see what I might do to lend your brother a hand."

"Don't . . . tell him," she pleaded quickly.

Again Hayden's direct gaze met hers warmly.

"As you wish, ma'am. Though I think he might bear it better than you suppose." He stepped back from Paloma and made a shallow bow before continuing purposefully down slope.

As Meg neared the north terrace, Major Trent and the head groom, Nichols, came tearing around from the stable yard, mounted on her father's best hunters. Had Meg not just seen Hayden she would have been shocked to see his brother. He intercepted her, smoothly capturing Paloma's reins, as Nichols shot on down the lawn to Bertie.

"Allow me to take her around back, Miss Meg," the major offered. "She has campaigned well today." His eyes held a light similar to Hayden's.

Meg slid from the saddle. Her anxiety was growing.

"He is well? You would not have left him if he weren't . . ."

"Chas is very well indeed, Miss Meg. I would not have

strayed a foot from him if he hadn't had strength to enforce it." He smiled. "You must rest awhile now, after such an effort. I shall be with you directly."

Meg relayed Bertie's request for the magistrate, and watched the major turn smartly to lead Paloma to the stables.

At once she felt strangely exhausted. Her legs seemed heavy as she walked across the baking flagstone terrace. Yet even in the sunlight she was cold. She pulled Bertie's coat closer and determined to go immediately upstairs to change.

In the hall Cabot was leaning against the doorframe to the rooms he had once occupied.

"Oh . . . ! You are . . . here . . ."

His dark gaze was furious.

"You should have raced up here away from him at once," he snapped. "Not risked so much."

Meg's chin rose. At once her blood warmed.

"Your cousins did not reproach me. Quite the opposite."

"My cousins, like boys everywhere, are impressed by foolish feats of derring-do."

"*Derring-do*? You *dare* to say that to me? After you . . . After a *duel*?" She choked on the word. "What was that, sir, but a 'foolish feat of derring-do'? At least I had the sense—to rely on a trustworthy animal, not the *honor* of a scoundrel!"

"I could not know he was that much of a scoundrel."

"Your cousins knew."

"They are exceptional." For a moment tension held them silent. Then his glance took in her tumbled hair and serviceable breeches and boots.

"I cannot argue with you, ma'am," he said at last. "Particularly as you appear to have endured your contest better than I did mine." As he raised his palms to her, Meg noticed a cane propped against his left leg. "Will you forgive me? My ill-humor was an unacceptable way of showing relief."

"Relief! That is no accurate description of your manner, sir."

" 'Twas an admission of feeling, Meg." His gaze now held hers fixed. "And I do not much care for 'sir'."

At a shout from outside, one of the footmen came rushing past them from the front door and on out the way Meg had entered. The activity reminded her that for many weeks the household had been readied for just such an alarum.

"Will you not step in here—out of the hall?" Cabot coaxed, lowering his hands and grasping his cane. "There is bound to be traffic, and I should appreciate a minute alone." He turned and walked, carefully and relying on the cane, but without a limp. She had been too angry to acknowledge it, but now her joy in seeing him upright and mobile asserted itself. She followed him into the parlor, where all the windows were open to the slightest breeze. Meg dropped Bertie's coat into a chair. Her chill had fled.

"You see that I am slow as a tortoise," Cabot admitted. He gestured to a table by one window, where four pistols lay ready. "We could not move out to him quickly enough. But had he pursued you he'd have met a firing squad."

"All of you were . . . waiting for him."

"Yes."

Meg turned to him and sought his arms. He dropped his cane and held her close against his shirt and open waistcoat.

She could feel the thickness of bandages against his left side. But they did not deter him. He kissed her hair as she clung to him. When she raised her face he sought her forehead, eyes and cheeks.

"I feared I should see you taken . . . right before me," he murmured against her temple. Then he gathered her even closer. "If you move," he breathed against her hair, "I shall fall."

"I shall not move—ever." But she trembled, and he felt the tremble. He maneuvered her the small distance to stand next to a sofa, then pulled her with him to collapse against it.

"I warned you," he whispered, "not to move." And even as she started to smile he caught her chin with one hand and raised her face to his. His gaze was so open she had to lower her own.

"You cannot know," she began carefully, "Mulmgren was—so badly injured, that Bertie had to—Bertie—"

"We saw, Meg. And we heard. Any one of the rest of us would have let the blackguard linger. For hours if need be."

"Bertie is not like that."

"No," Cabot agreed. "Your brother is better. But consider, dearest. When you drew Mulmgren to the ha-ha you knew what you were about." As she again looked down, he moved to kiss her hair. "You were so brave, my darling. And so very foolish!"

"Were you not the same?" she whispered.

He gave her a small smile as he caressed his injured side.

"It is a curiosity," he said, "that Mulmgren should meet his end in the *saut de loup*—the wolf's leap, Meg. For he was as close to a wolf as a man can come. And 'tis a strange justice as well—that one so cruel to others should die by an act of mercy." He was still caressing his side. Meg moved to stay his hand. But his small tug pulled her closer.

"Do you know I once thought to build a moat right 'round Selbourne—to protect you," he said.

"But you did protect me." And this time she stopped his hand. "You are still not well."

"I am fine. And I am improving by the minute." He turned up her hand, and stripping off her glove, soundly kissed her palm. Then he wove his fingers with hers. "We *are* married, sweet," he reminded her, noting her fumbling efforts to pull away.

"That is no excuse."

He laughed.

"You may be as severe upon me as you wish, my dearest Meg. As long as you permit me . . . to apologize as sweetly as you do."

"Stop, please," she said, ineffectually pushing against his chest. "We must talk."

"Have we not talked enough?" he whispered.

"We must think . . . of father."

"Just now? Even Sir Eustace would concede it impossible."

"That is not what I meant."

"Your father knows we are here. He plans to return to Selbourne tomorrow. We have his blessing, Meg."

"Then why did you not send for me?"

"I had no desire to be nursed like an old man—not by my charming new wife. Since I am *not* an old man." His close clasp proved it. " 'Twas trying enough to be tended by David. What a tyrant he is! I would never have imagined it."

"He must have lost . . . many men."

"You are right, of course. And I am obliged to him, for without his aid I never could have reached you here so quickly. I insisted we come the moment I could travel. But now I hope he and Hayden will depart as soon as may be."

"They care for you a great deal. They are welcome to stay as long as they wish." Meg's chin rose. "This is, after all, my home."

"I thought you told Hayden that Brookslea was your home?" He leaned closer. "You told him something else, sweet, that I had him repeat many times. May I believe it? It is no small thing. You might still have anyone. And I find—that nothing in life leaves me as uncertain as you do." His hold on her tightened. "I love you, Meg. Do not tease me. I must hear from you."

She could scarcely see more than his lips and chin—he was that close to her. But all else about him was clear, warm, strong, and urgent.

"Do you think," she breathed, "I would now have anyone but you? I . . . love you. I love you. I lo—"

He gathered her against him.

"And you are willing," he spoke above her head, "to let the marriage stand? I know I told you we should wed because of Sutcliffe—"

She placed two fingers to his lips.

"Do not say his name. Not now. It is too . . . perfect." He was stroking her arm and shoulder with a gentle, mesmerizing hand. With the other he interlaced his fingers with hers. His thumb rubbed her wedding band.

"I think I must spirit you away to Brookslea immediately. You have no idea how my cousins will plague us.

Though even Brookslea has its problems. For you would no doubt abandon me, and my convalescence, to rearrange the furnishings. Or paper walls," he spoke to her ear, "And plan kitchen gardens."

"I should think that would be more of a distraction for you."

"Never, Meg. I have waited too long for your company. Although, perhaps . . . I should consider employing you."

"Employing me! Is this the way husbands speak to wives?"

"I do not know," he said, touching his forehead to hers. "I have no experience."

"I should like to see my silverbell tree," she suggested softly.

" 'Tis now my silverbell tree. My gift was rejected. Do you not recall?"

She kissed the side of his mouth.

" 'Twas not rejected," she assured him.

"I am delighted. Because it is here. Do you think I would haul one sorry sapling about the countryside, because of a young woman's whimsy?"

"Where is it?" she murmured.

"You must find it."

"Why—that could take ages!"

"Not if one were systematic. Indeed, we must search— together." She felt rather than saw his smile. "As I cannot go to Abbey Clare just yet, I would as soon finish at Selbourne."

"Finish?"

"Some projects will, of course, be ongoing." He kissed her cheek. "Certain holdings require a lifetime's commitment.

And here at Selbourne, I doubt I have ever seen . . ." at last his lips met hers, "as fine a prospect."

Brookslea, Hants. 6 September 1814

Dear Louisa,

I hardly know how to begin. To say that I am happy beyond anything sounds much too weak. That Charles Cabot lives, and lives for me, is some state akin to heaven.

No doubt our attachment was the cause of our recent eviction from Selbourne. Father claimed that watching a newly married couple "court" under his nose was more than anybody could tolerate, for there could never be any mystery as to the outcome of our exchanges. This from father, who has always delighted in managing others' affairs! He did, in fact, imply to Cabot that the commission at Selbourne was principally to bring him into my orbit, a revelation to which Cabot took outraged exception. He told father such manipulation for "long odds" was a misuse of his time and abilities. But I know for a certainty that on my part the odds were never long—I loved him virtually from the moment I first set eyes on him.

Father says he never thought Selbourne needed alterations and that he is appalled the east lawn had to be so "chewed up." Cabot has offered to restore all and to return the daughter as well! You must see that it was best we removed ourselves, else I might have died of laughter.

Father cannot be too upset, as he has given Cabot Arcturus. He told me he believes my poor husband can use the advantage. In truth, Arcturus is speeding Cabot's recovery. That grand horse prefers no other rider. I cannot regret him. I shall always be true to my Paloma, who saved my life.

I thought I should never love another place as I do Selbourne, but Brookslea now holds my heart. Here is such a happy mix of water, walks, and woodland that I know I shall always be content. It is a dreamlike Eden, Louisa, and still new enough to Cabot that we might explore it together and plan as one.

Cabot's man, an elderly Austrian named Dietz, is a wonder at running the household. He does not speak much English, but he is teaching me German, which Cabot claims is the solution he would have predicted from Dietz. They have a most singular relationship, for Dietz always calls Cabot "mein Herzog" *or* "Graf" *and shows him the utmost honor, while being forbiddingly strict. I believe Dietz does not feel as responsible for me. With me he is most affable and indulgent. Cabot has told me the title, von Wintersee, is* "merely vestigial"—*the relic of a departed world—with what he describes as no rights and few privileges. But when I accuse him of stocking a fishing pond in Austria, he laughs and tells me that I will be surprised. He intends to take me to meet his father's mother in Vienna early next spring. I am exceedingly curious. Father may claim that married couples hold no mystery for him, but mysteries remain. Cabot intrigues me, as ever.*

Despite the happiness I describe, I still recall Lord Sutcliffe. Cabot will always bear scars from that decisive morning at Wimbledon. When I see them I am reminded, and both horrified and grateful that he risked so much. I loved him desperately in any event. It humbles me to recognize he loved me more. I am determined that he shall not surpass me in devotion in future.

I cannot face separation so soon as this fall, so he has arranged for me to accompany him to Abbey Clare in Kent next month. We are to stop with his Grand-mère in town both going and coming—I am all eagerness at the thought of seeing you and, with God's good grace, a little Ferrell. You know I shall enjoy being an aunt, Louisa. Cabot claims that you and Ferrell, and my most presumptuous maid Annie, aided him so immeasurably, at such critical junctures, that you have earned his eternal gratitude. I know that he looks forward to furthering the acquaintance when we are in town.

I must not forget to relay an invitation to Braughton for the New Year. The duke and duchess hold a house party annually and they have been kind enough to invite the entire family. Should you and a babe be ready to travel, I would welcome your company. It is the first opportunity I shall have to meet Cabot's uncle and aunt. If the magnificence of their son the marquis is any measure, their Graces must be most imposing personages. I do not mean to imply that I find Lord Hayden disagreeable—far from it. As you remember, he can be a most fascinating gentleman. And yet? I suppose I simply do not know what to make of him. I do know you will enjoy meeting Hayden's brother, Major Trent, Lord David. That is, if he attends—for the major has returned to Wellington in Paris, and Cabot hints that some discord in the family may keep him away. I am thankful father never ruled us too strictly, although of course there was never so much at stake!

I hope my raptures have not bored you as they did father and even patient Bertie. Imagine—they claim to be eager for Lucy's return from Brighton with the Wemblys! You recall father required she keep a journal for the year, that she might learn the value of words? I fear he will regret the assignment, for Lucy vows she shall read it to everyone!

Pray do write and tell me how you are feeling. I told you last spring, did I not, that Ferrell would stay in town with you, rather than decamp for the shooting? I wish you always as blissfully happy as I find myself with my own.

I hear him waking now and must to him.

Love,

Meg